DOOSRA

Also by the author

Unlawful Justice (2017)

The Mogul (2018)

The Heist Artist (2019)

Bhendi Bazaar (2019)

Lipstick (2019)

VISH DHAMIJA

A RITA FERREIRA THRILLER

DOOSRA

HARPER
BLACK
An Imprint of HarperCollins *Publishers*

First published in India by Rumour Books India in 2016
Publishers

This edition first published in 2019 by Harper Black
An imprint of HarperCollins

Building 10, Tower A, 4th Floor, DLF Cyber City, Phase II,
Gurugram Haryana – 122002, India
www.harpercollins.co.in

2 4 6 8 10 9 7 5 3 1

P-ISBN: 978-93-5357-281-5
E-ISBN: 978-93-5357-282-2

Typeset in 10.5/13.7 Adobe Caslon Pro at
Manipal Digital Systems, Manipal

Printed and bound at
MicroPrints india, New Delhi

‘Though seeing, they do not see’
— Matthew 13:11

AUTHOR NOTE

The idea of a diamond-heist-gone-wrong storyline came to me when I finished writing *Bhendi Bazaar*, but I waited to see how the readers reacted to the character of DCP Rita Ferreira. As the initial positive response to the book and Rita Ferreira started trickling in, I was convinced she would be the protagonist again, and *Doosra* was *born*. It's the second book in the Rita Ferreira series, and is quite different from its predecessor. Although it might have some references to *Bhendi Bazaar*, it isn't a sequel – it's very much a standalone story.

A lot of people helped me write *Doosra*, but it would be impossible to list all of them. As usual, my wife and biggest critic, Nidhi, was the first reader. After reading half the manuscript, she told me that the story lacked zing; it needed some more action. And hence I deliberated, altered some parts and added new dimensions to make the story come alive. Thank you, Nidhi.

My friend Patrick Whittick took a look at the final document and ironed out the errors in language, pointed out inconsistencies in the plot, and provided valuable suggestions, which I incorporated. Thank you, Patrick.

Thank you, team Siyahi and Story Ink, for having faith in my stories.

Thank you, team HarperCollins, for all the editorial support.

I hope you enjoy reading *Doosra* as much as I enjoyed writing it.

Love, lots of it,
Vish Dhamija
Find me on:
Facebook: www.facebook.com/VishDhamija
Email: vishdhamija@gmail.com

Doosra – aka *Googly* – is a term used in the game of cricket. It's a kind of bowling delivery that promises to go one way after the bounce, but goes the other. The primary reason most batsmen succumb to it is because they are misguided by the illusion that the bowler's arm creates. However, history is awash with batsmen who could look past that illusion by reading the seam on the ball. If any expert tells you differently, he is not adept enough. Remember – an illusion can only work till something eludes you.

What you can see, you know.

PROLOGUE

Antwerp, 2 April

Ron Jogani was ushered into Aaron Diamonds with genuine courtesy. The light pat-down by the jeweller's security was perfunctory. After all, he had been picked up by Aaron's personal chauffer right from Brussels Airport's arrival lounge that very morning and driven straight to Antwerp. He had only arrived in Belgium at 0750 hours from Mumbai on Jet Airways Flight 9W228 and unless he had surreptitiously arranged to pick up some ammunition or weapon from the immigration authorities themselves, there hadn't been any opportunity, as he hadn't stopped anywhere on the way or met anybody since. And, the Airports Authority of India wouldn't have let him on board with any firearms, would they? They wouldn't have missed it either, as there had never been any security lapse on any flight that had taken off from India in over fifty years.

Jogani wasn't here for the first time or the last, and he wasn't a novitiate either to attempt a burglary. In fact, Jogani was one of the bigger players in the diamond trade that had been dominated for decades by Jews and Indians – mainly of Gujarati ancestry – in Antwerp's Diamond Quarter. For someone in the diamond trade in India, a regular visit to Antwerp was sacramental; as such, Jogani had been here numerous times but the purchase on this visit would be the biggest he had ever done. The diamonds were for a syndicate back in India. Instead of individually flying to buy the polished stones, they had entrusted Jogani to buy and courier a few of them. This transaction could be in excess of €10 million, but it hinged on two dynamics: first, Aaron had to physically hold the inventory of the requisite stock – the specs had already been wired a month prior – for Jogani to evaluate, and second, and more significantly, Aaron had to be willing to undervalue the rocks to save on import duties and let unaccounted money change hands. Aaron had tentatively agreed to the conditions, but didn't want to discuss it any further on phone or online: the what-and-by-how-much was left open for negotiations.

Jogani was, of course, of Gujarati descent, but his clan had lived in Mumbai for generations. He was a large man, stood six-feet-one from the ground; he had recently celebrated his fiftieth birthday, and a bit of paunch had only started to make an appearance. He wasn't good-looking, no. But he was loaded. Single – divorced at an early age and decided he was better off single, given his predilections – and unapologetically promiscuous; diamonds and women were his only two weaknesses. His biggest skill was his knowledge of precious stones, especially diamonds. Even with a naked eye, he could price a diamond and it wouldn't be any more than five per cent away from the real value. Oh, he knew his diamonds. It was for this very proficiency that he had been picked by the diamond merchants back home to carry out the transaction on their behalf in Antwerp.

Jogani had been comfortable when his driver dropped him at Mumbai international airport at midnight the previous day. He had had a couple of drinks, and looked forward to some free Scotch before the steward made his little bed in the Première cabin.

So comfortable that he had missed some predatory eyes that had been watching him from the airport all through the flight, and he being picked up and driven out of the Brussels Airport to Antwerp. The sentience undoubtedly seemed lackadaisical; a consequence of having repeatedly done the exact job so often that it bred a false feeling of invincibility, the overconfidence. More notably, it almost tangibly heralded the carelessness to those watching and sinisterly lying in wait. His travel plans, his movements were being keenly tracked.

But now, clad in Ralph jeans and a white polo, Jogani was shepherded into the vaulted office of Aaron Diamonds and made comfortable in a cream leather chair across the large mahogany table – almost the size of an American pool table – inlaid with ivory and tortoise shell, an antique actually imported from India before Independence. It was apparent that Mr Aaron did not fancy making his affluent client wait for long. He arrived the moment coffee was served. Leonard Aaron, the tall, slim, pointed-nosed, silver-haired, aging diamond dealer, who had been around since after the war, solely owned Aaron Diamonds.

'Welcome to Antwerp, Ron.' Aaron forwarded his hand.

'Thank you, Leonard. And thanks for the pick-up at the airport.' Jogani smiled as he shook hands with the dealer.

'You're welcome. How was the journey?'

'As usual. It's a convenient flight, I had a good six-seven hours of sleep and then this drive up from Brussels was, as always, a pleasure.'

'Would you want me to make a hotel reservation for you here in Antwerp or Brussels?'

'It's already been arranged, thanks.'

Leonard Aaron was a respectable and honest man; Jogani trusted him, but he still wanted the camels tied. With a consignment of loose diamonds of the value that he was here to buy today, it was better that way. The fewer the number of people who knew his whereabouts, the safer it was. He would ask his host to get him dropped in downtown Brussels and then disappear into the hotel he was booked in for the night. There was no way he would share the name or location of the hotel with anyone, not even Aaron.

However, what Jogani didn't know was that some individuals had already identified the hotel he was reserved in. They even had a copy of his electronic reservation. They had waited till the hotel allotted the room to him in their register, at noon on the day of his arrival, and then the room in front – across the corridor – and both rooms on either side of Jogani's assigned room were booked. Of course, three rooms weren't necessary, but it was better that no one else stayed in them either.

Those booking these three rooms were cognizant that the morning flight that had brought Ron Jogani to Brussels was a shuttle – it returned to Mumbai after a few hours, after the usual change of staff, routine engineering checks and refuelling – and Jogani was booked on the same flight to fly out of Brussels in a little over twenty-four hours of his arrival in Belgium. Intrinsically, thus, they had less than twenty-four hours at their disposal to put their plan into action and get away.

'A man with a plan. I wouldn't tell you where I was staying with ten million Euros worth of rocks under my ass. No worries, I'll ensure my driver drops you back to Brussels safely.' Aaron chuckled.

'Thanks for that, Leonard.'

'Now, let's get down to business, my friend.'

'Sounds like a good idea. Have you been able to source the diamonds according to the requirement?'

'You know me better than that to be asking, Ron. All inventory is on site.'

'What are we waiting for then?'

'The preliminaries … I think it's best if we clarify what kind of discounted invoice you require before we get to the merchandise.'

'Oh right. We'd like you to undervalue the rocks so it saves us on import duty—'

'Which, on cut and polished diamonds is now a meagre five per cent …' Aaron had obviously read about the recent hike in Indian import duties.

'But which translates to quite a sum on a purchase of ten million.'

'What are you not telling me, Ron?'

'Well, OK. Custom duty is one thing. A lot of merchants in India – my clients – do not want to declare the total amount of purchase simply because a lot of retail sale happens without invoice. Ergo, some of the money I pay you for this transaction today is also unaccounted for. You know what I mean?'

'So what are you suggesting?'

'I buy ten million worth – provided they are what we want – and get billed for close to five million.'

'That's a whopping fifty per cent discount.'

'It's not a discount, Leonard, it's the value declared. It also helps you to get rid of the unaccounted merchandise you hold, so it's a win-win, isn't it?'

Aaron smiled. If he had thought he could swindle this Indian for extra money for under-billing, he had grossly overshot.

Jogani smiled back. 'Could I see the diamonds now?'

'Yes, of course.' Aaron nodded and, after both the men had finished their coffees, he pressed the buzzer under the table. The door to the dark wainscoted room opened and a blond girl walked in. She acknowledged Jogani with a smile before Aaron said something to her in French or Flemish, Jogani couldn't be bothered; he was intensely admiring the girl's pert rump. She scuttled out and returned almost immediately with a tan suede spread that she unfolded on the table and left the room once again.

Aaron waited to see her leave and then got up. He walked to the door, locked it. The switch to open one of the panels activated only after the room was locked from inside. A naked eye browsing through the room would have certainly missed that one of the walls concealed a vault. Aaron, too, kept his camels tied. Behind the panel was a substantial safe that required a key, a numerical combination and Aaron's fingerprints to open. He deftly opened the safe, not giving his client any opportunity to see what else was in the safe, removed a small pouch and shut it back. Locked.

Jogani withdrew his loupe as Aaron sat down again, opened the velvety pouch and let the sparklers roll out on the suede. In all, there were twenty rocks. If someone wanted to learn how to shrink cash, this was a crash course. Jogani was well versed with diamonds. Diamonds are valued on cut, clarity, colour and carat. And their imperfections. He looked for the imperfections first. He spent the next two hours in silence, studying the twenty diamonds – varying from a single carat to a little over six carats – with Aaron quietly watching him.

'Fantastic, Leonard.' He finally pocketed the loupe after he couldn't find a reason to reject any of the rocks presented. Aaron wasn't here to play games.

'It's always a pleasure to be at the service of my clients.' Aaron picked up the largest diamond – a six-point-something carat rock – and superciliously looked at it in light. The sparkle was worth killing for.

'What's the total price?'

Aaron kept looking through the rock he had picked up. 'I couldn't get the exact pieces to balance your order. These are worth hundred thou over ten mil.'

'I'll give you fifty over.'

'Done. Only because you're an old client, Ron.'

'And a loyal one at that. What's your account number?' Jogani pulled out his wallet and extracted a card that had nothing on it except a number embossed – the number of his relationship manager at his private bank in Switzerland.

Aaron scribbled a number on the pad in front and pushed it towards his client: his account details to transfer funds in.

Jogani was back in the car a little after 5 p.m.

The diamonds were in a black crocodile-leather briefcase – gifted to him by Aaron – biometrically locked and placed under the front seat, accessible only to him from the rear seat he sat in. The briefcase wasn't an off-the-shelf one, the leather was only a veneer; it was made from single-piece reinforced steel and the handle was an inherent part of the structure, not a bolt on. His little trolley-bag was in the boot of the car. Jogani asked Aaron's chauffeur to drop him at Hilton at Place Charles Rogier. He tipped the driver, picked up his briefcase and placing it on top of his luggage dragged it on wheels like a wayfarer. The insouciant driver in livery didn't even look back, but Jogani wasn't risking it. What if he did? He walked in and stood in the queue at the reception, waited a few minutes till he saw Aaron's car roll away, then briskly walked out of the hotel without looking up or causing any suspicion. He walked about fifty metres and turned left on to Bolwerklaan. Another hundred metres and he would be at his destination: Crowne Plaza. He checked-in at the reception, collected his key, whistled like a carefree soul and took the elevator up.

Jogani looked around before inserting the key card in room 513 to check if he was being watched, though he had no reason to be paranoid. No one knew he was here. No one knew about the diamonds. Nothing seemed odd, no one besides him in the corridor.

What he missed was an eye keenly glued to the eyehole of the door directly opposite his. The occupant/s of room 514 had been informed that the target was on the way. Those in room 514 had been busy since noon, when they had checked into the hotel. They had accomplished finding, and then distracting, the housekeeping-service maid long enough to exchange their room key for the master key, got into room 513, installed four high-sensitivity cameras in the existing electrical fittings to capture images in low light, unbolted the standard hotel-room safe and replaced it with the one they carried. If Jogani secured the diamonds in the hotel safe, irrespective of the code, they had the key. They had even chicaned the security cameras of the hotel. The digital security cameras had been frozen and were now replaying the live feed from exactly twenty-four hours prior. But unless someone compared them to the real scene outside, who was to know? The timestamp only showed the hours and minutes, not the date. When all would be accomplished and the diamond heist worth circa five million would get reported, they would have no one on camera to go after. Now, all that remained was to wait for the quarry to leave the room on his own for a drink or dinner or to ensure that he was somehow drawn out from the room for enough time for them to collect the diamonds, disconnect his room phone – they would also ensure the lifts wouldn't respond immediately – and exit the hotel before he could physically get down to the reception to raise an alarm. However, they had to wait for the darkness to fall, the traffic to wane for the escape plan to work.

The cameras installed in room 513 had started relaying activities of the room to room 514.

Jogani walked into room *513, closed the door, double-locked and engaged the door chain and looked around. It didn't appear that he had found anything off-kilter. It was reasonable to expect him to go straight to the – unbeknown to him, new – safe, extract the diamonds from wherever he had them and lock them there. So far so good, but the briefcase wasn't anticipated in the plan since Jogani hadn't carried any from Mumbai. Where the fuck had he got it from? Instead of heading to the safe, Jogani went directly to the bed, used his index finger to open the biometric lock on the briefcase and removed a pair of shiny handcuffs. He attached one cuff to the handle of the briefcase and clicked it shut, and then locked it with a combination – so even that wasn't a bare standard handcuff that typically had a universal key. He looked around the room, found nothing he could attach the other side of the cuff to. He moved into the bath – there was a camera implanted there too – and behind the commode, he found what he appeared to be looking for. He placed the briefcase on the floor and secured the other cuff to the chrome water inlet, and charily locked it with a combination too. He forcefully yanked at the briefcase to check if it was fortified. Holy fuck!*

1830 Hours

Jogani lay on his bed and the television was on. Fatigue had started catching up; he had been up since last night, save some sleep on the flight. He had looked into the drink cabinet but decided he should take it easy. He had to get up early morning to allow himself enough time to get to the airport. And although he had no reason to suspect that someone was watching him or the merchandise that he carried, it was still simply good caution not to be tanked-up when you were responsible for merchandise of that value. Having flicked through channels, he decided nothing was sufficiently interesting for him to pass time. He picked up the menu. The restaurants below had some appetizing French classics, but he wasn't keen to step out of the room leaving the diamonds, even though they were fastened. Carrying them around didn't appear a sound option either. Room service, like anywhere else in the world, listed appetite-subsiding sandwiches.

He glanced at his Rolex again. The entire process of securing the diamonds, channel-hopping and menu-thrashing had consumed all of fifteen minutes, and he had another few hours to kill till sleep knocked him out.

The drink cabinet suddenly looked appealing. Belgium, he knew, was famous for its beer: Hoegaarden, Leffe Brune, Leffe Blond, Rochefort all adorned the little refrigerator. Conscious that he hadn't tasted Rochefort before, he pulled out the bottle and came back to the bed.

It was nine-thirty and he lay on his bed in his boxers enjoying the late-night film he'd paid for, one that was graphically amorous enough to stir him. He had chomped on sandwich and fries ordered from room service, consumed six beers and was ready to tuck in. He called the reception and requested for a wake-up call at six in the morning, then additionally set the morning alarm for 6:15 on his bedside clock and dozed off with the telly on.

Jogani did not appear to have any inkling that the prominent flickering of light from the screen would indicate to the observers that the room lights had been switched off and that the target had turned in. Thank you very much!

Jogani woke up to his bedside phone shrilling. Coming out of his stupor, he read the display: Reception. He reckoned it was morning already and this was his wake-up call, till he looked at the time: 00:03. They better have a good reason for this, he thought, and picked up the receiver.

'Sorry to bother you at this hour, Mr Jogani, but could you come down to the reception please?'

'You got to be kidding me, it's midnight for God's sake.'

'I know that, sir, and I wouldn't have called you at this hour if it wasn't urgent and important,' the receptionist politely responded.

'What's the urgency? Is there a fire in the building?'

'Nothing of that sort, sir.'

'What *is* the problem then?'

'This is a reputable hotel, sir, and it's against policy to invite escorts into your room—'

'Excuse me? Who's called for an escort?'

'It seems that you called her, sir. We have here … a lady of suspicious character …' – there was a pause, like the receptionist was looking at the lady in question – '… somewhat inappropriately clad, and she is looking for you.'

'For me?'

'Yes sir, she asked for you by name.'

'There must be some mistake. I didn't call for any escort. You can send her back.'

'Mr Jogani, she even knew your room number, and our records show that you made a call at seven minutes past eleven …'

'I made no such calls, in fact, I didn't make any calls whatsoever.' Jogani could sense his temper and voice rising. Wary that he might disturb people in the nearby rooms, he lowered his voice. 'There must be some mistake. Listen—'

'I'm afraid, Mr Jogani, if you do not come down to the reception right away, I'll have no choice but to call the police.' The receptionist did not raise his voice but there was certainly a hint of menace in it.

'OK, I'll be down. Hold her there, I would also like to know who called her.'

'Certainly sir, she isn't going anywhere.'

Jogani rubbed his eyes. Was it some hooker from his last visit who had seen him in Brussels today? He thought about other possibilities as he put on his jeans and T-shirt and glanced in the bath. The briefcase was safely tucked away.

This should be a quick conversation, there seemed no need to unlock and carry the briefcase with him downstairs to the reception at this hour.

In room 514, they waited for the elevator door to close, and the moment it chimed, they knew the target was now away. They sprang into action.

No time to squander.

Jogani seethed as he rushed out of the lift on the ground floor and headed to the reception, only to find it unattended. There was a bell kept on the desk that he fisted repeatedly – till it sounded like a continuous trill and not staccato tings – to beckon the receptionist who had awakened him and roused him out of his bed just minutes ago, and had now appeared to have gone missing from his post.

'How may I help you, sir?' The receptionist yawned and sounded sleepy.

'I'm Ron Jogani – you just called me in room 513 and told me there was someone down here to see me.'

The receptionist looked perplexed. 'Sorry sir … *I* called you? I didn't call anyone.' He glanced around to see if someone was around who might have used the unattended phone at the desk. No one. The hotel's main entrance was locked. Anyone arriving this late needed to buzz to gain entry.

'Then, who called me?' Jogani gave a once-over. 'Who else has been manning this desk?'

'I don't know, sir. I'm the only one on duty and I made no calls.'

'The call was from the reception, I saw the display ...' Jogani realized mid-sentence that he had been deked. He had made a huge mistake by falling for – what now sounded like – some kind of a trap. The rage morphed into nervous energy as he turned around and ran to the elevators making his second mistake of the day, which he didn't realize, and it was a mistake he would never get time to regret.

He didn't think about the odds that someone who had deked him out of his room at midnight to burgle diamonds was unarmed? None. But his mind wasn't thinking how deleterious his next move could be. He could only feel cold tiny rivulets running down his back. Cold sweat.

He hurried out of the elevator car and darted to his room, swiped the key, opened the door and shut it behind him immediately.

But it was too late. The invader in room 514 had already been informed about Jogani's truncated visit to the reception.

Even when it is most meticulously planned, there are so many things that can go wrong in a burglary. Like, in this case, they hadn't planned to kill but there was no other way to jettison Jogani now. There was no other way if they were to finish their job. There hadn't been a plan B. There was no plan to eliminate Jogani, but the bald truth was that Ron Jogani was at the wrong place at the wrong time. Only this time it was fatal. The coda was as dramatic as it is meant to be – sepulchral sound of two bullets muffled by a silencer.

Hadn't Don Mclean warned about fire being the Devil's only friend?

The police would later discover that two bullets had been fired. One into the chest of Ron Jogani from close range – close enough to singe his T-shirt and skin – and the other one on a handcuff behind the commode.

THREE MONTHS LATER

ONE

Goa, India

There are, in living memory, two distinct periods in history: pre-9/11 and post-9/11. The rights enjoyed by individuals in any country could no longer be enjoyed if the world – in the words of Darwin – did not adapt to the new world order. 9/11 changed the world. Not all changes precipitated by it were bad – though no one in their right mind should even argue that what happened on that day was evil, sinister even – some changes were essential, and had these been in place before that dark day in human history, perhaps the disaster could have been controlled, if not completely evaded.

Then the November bombings in Mumbai in 2008 roused up even the sleepiest of governments. And now, DCP Rita Ferreira mused that despite being a senior police officer, she wasn't permitted to carry her service revolver on a commercial airliner. OK, the airport officials were polite enough not to pat-search her, considering she had been in the news all over the country after having chased down a serial killer only a few months earlier. Not to mention the two uniformed policemen who had escorted her to the security gate provided instant recognition. She was waved in with deference.

The flight took off on time. Rita reclined into the seat. Fortunately, as there was no one else in her row, she parked her handbag on the middle seat and contemplated on the past three months she had spent in Goa under the circumstances.

She had been shot at while nabbing the serial killer, and the bullet had grazed her shoulder. The physical recovery had been quick, but the psychological trauma – albeit unknown to Rita – needed to be dealt with. DCP Rita Ferreira had been discharged from her duty after the shoot-out in her last case. Much as she had wanted to carry on – she was chagrined when they had signed her off: 'official procedure', they had said – she was ordered to take time off. Having been taken captive or overpowered by a criminal – if only for a few minutes – and use of firearms usually mandated that the police officer involved be sent on statutory leave and psychological analysis. There seemed little point in challenging that. However, what had commenced as a two-week break had become a three-month hiatus as Rita's therapist disagreed to give her a clean chit to resume her position in the police force in the initial time allocated. Fortunately for her, Rita didn't have to live in her Mumbai flat. She had sojourned to one of her ancestral properties in a small village called Benaulim on the south coastline of Goa. Benaulim has been part of Goa lore for generations: Parshurama – the sixth avatar of Vishnu – had shot an arrow from somewhere above in the Western Ghats, and that arrow descended upon what came to be known as Banavalli: the village of the arrow. The Portuguese rechristened it to Benaulim. The place was full of natural beauty: the sound of the endless sea and the fragrance of local vegetation that Rita had grown up appreciating as a kid. It helped her recover a lot faster than if she had stayed back in Mumbai. In her mind she was ready to resume her duty, but she waited. No one in the bureaucracy, she knew, could or would override a psychological evaluation. The psychobabble of the therapist could never be vetoed. Hence she had lodged for most of those three months at the seaside villa she had spent her growing years in. It was a white, colonial house that had a huge garden in front, and the rear door unlatched on to a private beach for residents. Luckily the neighbours, too, used their properties for vacations, and hence Rita had the beach all to herself. She sunbathed in the day, enjoyed a drink at sunset, swam in the evening. She had spent days, weeks on this beach with her father. They had talked endless hours, late in the night, him telling her about growing up and looking for pastures beyond Goa: a guy, a family, maybe a career. '*Someone or something will take you away*,' he had prophesized. Robert Ferreira's little girl had finally grown up. An inadvertent smile passed through her lips reminiscing the days.

There were days she supposed that she could get used to this life. She neither needed the money nor the stress. Her parents had bequeathed their only child with more than she could spend in her lifetime. And with her history of broken relationships it still looked unlikely if there was anyone to inherit it after her. But she hadn't joined the police force for money; there were far better professions to make money if that was what one desired. Police was her calling, she always reminded herself.

However, three months and numerous sessions later, the therapist's evaluation was decisively complete and Rita was finally on a flight to recommence work. Vinay Joshi, her immediate supervisor and Joint Commissioner of Mumbai Police, had spoken to her about a case that Interpol had asked Mumbai Crime Squad to look into.

Thus began another one of Rita's chartless journeys.

It was almost getting to be a cold case, as far as Belgian Police were concerned, but they had found some new clues that had pointed them towards Mumbai. Joshi had provided no further information, and Rita hadn't yet looked up on the web for any news regarding the same. With such little detail it would have been a sheer waste of time: how could one look at all crimes that occurred in Belgium, and how far would one go digging for a cold case?

The coincidence of the two events – her successful evaluation and the urgency on the international case – was a bit baffling though. But when the bureaucratic machinery really decided to do something, she knew, it got done much faster than it took Tendulkar to score a century. Rita involuntarily smiled as the plane touched down at Mumbai. The flight had landed on the dot like it had taken off. The plane taxied for a little longer than usual, waiting for passengers from earlier flights to disembark before it docked on to the next available aerobridge.

As she collected her baggage from the carousel, her mind drifted to the case at hand. A cold case leading to '*some pointer to Mumbai*' could well mean that it would have provided the perpetrators with ample time to get away and move to Australia by now.

It would be frustrating.

It would be challenging.

But she was ready for it. She had had enough cessation from duty, and after a while it had actually grown into boredom. Her alcohol intake had also increased, which she had to consciously break the dependence on. Yes, she was ready, she murmured in her brain and walked out to her driver waiting for her, and who came running the minute he saw her exit and, mocking a salute, took her luggage and walked her to her new official white Volkswagen Jetta.

'How have you been, Kuldeep?' Rita asked as she climbed into the car.

'Very thank you, madam.' Kuldeep was a reticent man. He spoke very little and was uncomfortable whenever Rita made an attempt, but he responded, nevertheless, in his awkward English.

There seemed little point in labouring the dialogue further.

'Home.' It was late and Rita was tired. It was better to begin work from the next day, she reckoned.

Kuldeep just nodded and put the car in gear and drove to Bandra.

Whatever class of travel you picked in India, the car journey from the airport to the final destination ultimately coated you with a fine layer of grime, even if it is an air-conditioned car with windows closed. Rita unpacked, doffed her clothes and went straight into the shower. She stood five-six in socks, or without them, as she currently was under the jet flow of cold water that she needed to relax. She never considered herself beautiful – and conventionally, she wasn't – but she knew well she drew glances from men of all ages. Blessed with a great metabolism, she made the most of it by never restricting her diet. She was in fantastic shape for a woman of thirty-something; like most other women she, too, maintained ambiguity on her precise age. Whenever she missed gym for more than a week – normally when in the middle of a big case – she kept on with calisthenics at home: light yoga was best for toning the body. Tawny coloured body, with not an ounce of undesired fat. Flat stomach, not well endowed – certainly not the kind that was in your face – yet curvaceous enough. 56 kilos. And a God-gifted zillion-dollar arse to top that. Beauty can be an opinion steered by preconceived notion or your upbringing; sensuality was near absolute. Sensual: that was what she was if she were to be styled in one word.

They say a woman's intuition is far greater than a man's. Combine that with police training and years of experience: a perfect marriage of nature and nurture. And above everything else, DCP Rita Ferreira was a class-A workaholic.

Kuldeep had a set of keys and he had gotten the house cleaned and filled the refrigerator with fresh bread, milk and eggs. And ice. She unpacked and went around her apartment looking at all the things she had missed. It was mostly full of paperbacks and music. And there it was: a half-empty bottle of Jim Beam.

Should she? Shouldn't she?

She had, on too many occasions, witnessed her father get swacked, get into fits of laughter, get angry, get overeffusive and loud, then get all maudlin and finally get apologetic; all in one evening. He was never rude or violent, just noisy. All side-effects of Scotch. As a result, she never drank Scotch. Important precautionary measure, that. She was in love with Bourbon: Jim. *Sex, lies, and Bourbon.*

Should she? Shouldn't she?

What the heck! It was the last day of the three-month vacation that had been forced upon her.

A couple of large drinks down and she drifted into her unsuccessful love life. Where had she gone wrong? Yes, she'd had some relationships that didn't work – who didn't? – but she wasn't what someone would call rambunctious. Still single. As for life, so for love: you couldn't let your failures cling to you. Accept defeat or loss and then, breaking the old and unavailing ties, tightly shut the door on the past.

All relationships are mutable by nature, she now knew. You are permitted to believe otherwise at your own peril. There will always be spillages of memory now and then, but let them not dictate your decisions or future. Move on, Rita. You're not making any sacrifices; you're liberating yourself. And then, Ash Mattel, her buddy, the criminal-psychologist buddy, who had helped her in cracking the serial killer earlier, was travelling to India next month. Cheers! With that pleasant thought, she went into the kitchen, broke two eggs, scrambled them, put them on toast and called it a night.

Dawn was unfolding but the sun seemed to be on a late shift; no signs of it yet when Rita went for a jog. Mumbai, after a three-month sabbatical, is easy to dislike at first glance – the cloying traffic, the unruly crowd, the stifling humidity and heat – but having lived in the city before, Rita appreciated that it was even easier to fall in love with Mumbai and the people when you spend a few days in it again.

For some years now, fitted shirts and jeans were Rita's usual attire at work. And for a reason: she didn't have to be in uniform and she found any other outfit a little uncomfortable for the job she was in. She had got her hair cut shorter – they just sat on her shoulders, instead of falling down over them as before, which she tied into a pony sometimes – after the incident where a criminal she was chasing had grabbed her by the soft straight coffee-brown tresses. On the way out, she carried her powder-blue cotton jacket to cover the Smith and Wesson she knew she'd get back when she resumed office later. She ran her fingers through her hair. Short. They were still long enough to be gripped but surely not accessible from an arm's length.

Kuldeep was already waiting for her when she came down from her apartment.

Mumbai Police HQ is in the vicinity of a historic landmark called Crawford Market, and it is where the top brass of police and the crime branch are stationed. The travel from Bandra was about thirteen kilometres but it took them forty-five minutes to get there. Mumbai traffic had snarled up in the torrential rain that had started in the early hours of the morning. The pluvial waters of July had filled the potholes to the brim. Arrogant rain was still sheeting down like Arjuna's arrows and showed no intention of stopping. Its continuous thundering drops on the windshield sounded like a rap singer on steroids; the wipers struggled to keep it clear, but Kuldeep soldiered on. Rita mused as the car moved tardily through the traffic. Mumbai, she discerned, wasn't so different from Delhi as the media screamed at every given opportunity. In fact, no city was different from the other: the rich in their chauffeur-driven cars, the not-so-rich struggling in the weather on their bikes and scooters or on foot. There was, and always would be, without exception, an invisible line between the wealthy and those who aspired to be. Of course, you could win the lottery and cross over to the other side, but the not-so-fortunate inchoately existed on the sides largely because those fortunate needed them. Who else would clean their houses, run the laundry, repair their cars and bring their newspapers or milk?

Lost in her thoughts, she didn't realize when they arrived at the destination. Her reverie broke when Kuldeep opened the rear door for her to climb out.

'Thanks,' she said before walking into the building. A familiar opera of the usual office noises greeted her: photocopiers, telephones, mobiles, clacking keyboards and people talking. A lot of people went *hush-hush*. Most people working in the building knew her. Those in the vicinity exchanged *hellos* and pleasantries. Fifteen minutes after entering the building, she finally took the elevator to her office.

As she was in early, none of her team – the old team she commanded – were in yet. With her cafetière not having been plugged in for months, she picked up a coffee from the nearest vending machine and hurried to Vinay Joshi's office on the floor above.

TWO

Vinay Joshi, Joint Commissioner, Mumbai Police and the Head of Crime Branch, wasn't as submissive as he appeared or led people to believe, which Rita had only discovered after dealing with him in the previous case. He let people around him believe they were in-charge, but there was no mistaking him for a teddy bear. He delegated authority to his immediate subordinates but that did not mean he relinquished his responsibility. Gentle and balding, he could easily play Hergé's Professor Calculus in the next Tintin film. The only apparent difference was that Joshi was a lot taller than his caricatured twin.

'So, how's DCP Ferreira doing?' he started nonchalantly, getting up from behind his desk and walking up to Rita to shake her hand after she was done with her saluting. 'At ease, Rita.' He had always alternated between calling her Rita or DCP Ferreira depending on what he fancied that moment.

'I'm good, sir, thanks. How are you?'

'We're all fine. Though we missed you. Honestly.'

Missed me? Really? Or was it the cold case that made you miss me?

'It's good to have you back, and not working on anything or else. Commissioner Saxena had asked me for a favour and would have even issued a diktat for you if you had been involved in anything else at the moment.'

'What case is it, sir?'

'Though Commissioner Saxena would have liked to brief you personally, but he isn't in today so, unfortunately, you'll have to listen to my mundane voice.' Joshi attempted humour, at times. 'He's keen that you get involved in an international investigation. There was a larceny-cum-homicide in Brussels a few months back, and the investigators there believe the perpetrator is in India. In Mumbai.'

'Why me?'

'You are our best detective, India's best detective, and it's only right that you should be the one taking up this special challenge.'

So, if I fail it's me; if I succeed you're the sponsor? Clever, Sexy. Great move.

'Do you see any issue, any problems with the case?'

'Do I have a problem? Not at all sir. It's an honour that Commissioner Saxena and you have confidence in me to take up a challenging assignment.'

'But …?'

'But what, sir?'

'No, I could subtly foresee a "but" coming from the tonality, even though you have verbally accepted the offer. So tell me, what bothers you about the case?'

'Murder investigation – you know this more than I do, sir – is like snow on a steep slope of time. Even if you've lost forty-eight hours, all you find is nothing, and you just mentioned that the murder happened a few months ago?'

'A little over three months ago to be precise, but that ism is for amateurs. You see, Rita, I like you because you remind me of a younger me, taking up new challenges. I can see we're cut from the same fabric, as they say.'

Rita swallowed hard, and nodded. Was she being set up for disaster? But, why would *Sexy* – that was what Commissioner Sanjay Saxena was referred to in absentia, not derisively, just for fun: *Sexy* – or Joshi do that? It wasn't that she in any way threatened them. On the contrary, in the months ensuing the apprehending of the infamous serial killer, *Sexy* had been her foremost patron. He supported her on almost everything. Why would he, then, push her towards failure now? And why would Joshi second that.

'It's a significant case, if you solicit my advice. It bestows you exposure to an international case – many of us here never got the opportunity – and though this is no democracy that offers candidates to accept or decline cases, for you if you want to relinquish … because of your recent recovery, trust me it shall not be taken as insubordination.' Joshi's tone wasn't didactic like a supervisor's; it wasn't even cautionary, it was advisory.

'It's just that I wasn't expecting a significant case so soon after a break. Of course, I'll take it.'

'That's my bo … girl.'

As a woman in what has, around the world, always been a man's job, Rita was accustomed to being referred to as a boy/man. Joshi had, at least, graciously corrected himself.

'When do I start?'

'Monday.'

Rita hadn't cared about the days during her long break; it took her a moment to think what day it was. It was Friday.

'You mean …'

'Yes, this coming Monday. Some detective is coming over from Brussels to brief us, and I want you to be present from the start.'

'Yes sir.' Rita hunched up to move.

'Are you in a rush?'

'No sir, I thought this was it. I'm sorry.' She parked her arse back in the chair.

'Your usual team, Vikram and Jatin, will report to you. At this stage we are not sure who else will be required but we'll get more team members as and when needed. You report to Mr Saxena directly. I'll be here if you require any help with the bureaucracy, and I'll instruct the uniformed police to provide all back-up and assistance. Commissioner Saxena and I have no hesitation that you'll be successful again, DCP Ferreira.'

'Thank you for your confidence, sir. But, as they say, you've got to roll the dice to see the results.'

'I know you can roll the dice better than most. Any questions?'

'None whatsoever sir, thank you.'

'All the best, Rita. I'm not in office tomorrow, but feel free to call me on my mobile if you have any questions. Commissioner Saxena had to take a day off today for something important, but he'll be back in office next week.'

Sexy taking a day off meant he was booked on the golf course. *Sexy* on golf course meant he was playing with someone who fitted the *who's-who* list. He was a suave politician in uniform, a scratch golfer. Rita had no doubt he would brag on lending one of his protégé to an international case, as no one else had the talent. To use a word from his own advanced lexicon, he would be vainglorious at its sparkling best.

When Rita returned to her office, one of her man Fridays was seated on the visitor's side of her desk. Senior Inspector Vikram Patil, in his mid-thirties, was Rita's next in command. He had more experience in the police but was lower-ranked because he was a state police cadre. Taking Rita's position, when she moved or got promoted, was his aspiration, and with the mettle he had shown in the last few years, it wouldn't be a wrong or unreasonable replacement. Though not as sensuous, he was fit, six-foot-one, muscular and agile.

'Welcome back, ma'am.' Vikram stood up. Saluted.

'Thanks, Vikram. How have you been?'

'I'm fine, ma'am. Good to have you back.'

'So what are you currently working on?'

'Nothing consequential, just paperwork on my previous case and some court hearings.'

'Good. Whatever it is that you need to complete, please finish that or hand it over to someone. We have an important case. Where's Jatin?'

Jatin was her other go-to direct report. She had a brusque parting with him due to circumstances, but later, in retrospect, he had appreciated the reasons. He had called Rita while she was in Goa and insisted he still wanted to work for her and be in her team.

'He's on vacation, ma'am. He's back on Monday. What's this case that you know of already, and I have no inkling yet?'

'A homicide in Belgium. The murder happened a few months ago and they – the Belgian Police – have found evidence that makes them think that the perpetrator/s are in Mumbai, so they are here on Monday for a briefing. We'll take it from there.'

'Is that all?'

'Unfortunately, that's all I know at the moment.'

'OK. I'll get things sorted before Monday then, ma'am. And I'll send someone to clean and fill your coffee machine.'

'Is my caffeine withdrawal so apparent?' she retorted. 'Anyway, get the Operation Room ready please.'

The Operation Room was set up for any case that the crime squad handled. Over time, as the case progressed, it became a repository of all evidence and information and the assigned place for team meetings.

Before leaving the office, Rita signed for and examined a Smith and Wesson. It wasn't the one she had deposited before going on leave. She got a 2213 Compact. Small, not something that had a harsh recoil, but effective. Not brand new. Not a rusted one either. Picking up the gun wasn't challenging, but she knew she had to get to the firing range to try out the new gun. She could never trust a firearm she hadn't fired. No one in the police or armed forces did. You didn't want a surprise when you least expected. Rita made a note of calling up to book the practice range and go there as early as she could, possibly over the weekend.

THREE

The Belgian detective who came to Mumbai on Monday morning – Victor De Smet – was anything but the legendary Hercule Poirot, though he had the girth and the accentuated gait of the fabled character. Remove Poirot's moustache and add a head full of straight blond hair parted on the side and that was Victor. He was pleasant to look at and he spoke softly and carefully in his accented English. He met Rita and Vikram in the newly set up Ops Room. Jatin was still not in office; he had sent a message apologizing as his flight from Dubai had been delayed, therefore he would only be in after lunch. Handshakes, introductions, a bit of pleasantries exchanged, and the three got down to business.

Ron Jogani, Victor informed, was carrying diamonds of undisclosed value – certainly more than the receipt the police found in his hotel room – and got murdered. His corpse, cold and still unclaimed, lay in a Belgian morgue. Despite numerous efforts made through the Indian Embassy in Brussels, no one had come forward to collect it. Ron Jogani, apparently, didn't have any family: no parents, no siblings, no partner. His ex-wife had belligerently declined all requests; she didn't want anything to do with 'Ron' – whether dead or alive. The identification of his corpse hadn't been carried out by his kin, which is the standard legally accepted procedure around the world; the documents found in his hotel room had established his identity. The Belgian police had diligently investigated Leonard Aaron – the Antwerp merchant who had sold the diamonds that cost Jogani his life, and the driver who dropped Jogani at the hotel. Both had been cleared.

Jogani's autopsy report had little surprise unless one's curiosity extended to what beers and sandwiches he had savoured before he perished. Death was by a close-range shot. End of story.

Victor paused for the Indian detectives to digest all he had narrated. 'In the initial stages of the investigation we were certain someone on the inside – I mean the hotel staff – was involved, it had to be. There seemed no other way. I mean how else could someone circumvent all the security cameras and know about Jogani's booking in the hotel? The room numbers are normally allocated on the morning the guest is supposed to check-in. And the killer or killers knew the room number before Jogani arrived at the hotel to check in. They had access to his room key. They intercepted the telephone line to make the midnight call to Jogani like it came from the reception. But we found diddly-squat, and we checked out the entire hotel staff ... every single one of them was interviewed, investigated and cleared. We just don't know how it could have happened.' Victor raised both his hands animatedly in despair.

Rita waited till he stopped. 'Somehow the crime scene does not add up to a premeditated killing. Of course, the perpetrator or perpetrators knew about the diamonds – why else would someone break into a hotel room of all places? – but cold-blooded murder is an altogether different crime. Most human beings do not plan to kill another unless there is an agenda.'

'Then why murder Jogani?'

Rita had anticipated the question.

'At the end of the runway the pilot only has one choice – unless of course, he wants to commit suicide and take all passengers down too – and that option is to go airborne. *If* Jogani had seen the killers or intercepted them, they had no option but to off Jogani.'

'Interesting way to put it,' Victor said.

'But it's still a theory and it's still one big *if*…' Rita surmised. 'But then, all investigations have to begin with a theory. In time, the theory could be proved correct. Then again maybe the evidence could cite that the direction was totally wrong. But we need to start somewhere.'

Victor nodded to the rationale.

'So, Mr De Smet …'

'I think we should let go of the formalities. Call me Victor.'

'Likewise Victor.'

'So, how, after over three months and change, did the Belgian police determine that Jogani's killer could be in India?'

'Very good question. In fact, I was expecting it sooner. We got video footage from the hotel. You see, whoever masterminded this had planned for everything. They froze almost all hotel cameras connected to the main control room and ran a film that was basically from the night before. When we juxtaposed the two footage, they were identical …'

'Then how did you get this footage?' Vikram sounded interested.

'As I said, *almost all*, there was a concealed camera in the elevator that wasn't connected to the control room. In fact, even the hotel personnel didn't know about it. But the hotel chain's central office that had implanted it released it to us. We've been analysing the same for weeks now. I'm carrying a copy, should we play the footage?' Victor took out a CD from his bag and handed it over to Vikram who put it into the computer and tilted the screen a bit so all three could see.

A camouflaged reminiscence of George Eastman's invention, albeit in moving frames, had done the trick in the elevator. The surveillance camera was obviously placed high and most of the shots were a bit blurry, grainy. The time count on the camera proved the pictures were in the time frame that the Belgian police had ascertained as the time of the murder. The Belgian police had done a professional job of cleaning it up, zooming and enlarging to make one perfect 6 × 8 candid-shot from one of the frames.

However, if you showed the picture to a hundred people, only fifty *might* have agreed that the guy was an Indian.

Rita and Vikram looked at the picture.

A strikingly handsome man from what Rita could see.

Photograph would help in identification. But you've got to find the person first to identify him. Who was it? Rita's mind was already churning.

'Our intelligence – and our government's sincere apologies that we didn't follow protocol and carried out investigation without proper authorizations from the Indian government initially – has not been able to track down the individual, and hence we need your help. Our experts estimate the person in these photographs to be male, height 6'2 or 6'3", about a 100 kilograms, a head full of straight dark hair – the pictures are too grainy to discern the exact hair colour but who knows if he wasn't wearing a wig?'

'And he carried a Blackberry.'

'I must compliment you on your sharp eyes, Rita. Yes, that *is* a Blackberry he has in his hand.'

'Thanks, Victor. However, looking at this footage alone, there is no certainty this man is an Indian. I mean … he could be anyone from Southern Europe, Northern Africa or even from the Middle East.'

Recognition across races is known to be pretty appalling. Ask an Indian witness about a Caucasian or an African or a South-East Asian and they'll be at a loss. Wouldn't it be the same for a Caucasian in identifying an Indian? Didn't Ash Mattel tell her that every Indian girl looked like Shilpa Shetty to the Brits after she had won some *Celebrity Big Brother* in the UK?

'You have a point there, Rita but after we got this footage, the hotel front-desk personnel confirmed they had seen the guy, spoken to him and he was positively identified as an Indian. After all, they had checked him in. He couldn't have eluded that. He checked-in with the name …' Victor scrambled through the pages … 'Sishir Singh.' He passed on the papers to Rita.

Rita looked at them for a few minutes, and then passed them to Vikram.

Vikram looked at the papers. 'I can appreciate why you're here now.'

'I'm glad you both agree with me. Now, how do we find this guy?'

'Hold on a minute. Even if we concur that he is of Indian origin, that is no harbinger that the guy lives in India.'

'Well, the airport authorities gave us their surveillance tapes too. Let's look at them first.'

The guy who could possibly be Sishir Singh was on camera for a fraction of a second and then, poof, vanished. No other surveillance camera anywhere at the airport picked him up again. In the only spotting, the guy was of same height and body proportion as Sishir Singh, and hence the possibility. The guy wore a baseball cap with the shade guardedly pulled down till it almost covered his nose. The airport cameras worked 360 degrees. They rotated such that each one covered the same spot every fifteen seconds. There was only a brief time when one camera arrested Sishir Singh when he went to the check-in desk. It was evident that the guy knew the location of airport cameras too. You had to know the camera locations and their movements in entirety before you could outfox it. Sishir Singh certainly knew the CCTV blind spots. There was no other way. He should be given full marks for the research.

'The image was dark and hazy, as you can imagine, but our experts, after enhancing and enlarging, have compared and confirmed with statistical confidence that the image was of the same person that was in the elevator,' Victor began after the short video ended. 'Moreover, our airport authorities confirmed that a guy named Sishir Singh flew from Brussels to Mumbai on the morning after the murder. That was the same flight Mr Jogani was booked on. Perhaps, if he had failed to get the diamonds at the hotel he had planned to take them someplace else. Who knows?'

'OK, that's too much of a coincidence to accept. That settles it, if Sishir Singh flew to Mumbai ...'

'They hadn't thought the plan through. How do you steal diamonds from the merchants and sell them back to them in India?' Vikram questioned.

Rita could explain it but she let Victor explicate.

'In our experience, art, antiques, collectibles or merchandise, like precious stones over a certain value, are stolen only after they are sold. The buyer is already there. The diamonds would have changed hands before our police got Mr Jogani's body bagged and tagged and got it out of the hotel. The buyer, of course, hadn't ordered blood diamonds, but who would have known about the murder when the deal was sealed?'

The hypothesis made sense.

'And in any event, selling the diamonds – I guess that worry would pale before the reward,' Rita explained more logically. 'And I know it's only an assumption but in my opinion, it's a calculated hypothesis.'

'It's more than a hypothesis actually, as one of the diamonds stolen from that heist turned up in Antwerp again, and the origin of that stone was given as Mumbai. So, some of them have already changed hands once, at least.'

'And is there no way to track the last sale and then work on the chain backwards to its origin in Mumbai?' Vikram asked.

'No.' Victor wagged his head. 'Diamond trade is more guarded than you imagine; almost the same secrecy is awarded to it as to drugs trade for some reason. Nevertheless, that aside, we did try but got nowhere. The search was futile.'

'How do you want us to proceed?' Rita asked.

'As I mentioned before, first of all we need to contact Mr Jogani's office, house, friends, and track down Sishir Singh before we can even begin. As the murder happened in a hotel, a public place, you can well imagine we have picked up more fingerprints – latent, impressed and patent – than in any other case that I've been involved in. We've ruled out all the hotel staff, and whoever we had on the file, but unless we find a match, all that remains is unusable.'

Victor was correct. Finding prints in a hotel room were always a bitch, considering the number of people who'd have lived in the room before and touched the articles, equipment, walls, fittings and whatnot. And then, be it prints, hair, blood, skin residue, evidence per se was impotent. It had little value till it could be found. Once found – like Victor's team had – it should have been recovered from the crime scene and examined to establish its legitimacy, which Rita couldn't imagine could be the case in a hotel room. Nevertheless, even if they were, there should be something or someone that it could be compared to. Only then it could give any direction to the investigators. Otherwise, a drop of blood is only a drop of blood. Nonetheless, Rita was convinced the intruder – Sishir Singh or whoever – wouldn't have left some such evidence behind that could lead it back to him. The whole incident was indeed a well-planned operation. And whoever masterminded it had enough IQ to recognize that was the first thing the police would look for: murder or burglary.

'Witnesses? Not one,' Victor concluded.

'If Sishir Singh is in Mumbai, we will find him – it won't be easy, but it can't be impossible either.'

Reasonable assurance without a promise but what other surety could Rita offer at this stage?

'Thank you for the confidence exhibited. What do you need from us?'

'Could we have a copy of this surveillance-camera footage and the pictures please?' Vikram asked.

Since Rita had known Vikram he had been a meticulous officer who was conscientious and focussed. He sounded like he was already imbibed into the case.

'Of course … we made a copy of everything, you can keep them.' Victor opened his case again and took out a red-coloured box file – in the manner he lifted the heavy file Rita could assess that it weighed a ton – and placed it on the table. Neither Rita nor Vikram rushed for it. It lay between them like an orphan. What was the rush? The file would be with them now and they could sink their fangs into it at their earliest convenience. 'I'm cognisant that you will have questions when you read the file,'

Victor carried on, '… and watch the footages and picture a few times, so if you want to ask or discuss anything, I'm in Mumbai till Thursday, then I need to return. However, I'll be contactable twenty-four by seven on phone and email should you need me.'

With a few other sundry details and a plan to meet a day after, giving the Indian contingent ample time to swallow the details and work on a blueprint, the briefing finished around 2 p.m. A police driver from the pool had been allocated to Victor for his stay in Mumbai and he left for the hotel. He had only flown the night before, ergo he was well past his bedtime according to his body clock.

Vikram sat opposite on the visitors' seat in Rita's office when Jatin came in. Inspector Jatin Singh had moved into Rita's team only since the last case that had brought the three of them together. He was just proving to be a prized asset when the misfortune of getting involved with some wrong people almost destroyed his career. But he was back. Rita appreciated his high levels of energy and his sharp intellect; he was much younger than Vikram and herself though. The fact that he succumbed to something stupid once did not alter Rita's attitude towards him. Hadn't they all been taken for a ride by the crafty murderer in the infamous *Bhendi Bazaar* case? Why, then, isolate poor Jatin for his recklessness? He had, after all, been her other man Friday. Taller than Rita, but shorter than Vikram, Jatin was five-feet-eleven, and he was always well dressed. In her mind, Rita thought of him as eye candy: innocuous pleasures of life.

He seemed irked. 'I'm very sorry, ma'am. The flight got delayed …' he started.

'It's OK, Jatin. As per usual protocol we've allocated the most horrible tasks to the absent member.'

'Welcome back, ma'am.'

'Thanks. You too. How was the vacation?'

'Fantastic.'

'Vikram will brief you on the case. And then we have this huge file to go through. I think we should get copies made for all of us, as we can't lose any more time reading it sequentially.'

Vikram nodded, and in his usual manner jotted it down. He wrote down everything that Rita said. Sometimes she wondered if Vikram was as meticulous at home as he was here. Did he note down every task his wife asked him to carry out too?

'Is there anything you want to discuss about the case?' She got up to indicate the meeting was over. 'Please give the original file back to me after you make the copies. I'll try to read the case file tonight. And we should come in and discuss our summaries and strategy tomorrow afternoon. Depending on the task at hand, I'll see how many people we need in the team to manage this investigation. Have a good evening, you two.'

As she walked out and waited for the lift she observed that the phones rang more than they did before she went on medical leave or so it seemed. Maybe it was simple mathematics: there had been some redundancies in her absence and perhaps there weren't enough people to attend all the calls. She smiled at the irony. Not enough people to man phones in a police headquarter and here they were looking at a case that didn't even happen in their jurisdiction. *Welcome to shit extraordinaire*, she murmured.

She had messaged the driver and he brought the car around. A constable had lugged the heavy file for her and was putting it in the boot as she stood there mulling over the day.

Sishir Singh. Not a common name.

FOUR

It had been a long day. More than the case – though the case, Rita could tell, would turn out to be a real pig very soon – the routine of being in office for long hours once again had drained her. Chugalugging a generous sip of Jim Beam from the bottle, she went for a shower.

As she changed after the shower, images of the blurry film footage that Victor had shown ran through her mind. She had an eidetic memory. Nothing escaped her mind. Image. Sound. Names. Scent. She was born to be a detective. Something bothered her. Had she missed anything that could provide a clue to the person in the elevator? Sishir Singh was definitely an alias. One didn't need a Sherlock to tell her that. But that was logic, not evidence. No one would have given their real name at the hotel where they were about to steal diamonds. Which also meant that the perpetrator had access to fake documents. Not an impossibility either.

Catching a criminal is like one side playing the game with ever-changing rules. The police have to adhere to the guidelines, the criminal can change course any time: name, identity, MO …

Jim was beginning to take the weariness of the long day away. It was only seven and the day was still bright. She thought of going out for a bite, but dropped the idea. She didn't know anyone close by to go out for dinner with, and sitting in a restaurant alone was not something she was in the mood for.

She knew Jim, her best friend, was always there for her but, she also understood that some more intimate kisses from the bottle and he could easily become her worst enemy. She had seen her own dad – an alcoholic, though he never admitted it. Who does? – kissing the enemy to death. History, it is often quoted, had a penchant of repeating itself by calling itself genetic and Rita knew when to stop. Good night, Jim. She had three drinks and went into the kitchen to raid the refrigerator.

She thought about reading some material that Victor had given, but she was exhausted and it was the weekend.

Tomorrow, she promised herself and switched off the lights.

Birds sang. Sun rose. Leaves were still green. Ground was wet from the overnight showers. Rita savoured the breakfast of eggs, toast and baked beans, when her mobile rang. She finished the large morsel in her mouth as the caller ID showed up: Commissioner Saxena. She looked up at the clock: 6:30. Wow, impressive, *Sexy*!

'Good morning, sir.'

'A very good morning to you too, DCP Ferreira. I was wondering if you had some time to update me on the Belgian case.'

There was hardly any update. All they had had was the briefing from Victor less than twenty-four hours ago.

'We've just got the files now, sir. Give us a day or two, please.'

'No worries. When you're in office, please come by to see me.'

The line was dead before Rita could respond.

No one was in office when she arrived at work; it was still only 7:30. Coffee in hand, she settled in her office and took out the video-footage DVD and put it in the computer.

After so thoroughly planning the operation, how had the murderer missed this lone camera in the elevator car?

Next she slid the red box file towards her. It was indeed bulky. But unlike body weight, in a murder investigation it was better to have more, than not enough. As always, Rita's next step was to discern what fat to cut when she didn't know what could be rewarding and what was unavailing. But because there weren't enough number of hours in the day ever, every detective had to make a choice based on the preponderance or imbalance of evidence. Oh yes, of course everything could go wrong with that choice. She sifted through the papers for over an hour. Reports. Memos. Tips. Witnesses consulted and cross-referenced; alibis corroborated by friends, associates and acquaintances. Most of the documents were what Victor had narrated, the documents were detailed, analysed and evaluated. Everything hinted it was a big case for Belgium where homicide rates were low and they took them seriously.

Subsequently, she focussed on photographs and maps of the crime scene. Jogani lay in a pool of congealed blood. The hotel personnel only became aware of the murder when Jogani didn't respond to the alarm he had requested for early morning to catch the flight to Mumbai that he was booked on. The hotel employees obviously got worried when the cabbie arrived and Jogani had neither responded to the alarm nor come down to settle his bill. They called the police.

The night porter, who had attended to Jogani when he had come down for a fake call from the reception, had given his account to police. He explained to the police that Jogani appeared stressed and that he had raced back once he found out that no one from the reception had actually called him down.

That was unquestionably a ploy to get the quarry out of his room.

Adding up his evidence and the postmortem report, the Belgian police had narrowed down the time window of death. Then the time stamp on the concealed camera in the elevator confirmed the *lone* murderer leaving.

The time of death was thus further contracted down to a precise period between those fifteen and twenty minutes. There was nothing in crime-scene photos that gave anything. The police had summed up that the bag was missing. Two things fascinated Rita in the documents. One that the lock on the entrance door to Jogani's hotel room had been tampered with, and second – even more bizarre – the safe in Jogani's room had been replaced with another one. The police had discovered the original safe from the adjacent room, which was one of the three rooms booked by Mr Sishir Singh. Victor had forgotten to mention that Sishir had booked three rooms, but no one in the hotel had seen any other guests but him the whole time.

How was that possible? Did they manage to give a slip to the receptionist? Surely, they should have been caught on the solitary camera in the elevator at some point or did they never use the elevators at all?

The floor plan of the hotel strongly suggested that whoever was along with Sishir Singh in accomplishing the caper had used the fire escape, the stairs that were at the opposite end of the lifts and they had – for health and safety reasons – an unlocked exit directly leading to the street.

Even transcripts of the interviews carried out by Belgian Police had been included in the box file, which Rita decided to delve into later. She wanted to mull over the info she had consumed so far. Bite-sized processing.

Sadly, in an investigation, she knew, questions and answers did not come in a sequence. Sometimes you got some answers first that you had no use of. Later came in the questions that bridged the gap. It was like putting the scrabble tiles in the box again and juggling them. You never knew when the winning word would pop out. You had to keep looking at all that you've found before, whenever you got some new material. Put together it might make sense. Conscious of all that, she made mental notes as she processed the gen she captured from the file. Jogani must certainly have friends and business associates in Mumbai. And what about his home, his company, his employees? Did he operate alone? Shouldn't someone in Mumbai be the first point of contact? Perhaps someone knew Sishir Singh or someone who looked like the guy who allegedly called himself by that name. That the burglary was the principal plan and unfortunately culminated in murder was one theory – most palpable one too, possibly – but there could be numerous other motives for murder. Finding diamonds in the room might have been like winning a lottery without buying the ticket, though it didn't appear such: the murder might have been an improvized plan, the break-in was indeed thought-out. Well thought-out. Eliminating Jogani with a gun didn't require changing the safe in the room or tampering the lock of the hotel room; it could have been accomplished by whacking Jogani in the street.

But she was at a major disadvantage, she realized. Most homicide investigations started with a dead body. Here they had a picture of one. She looked at the photographs of Ron Jogani's stiff again.

Rita concluded that someone had followed Jogani to the hotel. It was mere gut feel: nothing to support it, nothing to dismiss. How else would someone have known about the diamonds, the precise hotel room number and the call that was made to Jogani in the middle of the night to get him out of the room? But from where – from somewhere local in Brussels, from Antwerp or did someone trail him all the way from India?

And how had Ron Jogani – carrying diamonds worth millions – missed being shadowed? Wouldn't he have taken due care not to divulge his plan? Maybe someone knew the itinerary. And how could someone know that? Every case, in Rita's experience, was a series of endless conundrums. Sometimes, all one needed was to untangle one element and, like the weakest link in the chain, the rest of the mystery laid bare. Not always, but there was always a good probability.

She was convinced someone evidently knew Jogani's itinerary. The question was: who? And how?

Despite being aware that Sishir Singh was, in all probability, his *nom de guerre*, Rita logged into the central information database to look for Sishir Singh. Dozens of them in Mumbai but none – not a single one – had any conviction or police cases filed against them. They would have to loan this one out to snitches to snoop around. There existed – and always would remain – an ironic symbiosis between the police and criminals. Without criminals there would be no need for the police and without police the criminals wouldn't be in any kind of check. The mutualism didn't end there. Far from it. More often than not, snitches were petty criminals at one time if not currently. Having been caught out or being on the police radar after a few warnings, some snitched for favours, some snitched to save their own skin, some others snitched for vendetta or jealously: to let police handle whom they weren't equipped to button down themselves. She went over to the scanner-cum-printer and took a few printouts of the candid-shot of the alleged Mr Sishir Singh.

Picking up her Blackberry, she walked around the desk to close the office door and called Senior Inspector Rajesh Nene. She knew she would have to speak to her superiors to engage Nene full time, but she didn't bother waiting for the approvals at this moment.

Rajesh Nene sounded happy to hear from her.

It was a quick conversation and Nene simply wanted a couple of hours before he came in with a list of the best snitches for the task at hand.

When Rita put the phone down, she was confident Nene would be in her office before the two hours ran out.

The case was all menacing and threatening her now. But threat can work two ways: it could either shut you down due to fear or it could concrete your resolve. Till only a few days ago when she had been asked to report at Mumbai, Rita had anticipated she'd need to make a few enquiries – it being a cold case of a homicide in a foreign land – but as she read the file and got grips with the whole incident, the case had begun to get under her skin. She recognized she wasn't brought back in to nidificate and lay eggs; she was entrusted with a case that carried national pride. Bring it on, *Sexy*. She was ready.

Vikram arrived before Jatin. He had bloodshot eyes that indicated to Rita that the man had been up all night and read each leaf in the copy he had made of Victor's colossal file. She could have asked him to write an exam and he would have passed. There was no question in Rita's mind that part of her success was due to the dedicated and loyal team she had.

'I am confident you've read the file cover to cover,' Rita mused.

'You're correct, ma'am.'

'I have a meeting with Mr Sanjay Saxena first thing this morning. He wants an update.'

'Already?' Vikram seemed as surprised as she was when *Sexy* had asked for it.

She just rolled her eyes. 'He's the boss.'

'Anything you need from me for the meeting?'

'No, I guess it will only be a preliminary one with him to outline what we know so far and what chances we have in cracking an old case like this before he goes ahead and communicates to the powers that be.'

'What time is the meeting?'

'As soon as he's in.'

'He's in. I saw his car when I came in.'

'OK, here I go.' She got up and walked out from behind her desk, out of her office and towards the elevator.

Rita was a Goan, Portuguese ancestry, born a Catholic, but she was a deist – she believed that God or the higher power did not intervene with the functioning of laws of nature. He wasn't there to get you the next promotion or invoke rainfalls or stop fires or accidents or murders or burglaries or to help catch the perpetrator or solve office politics or save from *Sexy*'s wrath or questions. That wasn't *his* role. She looked at her watch. It was nine when she walked into *Sexy*'s opulent office and offered a proper salute.

Sanjay Saxena, the Commissioner of Mumbai Police, of course, had asked her to see him this morning. *Sexy*, customarily, didn't ask for people to do something because he didn't need to; he just demanded what he wanted. He had been a right arse when Rita had taken up the case of Mumbai's first serial killer, and showed no signs of warming up to a female IPS officer up until it was she who cracked the tangled case. Since then, despite Rita's attempts to include her line manager, *Sexy* repeatedly disregarded the chain of command and involved her directly in cases that weren't even remotely connected to her. And he had, once again, asked her to see him without Joshi, her immediate supervisor.

Sexy, like his two generations of forefathers, had been born with the complete set of silver crockery in his mouth. Educated at the prestigious Doon School, his English teacher had made him absorb the entire word list. Ergo, his communication was always peppered with some of the biggest words there were in the dictionary; adjectives and adverbs he hurled at his subjects to forever stretch their vocabularies.

'Hello, DCP Ferreira, and welcome back.' *Sexy* didn't make any attempt to stand; he was in mufti; cerulean linen jacket and blue chinos, which were darker blue than the jacket. White shirt. No tie, of course. Through the gap under his snooker table-sized desk Rita saw that he wore tanned moccasins and no socks. He always looked like a stylish villain from Hollywood's bygone black-and-white era.

'Good morning, sir,' Rita barely uttered, not knowing if she should be cheerful or not, considering she wasn't prepared to update him on the case at hand.

'DCP Rita Ferreira, you are the foremost detective in the country today.'

Where was this headed?

'Please take a seat.'

'Thank you, sir.'

'DCP Ferreira, I'm sure you are already aware that this case has national pride attached to it, and hence I specifically wanted you to take it up.'

As Rita had anticipated, it was no more than a customary pep talk.

'Thank your for the confidence shown in me, sir.'

'Is your consultation over?'

Sexy was obviously referring to the therapy for trauma that Rita had to undergo after the ugly shoot-out. The therapist had checked if the brain was still in its usual place. However, the question, and hence the episodic memory, reminded Rita of it again.

'Yes sir, I got the green light.'

'Good, I forgot to ask that before I assigned you to this high-pressure case.'

'I hope I don't fail you.'

'Life is no more than a profit and loss statement: and profits and losses are always "as on" a date, a point in time, since the actual profit or loss can only be determined when the enterprise closes. So is with life. So you're a winner till you actually lose.'

'What happens if you lose ...?'

'In the end?'

'Yes.'

'Why in the world do you care once the light goes out? You're gone, the game is over.'

Philosophical, Sexy, very philosophical!

'Anything else, before I go?'

'I appreciate it is a Sisyphean task, and as I alluded to Mr Joshi before you were reinstated into the department, I'm convinced that you, and only you, can disentangle this Gordian knot and bring the perpetrator to justice. On this case you report directly to me, so you don't need to supplicate permission from ACP Joshi on anything. I'll be here if you require any succour with the bureaucracy. Should you require assistance from any of the uniformed forces across the country and if they don't comply, just call me and I'll have them imbeciles on the run within minutes.'

Territorial skirmishes just wilted and died in *Sexy*'s presence. No one wanted to appear petty or dared go against him.

'Thank you, sir,' she said, noting the unusual words used in the discourse.

As she walked to her office, she thought about the meeting. *Sexy* had, in as many words, made it amply clear that Joshi was out of the equation here. She made a note to let Joshi know. She might have to work with him again in the long run and she knew how the police machinery worked. Joshi was a fine and reasonable man, she was sure he'd understand and support her.

And for all the frippery, the flowery language, and the initial resentment he had shown towards her, even *Sexy* wasn't a bad guy, she realized. If nothing else, *Sexy* was known to be overzealously protective of people who were loyal to him. Plus, she now knew it was a Sisyphean task and, also, there was something called a Gordian knot, which wasn't in everyone's remit to disentangle.

Conscious that nothing consequential had been done on the case in the past twenty-four hours, Rita found the number and called Victor. He was at a meeting over tea at the Belgian Embassy.

Rita apologized for the delay, but he wasn't irked. If the Belgian Police hadn't caught the murderer in over three months, he hadn't expected an overnight arrest. He was polite. Rita updated him that a taskforce had been put in place with her as the lead, and that the Indian Police was taking the case seriously.

Victor, with regret in his voice, told Rita that he had to return to Brussels earlier than scheduled, due to some crisis, but he shall be available twenty-four/seven, as he had promised.

'We'll be in touch soon, Victor. Have a safe flight.'

FIVE

Honey Singh. Yes, Honey was his name and he was a six-feet-three hunk of a male and as good-looking as they come: *strikingly handsome*. Long straight black hair – a bit of salt had prematurely commenced appearing – swept back or tied up in a small ponytail, muscled body of an athlete that he was when he was at college. A *mona-Sikh*, for which his mother never forgave him; an *apostate* is what she called him – traitor to the faith for getting his turban cut. But she loved him. Loved him more than most mothers love their thirty-one-year-old sons and a son who revered his mother – a mama's boy totally – he lived with her. Still apparently single, he was dating an upcoming model that his mother wasn't acquainted with though his friends and co-workers were aware of his clandestine relationship and the confidentiality they were expected to maintain when dealing with Mrs Lucky Singh. Occasionally, he arranged surreptitious sleepovers or weekend getaways with his guy-friends – at least that is what Mrs Lucky Singh was told. She was a virago in a loving sort of way, an archetypal doting Punjabi mother of a single fatherless child. The concern was genuine, overwhelming, even suffocating at times. Honey's dad was an industrialist who passed away when he was four, and the business partners – mainly distant cousins – cunningly cut off Mrs Lucky Singh and her son from the business and the money. From a lavish bungalow in Ludhiana, the duo managed to cash in on Honey's dad's life insurance and bought a two-bedroom apartment in Andheri East, which they currently resided in. The interiors were a lingering vestige of old money, all but gone now. Honey had started working a few years back and modest prosperity had gradually started finding its way back into the household. His mother wasn't impressed with him starting a computer-repair store; she had expected him to work for some multinational corporation after his degree in electronic engineering, and not become a computer mechanic, as she told everyone.

'You're a computer engineer, Honey. Why do you want to repair godforsaken broken computers?'

'I want to be my own boss, and I love being my own boss, an entrepreneur like Dad.'

'You are no longer a kid ...'

In her view, her once-shining son had turned out to be anything but.

But she still loved him.

It was on the day he completed graduation, Honey Singh, much to the chagrin of his doting mother, had got his tresses cut.

In every locality, there resided an *auntie* who kids were scared of and loved at the same time; scared because they knew they dare not mess with her and loved her because she was the only person who could save them from their mother's wrath when they had fucked up. Mrs Lucky Singh was that auntie and Titu

– the neighbourhood barber who cut Honey's hair – had, albeit unintentionally, messed with her son. The poor chap owned a small shop outside Takshila, the apartment complex Honey Singh resided in, and had no inkling that he'd have to deal with Mrs Lucky Singh. After facing her virulent rage – yes, he was slapped on the face, inside his own shop with other customers as witnesses – he decided to give up his tonsorial career. He was so embarrassed and so much in shock that he disappeared from the locality to set up a shop elsewhere.

What Honey Singh never disclosed to Mrs Lucky Singh was instead of opening another barbershop, Titu was a full-time employee in his small and growing business.

Honey's office was in Bandra Kurla Complex for obvious reasons: with rapid expansion in the past decade, the corporate houses needed someone to support the day-to-day running of their computers, mainframes, networks, and it was much more economical to outsource maintenance to smaller firms than run their own army of in-house engineers. Honey Singh was charming enough to procure annual maintenance contracts, and he delivered the results. Once he got his foot in a company, the competition had little chance when the contract was up for renewal. His back office comprised six cubicles, three rooms – the largest one being en suite with living arrangement where he occasionally slept and on other occasions romped with his model girlfriend Kitty Varghese. It was housed in the top floors of just another one of the ubiquitous glass buildings, as there wasn't any requirement to spend money on premium office space on the ground floor: it wasn't any retail operations and the clients never visited him. He had a twelve-member team that was perpetually on the move for on-site firefighting at client locations. Something virtually broke every day at some office. The staff came in only when they required expensive parts, salaries or something that needed expert advice, help or guidance of their guru. The only other person who attended the office daily – he actually lived in the third room on the premises – was Titu, the barber turned confidante. He was *Mister* office boy, deliveryman, telephone operator, receptionist, all rolled in one. And, he was loyal to Honey Singh like a mastiff.

Preternaturally brilliant at computer programming, Honey remained locked in his office for most of the day. He told everyone he was currently working on some accounting-software package which if he succeeded in programming, he'd patent it and sell it for millions around the world. Initially, everyone believed him, but as weeks, and then months passed, everyone – his clients, even some employees – thought he was just delusional. Only two people believed in him: Kitty and Titu.

With his good breeding and reasonable bread-earning skills, Honey Singh's life was sweet and fun, and looked promising. Even without the new programme that he was working on, current business showed potential, and he was still only twenty-nine.

But there was a glitch.

The strikingly handsome man caught on the camera in the elevator of Crowne Plaza hotel in Brussels, the night Ron Jogani got murdered, had an uncanny resemblance to Honey Singh.

SIX

The team sat around the round table in the Operations Room after lunch. Jatin had, once again, been given charge of the room, and he had, yet again, been spectacular in covering all the minutiae he could dig out from Victor's file. The local investigation file being pulled together on Ron Jogani's murder was also two-inch thick by now. The walls were plastered with scene-of-crime photographs, pictures of Ron Jogani, list of his close associates, details of his ex-wife – the one who had refused to have anything to do with him or his corpse – blueprint of the hotel Jogani was murdered in and maps of streets surrounding the Crowne Plaza hotel. Rita acknowledged that Jatin must have laboured throughout the day to come up with all the important info. It was good to note that just one anserine incident hadn't damped his investigative spirit.

Rita, Vikram and Jatin sat reading the reports again, sipping coffees when Nene arrived.

Senior Inspector Rajesh Nene: a local from Mumbai, Nene was the most experienced Inspector in the crime branch. He was nearing fifty now, but he refused to lose his youthfulness or agility. He had forgone all promotions and stayed in Mumbai – family obligations – and hence knew all the dugouts, and the farragoes of crime and criminals. A full, curly, raven-dyed mane – not a strand of grey – sat on top of his five-feet-eleven frame that was terminally unbowed. Like some other cynics in Mumbai Police, even he wasn't pleased when DCP Rita Ferreira had taken charge of the crime squad, but had put his ego on the shelf, and now, having worked with her, he too was a loyalist.

It was time to get to work.

Rita narrated briefly about her meeting with *Sexy*, emphasizing how important the case was and spent the best part of an hour briefing the three.

'Don't risk writing off the intelligence of the perpetrators. They're clever, they're smart, and they think on their feet. They have the ability to optimize their plans as they go along if the circumstances change. Remember they were there only to steal the diamonds but improvized and ended up killing the subject because the situation demanded it. This is a homicide investigation and everything is important until proven otherwise. Capture everything, every minute detail and run it by your colleagues before you discard it. If you need anything – back up, vehicle, technical support, or just cooperation with other departments – you can call me anytime twenty-four/seven.'

Nods.

So much for pep talk, it was time to assign responsibilities.

'Here's my plan: we look into Jogani. We begin with his residence and the office – what happened to the entire domestic and business set-ups when he didn't return? I want to know everything about Ron Jogani: age, place of birth, school, colleges, friends, medical history, financial status, bank accounts, properties, anything and everything. We need to comb through everything. At this stage, we simply don't know what wouldn't add up and we'll keep digging till we find something.'

'What about his ex-wife?'

'We need to check her background thoroughly too. Though everything indicates that she has nothing to do with Jogani, we need to clear her. Her mobile number is on the file as Belgian Police had contacted her, she shouldn't be difficult to track down.' Rita pointed towards the photograph of the alleged murderer on the wall. 'We need to find this guy – Sishir Singh, obviously not his real name, but we need to work with the informers. Someone has to know him.' She turned to Nene. 'Did you get names of some informers?'

'No dearth of them, ma'am, leave that to me. I know a lot of them, I'll ask around.' Nene was ready for action.

'Good. Let's divide the tasks then. We should split into two teams. Jatin, you come with me. Vikram, you partner with Nene – both of you take charge of the snitch network. We have to find Sishir Singh.' Rita knew from experience that neither of the two senior inspectors required any supervision.

'If he is in Mumbai, consider him found, ma'am.'

It was fortunate to have a loyal team, but it was even luckier to have a confident one. Rita thanked her stars.

The pairing seemed agreeable to all.

'We move to Jogani's house, you guys carry on to brief all those you think can help identify Sishir Singh. We keep in touch, and if there isn't any emergency we meet back in office tomorrow morning. Any questions?'

None.

'Watch your back, guys.'

Rita and Jatin came out of the office building. Rita asked her driver to go home. She told him not to switch off his mobile in case she needed him later though.

'Keys, ma'am?' Jatin requested, his hand stretched out to receive the car keys.

'I'll drive.'

Rita drove calmly. They turned left on Lokmanya Tilak Marg and waited on the traffic lights to turn right on to Ramabai Ambedkar Marg. Mumbai had the quintessential distinction of a twenty-four-hour rush-hour traffic. A river of vehicles of every size and shape and colour and brand, on two, three and four wheels stopped and moved at various speeds. Driving was by pure instinct. Everyone had a gut feel for who to let pass, who to rush ahead of. Horns blaring, music streaming out of open windows, smoke and pollution further begriming Mother Nature. As they idled at the junction, they heard a thundering motorcycle roar from the rear. It was as if someone was travelling towards them from behind. Rita looked in the wing mirror and saw a leather-clad figure – who, presumably, hadn't seen that the traffic light was red – racing towards the junction. As the roar got louder and the motorcyclist got larger in the wing mirror, Rita wondered how did the idiot plan to brake at the last minute, as the signal still read thirty-one seconds to *go green*.

The motorcyclist didn't decelerate. With a helmet covering a brainless head, the rider jumped the signal at a speed that – God forbid – if it crashed into anyone, the rider's DNA would have to be scrapped from the tarmac on the road.

'Idiot,' Rita shouted aloud, not realizing that windows of the car were up. 'Did you just see that?'

'Nutter. There are many like him in the city these days, ma'am. Since these imported large-engine motorcycles have come to India, and you know how we mete out driving licences in our country.'

The signal turned green and they turned right.

'He could have died ...'

'Or killed someone.'

'That too. Did you read the registration plate?'

'5-7-6-4. I couldn't catch the series, but I'll figure out a way.'

'Please. I want to meet this person, and some others like him. We should send out a notice to the local police stations. These guys shouldn't just be fined, we should take away their driving licences.'

Cuffe Parade is one of Mumbai's crowned jewels: luxurious, posh and la-di-la. Industrialists, businessmen, bureaucrats, politicians and corporate moguls reside here; it isn't a much-favoured residence address for Bollywood fraternity. Named after one Mr Cuffe, it is a dazzling example of human greed annihilating nature. 75,000 square metre of land was reclaimed from the sea in the sixties to provide waterside residences and office to those who could afford. Of whatever Rita had read this far about Jogani and his philandering accomplishments, apparently Ron Jogani's apartment was described as over 3,700 square foot in one of the India's richest housing society: Jolly Maker One, where the societal reserve fund is so large the residents get interest instead of paying maintenance. Jogani's apartment was on the fifteenth floor overlooking the sea. This was one of the primo residences in the country, not just in Cuffe Parade or Mumbai.

Money, diamonds, luxury apartment, fancy cars and a lot more besides, and then a bullet – a mere two-centimetre metal shell – takes it all away. Kaput!

As neither of the car occupants was in uniform, and there was no red light on the car, the security at Jolly Maker stopped Rita's unmarked car at the barrier. The skinny uniformed guard came towards the driver's side as Rita lowered her window.

'Yes, madam?' the guard spat out. 'Who you want?' He quizzed in his English-patois and peeked into the car to see if there were any more occupants besides the obvious two. He had his talkie ready to call the apartment resident and seek due permission before letting the visitors in.

'Mr Ron Jogani's apartment,' Rita responded politely.

The look on the guard's face was sceptical for a split-second.

'He no live here anymore. He gone.'

'Gone? Where?' Rita wanted to know if the people at this posh tower knew about Jogani's demise.'

'He go to heaven. Who you?' The guard looked doleful but carried on in his vernacular.

'Mr Jogani is no more?' Rita feigned a surprise.

'No more. Who you?'

Rita ignored him the third time. 'So who lives in his apartment now?'

'Madam lives. Who you?'

'Madam who?'

The guard, realizing his questions weren't getting any response from the visitors, decided he won't answer any more. 'First you tell, who you, then I tell.'

'I am DCP Rita Ferreira, and this is Inspector Jatin Singh. Does that answer your question?' Rita looked at Jain who showed the ID.

'Yes madam …' The guard looked disappointed and impressed simultaneously. His hand went up to his forehead to salute. Pure reflex.

'So who lives in Mr Jogani's apartment now?'

'Madam lives.'

'Which madam?'

'Madam Jogani.'

'Madam Jogani?' Hadn't Victor mentioned Jogani was divorced, single? 'But … Mr Jogani wasn't married.'

'He was married before the divorce,' he explicated innocently. 'Mrs Jogani come back to apartment.' Despite his grammar, he conversed in English.

Horror vacui, Rita pondered. Nature abhors a vacuum, doesn't it? Dig a trench and the river fills it in, pull out a shrub from its roots and the weeds appear within days. Depose a dictator and coup leader becomes the next tyrant. Vacate an apartment in Cuffe Parade and Mrs Jogani – ex Mrs Jogani – gravitates into it before rigor mortis sets in Ron Jogani's corpse. Rita and Jatin exchanged glances. This was getting interesting.

'OK, let us in, we need to see Mrs Jogani.'

The guard didn't flinch; he jinked and raised the barrier for the car to drive in. He courteously pointed towards the visitors' parking spot. The building, for all its financial value, looked worn out due to the harsh Mumbai weather. Being close to sea – like Rita's own Bandra apartment –the salt and moisture had played their part too despite the large reserve funds in the kitty to upkeep the same. However, given the breadth of the towers it was evident that the apartments were leviathan by Mumbai standards, where builders could sell a one-bedroom apartment in 400 square feet and a family of four could dwell in it. Certainly lavish. Considering the gentry that resided here, anything smaller would have been embarrassing anyway.

Rita and Jatin didn't speak. Rita wondered if the return of Mrs Jogani was a coincidence or a consequence of Jogani's death. She leaned towards the latter. They silently took the elevator to the fifteenth floor.

Wouldn't Jogani have alarmed the apartment before he left for Belgium? If so, how did ex Mrs Jogani get into it?

Jatin Singh rang the bell and the maidservant opened the door instantly, like she was waiting for them. In all probability the pint-sized security guard would have called in to inform about the visitors. Jatin introduced themselves and showed the maid his ID. She ushered them into the house. They walked behind the maid into a broad entrance lobby and into the living room. She requested them to sit and informed them that 'madam' would be out within minutes to see them. Before leaving the room, she asked if they needed a drink.

Both asked for cold water.

The furniture in the living room was upholstered in beige and raw silk and tan leather. A potpourri of artefacts filled up every available space in the room. The living room had an unusually high ceiling that provided space for all his paintings to be displayed on the cream walls. Full marks for aesthetics. Almost zero on personal touch. It was the kind of house that screamed that it was done up by an interior designer, the kinds they featured in magazines. Maybe some designer magazine had already covered it, but Rita didn't know. She had done her apartment herself in minimalistic design.

Rita had no doubt that ex Mrs Jogani would be unforthcoming, if not utterly inimical. But she was keen to know the how-and-why. The alternative theory was, once again, beginning to spin in her mind: was Ron Jogani actually killed for the diamonds?

'It took you quite some time to come by.' Ex Mrs Jogani arrived. An upright, tall woman – marginally taller than Rita – in her late forties with certainly more make-up than Shahnaz Husain would recommend, but not too distasteful. She would have certainly been a stunner in her youth. She was casually attired in a white round-neck T that had The Beatles crossing the Abbey Road on the front peeping out of the knee-length denim dungarees. She didn't appear to be mourning. She didn't appear defeated. Or lost or bereaved.

'Hello, I'm DCP Rita Ferreira, and this is Inspector Jatin Singh. And you are ...?' Rita wanted to avoid calling her *Mrs Jogani.*

'Anita. I was once married to Ronnie,' she said glumly.

Were you a widow if your spouse died after the divorce?

'Hello, Anita, sorry I couldn't connect – what did you mean when you said it took us some time to come by ...?'

'Oh, nothing. Ronnie died ... I mean he was murdered,' Anita corrected herself, '...some months back. I'm surprised no one came around back then.'

'Wasn't the Indian Embassy in Belgium in touch with you?'

'They were, but no one came here personally.'

'Well, all I can say is we got the case only when the Interpol got involved. But the information we have is that you declined to identify or take custody of the body, which is still freezing in some drawer unclaimed in a morgue in Brussels. Am I correct?'

'You are. Ronnie ... I mean Ron and I divorced over a decade ago, and it was because of his cheating on me. I have no feelings for him – dead or alive – and I don't want to have to do anything with him. Shouldn't talk bad of the dead but isn't it funny how people get what they deserve and, in my humble opinion, some people deserve a bullet.'

'So, if you don't mind me asking, how are you living in this apartment?'

'Well, I know Ron has no relatives, so when I got the news that Ron was no more, I thought I should come and take care of this property before one of his cunning whores got into it. We lived in this place, so I moved in.'

'Did you break the locks?'

'I didn't have to. I still have my set of keys.'

'What about the alarms? Surely, Mr Jogani would have alarmed the house before he went abroad …'

'That was the problem with Ron. He was so predictable. When we lived in this place together the alarm code was our wedding date. I was sure he changed it when we got divorced and I moved out, but I could guess what he would have changed it to. It was the date we got divorced. Easy.'

'Do you know of anyone who might have wanted to harm Mr Jogani or threatened him?'

'Don't know anyone else besides me.' Smirk. Wiseass.

'So I take it that your divorce with Mr Jogani was … acrimonious?' It was best to ask for it to be on record.

'The man couldn't keep his pants zipped. I caught him here, in our home, with a young bitch.'

'And you let him have this apartment at the divorce?' Rita rolled her eyes to emphasize the valuable property.

'I didn't want to live here visualizing him with some whore all the time.'

'So you took the cash and moved out?'

'I suppose you can say that.'

'And now you're back in this very house and that doesn't bother you?'

'For one, he's dead, and after so many years … I guess it doesn't matter anymore.'

'Do you have legal right to be in this property?'

'Possession is nine-tenths of the law, isn't it?'

Gold digger. Either Anita was a smart woman or there was a brain somewhere who was feeding her the intelligence.

'Am I a suspect?'

'Everyone's a suspect till the murderer is caught, so to that effect you are in the pool too, but you aren't convicted. Are you planning to leave the country in the coming weeks?'

'No, but are there any restrictions?'

'No, but it would be good if you let us know in case we need you for any questions that would help us get to Mr Jogani's killer.'

'But the murder happened in Brussels in some hotel, and I was told it was a burglary that went wrong ...'

'You're right about the location, but whether Mr Jogani's murder was a collateral damage to burglary or not is something we're re-evaluating, Anita.'

'No, I'm in town, and though I said I have no feelings left for Ron, I now think I should at least give him a decent send-off. How can I initiate to bring his body back?'

Rita noticed some moisture in the other woman's eyes. Maybe, the hurt of being cheated ages ago was over, maybe she was redeeming Ron. Who knew?

'That's nice to hear. I'll let the Belgian authorities know, and they shall be in touch.'

'Thanks.'

'Where is Mr Jogani's office?'

'He worked from home. The office is one of the smaller bedrooms.'

'We'll need to search the place, specially his computer, for anything we can find that might lead us to the murderer.'

'Of course.'

'Have you been in the office yet?'

'Once, yes, but I'm not into computers or diamonds, so I had no reason to rifle through. Happy to let you guys in to search the place, whenever.'

Was there any point in sealing the place now before the team combed the place, bearing in mind that the chain of evidence had already been breached?

'I have some equipment in the car, Jatin.' Rita turned to Jatin who had been sitting quietly jotting notes on his pad all this while. He immediately got up.

'I'll get it.'

'We shall seal the office, at least.' She turned to Anita. 'Anything you remember after we go, please call us immediately. The team that comes for the office search shall also go through the whole house, just in case there's something that can provide us with any clue ... hope you are OK with that?'

Nod.

'And I'd like to speak with whoever was living with Mr Jogani before he left for Brussels, whoever worked here.'

'Most of the people here are the ones who worked for him even before I walked out on Ron, they've been around for years and, if you ask me, none of them could have been involved.'

'I wasn't thinking about that, I wanted to know about people who visited Mr Jogani here, people who visited Mr Jogani in the last six months or so.'

'Oh, that? Of course. When would you want to do that?'

'I'll ask someone to organize that tomorrow.'

'I'm home, so no problem.'

'And please don't ask them anything what we've talked about today. I don't want these people to be prepared.'

'Sure.'

Jatin, in the meantime, had fetched the police tape and sealed the office as they had just agreed upon.

Before leaving, Rita asked Jatin to leave a card in case Anita wanted to be in touch. As they walked out of the Jogani residence Rita wondered where did her tête-à-tête, with the gold-digging wife, leave her: nowhere. She might as well have spent time looking for UFOs. Could they possibly find something in Jogani's office so late into the investigation? Doubtful. But it was worth a try. And it was the procedure.

It was six. The sun had still not finished its shift, and the sky was still bright. Was there anything that they could accomplish now? They had given themselves two tasks for the day: Jogani's residence and office and his ex-wife. And they had struck both the proverbial birds with one stone.

'I have a request, ma'am,' Jatin said as they sat in the vehicle. 'I'd like to lead this search, and look into Jogani's computer.'

'Since when have you become a computer geek?'

'Always was, ma'am.'

'Great, let's see what we find.'

The mouse-sized guard gave them a salute as they drove out of Jolly Maker building complex. As the motor wafted away, Rita looked at the city. Mumbai wasn't so big geographically, but it was extremely complicated. It was a corporate metropolis. The corporation was India and the challenge with India Corporate – Rita compared it to her Goa – was that everyone was someone or at least pretended to be someone. Maybe Guinness should have recorded the city with the highest VIP to common-man population. She smiled.

SEVEN

Seventeen. It took the best part of the day for Vikram and Rajesh Nene to contact a total of seventeen snitches between them. Seventeen police informers were not ample to cover every inch of Mumbai, but they had their own sources. It was like fuelling a fire in a maze; the flame would certainly find its way. Someone, somewhere always knew something. It wasn't funny how many cases had been cracked because someone squeaked, or sold out, or blabbered after a drunken night, or toasted to boast regarding the booty, or felt chicaned enough to report with an intention to relay the info. Endless possibilities. Unvarying result. It eventually seeped through to someone who could trade it for a favour or pay off a debt. The seventeen copies of Sishir Singh's grainy candid-shot would be reproduced umpteen times and travel into the corners of Mumbai that did not even feature on Google Maps. Lanes and dusty by-lanes that even Mumbai Police could not find, forget carrying on a search. This would all be in undercover, of course. When – and not if – the guy was spotted, the orders were clear: just report whereabouts, do not make any contact. Exhausted from making those calls personally, the two senior inspectors split for the day.

Teams were briefed and dispatched to the Jogani fortress before Rita arrived in office the next morning. Jatin turned out to be even more efficient than before. Essentially, all the three subordinates in her team – Rita had got Rajesh Nene signed off for the case – were competent. Good sign that no one consciously or inadvertently throttled the progress out of competitive jealousy or idiocy. Rita had been up late the night before, searching for archived news from metrotime.be portal: news items available in Flemish or French, which Google Chrome effortlessly translated into English for her. She found nothing on the web that wasn't mentioned in Victor's report. Perhaps the dailies in Belgium didn't do much digging themselves and relied on whatever info police provided them with to report or that the case wasn't significant enough to deploy their resources on a random, one-off murder in the city – a foreigner chilled during a heist wasn't exactly WW III.

Rita wanted to bond with the guys, rebuild the sodality with them after the brief break. She gave a shout and the three men were happy to join her for lunch. The foursome walked out to a nearby pav-bhaji, nothing fancy. Jatin left for Jogani's swanky residence after lunch.

Back in the Operations Room, Rita updated Vikram and Rajesh Nene on the interesting meeting Jatin and she had had with Anita, and that troops had now been dispatched to scour anything they could get their hands on after a significant gap of time, and numerous people that might have handled any possible evidence. In any event, a break in the chain of evidence would not be acceptable in a court. In short, counting on anything received from that search would be amateur. They should be contended if they get some pointer. The two senior inspectors filled her in on the contacts they had made with several individuals. If Sishir Singh looked anything like the guy in the picture they had, he should be identified soon.

Like a kid who had just seen Santa Claus, Jatin returned in a state of excitement. His exuberance was powered by the fact that the date logs on Jogani's computer had established that it hadn't been used after the evening he had flown out of India. And thus, he sounded confident anything and everything that Jogani had worked on – emails, accounts, bank details, and airline and hotel bookings – could be traced even though the cache had cleared after thirty days as per Jogani's computer settings. He told Rita that most computer users don't realize that deleted history from a hard drive can be retrieved in three steps even by some dubious expert: search for it, copy the .dat file, and using a specialized reader the entire web history would be revealed unless, of course, some expensive software has been installed to break the deleted files.

But why would Jogani have bought something like that?

Nothing significant was discovered in the interviews of Jogani household staff conducted so far. They were still in progress, but Rita didn't have much confidence in achieving something that might break the case. Even under ordinary circumstances, Rita knew that very few witnesses could narrate anything consequential after a critical event. It's not that people intend to lie, but they falter, and the more serious the crime the more the duress and anxiety, and anxiety was a known bitch. It frequently lapsed memory. History is packed with victims who'd seen their own attackers close and personal but the trauma dwarfed their memory; where people failed to identify the perpetrator correctly, remembering the events or their sequence was a big ask. Police largely worked through the inconsistencies in witness statements; if they found a slight gap they jumped into it and ploughed in big enough holes for lying witnesses to bury in but, what were the odds that any domestic help in Jogani's household would remember anything that could be of any authentic value over three months post the event? But it was the procedure and it had to be done. There's nothing that bothers bureaucracy like a miscarried procedure. Do anything but don't break the rules and procedures irrespective of how ridiculous or obsolete they are.

'So let's focus on what do we know until now ...' Rita began when all four were seated in the Operations Room. 'By all means Jogani had died where his body had been found by police, no doubt about it. The Belgian Police investigated and documented that.' She pointed towards the red box file. 'The foremost doctrine of homicide – to look for the killer within the family – doesn't seem to hold here. Spouse. Siblings. Kids. Jogani isn't survived by any. Ex-wife, yes she is a flagrant gold-digger but this murder doesn't look like her doing. And before I forget, I need a watch put on her for at least a month. Who she calls, who calls her, where she goes, who comes visiting, everything.'

'What about acquaintances?'

Impatience is a virtue in investigation. It establishes confidence that someone else was thinking about the case too. Vikram already looked embroiled in the investigation.

'You're spot on. Business associates. Then friends. And then all acquaintances who could have had the information regarding his travel. We'll find people to look out and provide us with a list.'

Vikram noted it down in his usual fashion.

'What we also know is that someone knew about the big deal happening in Antwerp, and the hotel Ron Jogani was booked to stay in. It certainly doesn't look like someone broke into Jogani's hotel room at random and found the diamonds. All evidence points to a planned heist – the adjacent rooms booked, the locks and safe tampered with, the midnight call rousting him out of the room … what we need to figure out is where did someone get on to the trail of our victim? My analysis is that someone got on to him from India itself, if Sishir Singh was the person identified in the hotel, and then at the airport on the flight back to New Delhi. Are we all in agreement on that?'

Nods.

'So the first question on the point we all just agreed on is how did that someone know the detailed itinerary?'

'Ma'am, we've got to figure out who knew about the travel.' Nene.

'Many … considering that Jogani was there to buy diamonds for a cartel, everyone who was involved in the deal knew about his travel. And maybe even their associates.' Jatin.

'But, why would he have shared the exact itinerary with all?' Vikram.

'He may have or may not have and we have no way of knowing that, unless he shared it by email and we go through that when the lab breaks into his computer.' Nene.

'However, even if he shared the travel plan, there is no way he could have known the room number he was going to get allotted when he actually walked into the hotel in Brussels, would he?' Rita pointed out.

'I have a hunch that someone from the hotel was involved.' Vikram.

'That is, of course, one possibility.' Jatin.

'What is the other possibility?' Rita.

'There is always this chance that the Blackberry we saw with the killer in the picture actually belonged to Ron Jogani and he had called someone before his death that left a trace for the killer.' Jatin.

'You have a point … though he could only have known the room number he was allotted once he was already checked in at the hotel, and that was too late. The rooms adjacent and opposite to him were already booked at midday. So says the Belgian report.' Rita brought Jatin's hypothesis to a halt.

'So maybe his BB was hacked into?' Jatin persisted.

'Same logic applies, Jatin. How did the killer or killers know the room number before Jogani checked in, when Jogani, himself, couldn't have been aware of it?'

Jatin looked deflated.

'Have you guys got your teams ready?' Rita referred to the subinspectors that worked for both the senior inspectors. The foot soldiers. Unfortunately, Jatin had no team at the moment.

Nods.

'So here's how we divide the investigation: Mr Nene …'

'Ma'am, please stop calling me Mr Nene. You call Vikram and Jatin by their names, why should I be different?'

'I'm sorry, Rajesh.'

'I'd be happier if you called me Nene. That is what everyone addresses me as.'

'OK. So, Nene, as you know the informants best, you lead the search for Sishir Singh. Vikram – you take the charge of tracking down all Jogani's associates, personal and business, and also see if you can ferret out who, eventually, bought the diamonds after the murder. It has to be one of the big merchants, and my guess is it just might be someone who was in the cartel that had appointed Jogani for the deal. But I might be totally off the mark here. And I'm not at all suggesting that this person or persons are involved in the murder, but who knows?'

'And me, ma'am?' Jatin asked.

'You're responsible for breaking into Jogani's computer. And find out who was Jogani's mobile-service provider. Ask them for all Jogani's calls and whatever data they have for last six months. Make that a year.'

Jatin felt good. Rita having given the responsibility he had asked for made him feel that his boss had ignored his past folly. He knew he had to be extra careful this time around. It was OK to make a mistake once, but second mistake would be a career suicide.

When the guys left, Rita sat down to ponder. There was still a web of unanswered questions or rather, unknown questions. Contrary to what most people think, the police didn't merely look for answers. The foremost search was always for the correct questions. Correct questions get correct answers. Answers to non-existent questions are useless.

It was 4 o'clock Friday afternoon and if nothing gave way, she knew she'd have to spend the weekend alone. Bored. Of course, she had the case, but in absence of even a slight breakthrough, what would she do for the next forty-eight hours? Ash was supposed to be in India the next weekend. Was Mumbai in his itinerary? He usually travelled to Mumbai though.

Ash Mattel – Ashwin Mittal originally, but Microsoft Word forced him to change his name rather than correct the spelling each time – was Rita's reunited college friend. Not her boyfriend. Not her lover. Not just a friend either – friends who were *just* friends didn't sleep with each other. However, here wasn't a past or future of the relationship. Heck, there was no relationship. He was a divorcee, criminal psychologist based in the UK. Rita and he had been in college together barely a year before he went to the UK for his medical studies. They weren't friends then. Years later it was pure stroke of luck that Ash was in Mumbai, and her boss, Vinay Joshi, reintroduced them. Rita was looking for an expert to break the serial-killer pattern and Ash turned out to be a real blessing with his experience in the field. Of course, they exchanged more than their opinions on the case. It wasn't love. It wasn't lust. It was merely that they enjoyed each other's company and a lot more besides. Ash was tall. He was big. He was dark. The dichotomy was that he was ugly and handsome at the same time. Rustic … manly?

Rita sat wondering if she should call him to let him know she actually missed him and his cheesy one-liners when Nene walked in.

'Sishir Singh has been spotted, ma'am.'

It was not even a complete twenty-four hours since the information had been farmed to the informants.

'Wow! That was quick. Tell me about him.'

'His name is … Honey Singh.' Rajesh Nene chuckled as he read from the piece of paper he held. 'Facial and physical description – ditto as in the pictures from Belgium, except Honey Singh has longer hair, but they could have easily grown in the last three months. The suspect lives with his mother in an apartment complex called Takshila in Andheri East. Lucky Singh, her name is. Honey Singh has a girlfriend, Miss Kitty. Miss Kitty Varghese is a model by profession.' Nene giggled like a schoolboy, and Rita understood why. Most so-called models were also escorts, though that might not have been the case with Kitty if she had a serious boyfriend. 'We don't yet know where she lives. Honey Singh runs a computer repair-contract business in Bandra Kurla. That's' all we have for now. Should we bring him in?'

'No. Let's think a bit. Where are the others?'

'They must be out on their jobs, ma'am. Want me to call them?'

'Nope. Take a seat.'

Rita could tell that Nene was not happy about the order for inaction when he appeared hungry for it. If it were left to him, he would have sprinted out and busted Honey Singh and thought about anything else later.

'Does anything indicate that this Honey Singh has recently acquired wealth like the burglary we are investigating?'

'He drives a Honda Accord ...'

'And lives with his mother in Andheri East. And he still hasn't fled Mumbai. All we know is a guy called Honey Singh looks like Sishir Singh. Have you seen a picture of Honey Singh yourself yet?'

'I'll ask someone to take his picture and send us.'

'I can't believe that this guy didn't even take the trouble of using a different family name, from the one he used in his alias: *Singh*. Strange, don't you think?'

'Now that you say it.' Nene looked relaxed but only a bit. Rita could tell that he wasn't biting her logic a hundred per cent.

'OK. Let's do this: let's place him under watch for the entire weekend. Ask your guys to take photographs, log his travels, who he meets, who he calls, where he eats. Everything.'

'I'll arrange that immediately.'

'We don't have time for getting any court orders before tomorrow, so let it all be under the radar.' It had been one of the rare times she was stepping over the line. Ends justified the means, didn't they?

Nene smiled. It was understood.

'He shouldn't even suspect a tail, but the tail shouldn't lose him even for a minute. If Honey Singh is our man, he would in all probability be looking over his shoulder all the time. And taking into account the immaculate robbery, he should be able to spot a tail faster than most.'

'Right.'

'Ask everyone not to approach Honey Singh under any circumstances. Please use your best guys. Although, if this Mr Honey Singh is seen travelling towards the airport or driving out of the city, arrest him for some innocuous reason. He should not leave the city over the weekend. Not now when we're this close.'

Making an arrest in Mumbai is simple. The police could find one hundred and one reasons: some error or missing documents in car registration, insurance or diving licence. Simple.

'We need to see his picture before we start tailing him. See it to confirm it yourself. Send me a copy too. And ask someone to dig up his life history from the day he was born and email the same to me please. Encrypt it.'

'We'll get that over to you as soon as I get it, ma'am.'

'And … thank you, Nene. I really appreciate how quickly you've cracked this.'

'Only doing my job, ma'am.' He looked embarrassed.

'Thanks, and have a good weekend. Be in touch.'

'You too ma'am, if you need anything over the weekend, give me a call. My mobile is always on.'

'Same here. Thanks.'

Rita sat in the office for some time after Nene left. Was it just fluke or were the snitches in Mumbai faster than the person she had seen on the motorbike in the afternoon? That reminded her of prompting Jatin to find out who that reckless rider was.

Later that night Rita poured a civilized belt of Jim and let the aroma fill her nose. She sat thinking about the case. Police work was a lot about deduction. Quite like mathematics as a matter of fact. Not plain arithmetic that everyone can add or subtract, but not unlike a complex set of equations. But here is the catch: unlike a complex set of equations, the real-life equations could have more than one solution, and they were ever-changing, so one also had to take into account the unknowns. One of the jarring overlooks in Victor's file had been that if the Belgian authorities had established when Sishir Singh left Brussels for Mumbai, why hadn't they traced and confirmed when he had arrived in Brussels? He couldn't have just walked in behind Jogani. She bet he was there a few days in advance or, at the very least, some of his accomplices were. He couldn't have carried the gun from India. He required tools, gun, and other help; it would have taken time to arrange those things in a foreign country. She had no doubts that there was more than one individual to carry out the task: if not physically present in the hotel, at least in the planning and in keeping a watch on Jogani.

Finishing her small drink, Rita switched off the lights. Her bedroom window was open and she could feel the moisture in the air. The light wind brought the promise of rain later. It was already there somewhere in the distance. A few hours away, maximum.

But when she got up early morning to go for her run, she realized that the clouds had passed them by without obliging. Perhaps they obliged some towns and villages in Gujarat.

When she got back, her Blackberry beeped. Nene had sent the picture of Honey Singh. The picture was clear enough to exhibit that Honey Singh was a doppelgänger of Sishir Singh. Identical twins?

EIGHT

Criminals don't work nine to five. They don't stay away on weekends. Ergo, the police workforce never has enough hours in a day or enough days in a week. Weekend? Well, it was a busman's weekend, and more so if you were selected by your supervisor to be part of a clandestine surveillance on someone who was being investigated for homicide. Even more so if it was an international case and, apparently, the nation's pride was attached, however tacitly. Four teams of two plainclothes ASIs each were deployed to tail Honey Singh. As he had been made responsible, Rajesh Nene was leading the whole undercover operation. The eight Assistant Sub-Inspectors he had handpicked were people he had worked with in the past. It was all about efficiency. And trust. He knew they could carry out the task discreetly. One team was stationed at Chhatrapati Shivaji International Airport. If Honey had any plans to fly out of the country, this team would become paramount in the operation – it would have been amateur to presume any tail could keep up with the target in Mumbai traffic. There was always a chance one couldn't keep up with the suspect. It was a chance no one took. It was a chance Nene wasn't taking either. If Honey Singh flew out of the domestic airport it would a simple call to the local police in the landing city to apprehend him at the tarmac and put him back on the return flight.

Takshila wasn't an enormous housing complex like some others in Mumbai. Any rational person could take two routes out of the housing complex, and at this point it was deemed that Honey Singh wouldn't behave unreasonably. There seemed no cause to assume otherwise unless, of course, Honey Singh suspected anyone following him or watching him. There was no reason to consider that Honey would jump out of the balcony of his first-floor apartment in the building and run on foot or use a camouflage. Working with the informants, Nene had figured out that Honey Singh's model girlfriend, Kitty Varghese, lived on Yari Road in Versova, which could well be where he might drive to over the weekend.

If he drove out of Takshila, Honey Singh could either turn right on to Mahakali Caves Road that passed Holy Spirit Hospital, and then join or cross Western Express Highway depending on his destination: if he were to go to his office on Saturday, he'd join the highway; if he went to see Kitty, he'd cross it. Conversely, if he turned left when he came out of his apartment complex, he'd take JVLR via Vallabhbhai Patel Marg to get to the same Western Express Highway. Obviously, there could have been another ten destinations he could drive to, but given the resources Nene had at his disposal, they would have to improvize if Honey altered his route. In any event, they'd follow him till the highway and then radio each other.

Though it can chase down anything that moves, surveillance couldn't be carried out in a Ferrari: you needed a camel in the desert, not a cheetah. You want anonymity and not a jarring sight that begged a double take. Or worse still – the target stopping to have a look and chat-up with the driver about cylinders or BHP or fuel consumption. Team One's unmarked car – an old white deceptively derelict Maruti Omni, still one of the most inconspicuous vehicles on Indian roads – parked at the corner of Mahakali Caves Road as it curved right. Team Two was parked on the other side, in what was visually an equally hard-bitten Tata Indica. These two vehicles would spring into action when Honey drove out. Team Three, the blessed ones, had Ford Escort from the nineties, and their task was to burn fuel, take rounds around and broadly encircle the target location.

Of course, the police station at Andheri East was on high alert. If required, they would dispatch uniformed patrols within minutes.

Nene had deliberated on scanning Honey's Singh's office on Friday night but gave up the idea. Surreptitiously following someone was one thing, breaking into an office was an altogether another level. If you were spotted tailing someone, you could very easily manipulate the situation, turn around and disappear, making it look like a coincidence. How would you elucidate a break-in? And also, he hadn't come up with the idea earlier in the evening to discuss with Rita, and calling her late on a Friday night for something like this? He killed the idea.

The four teams would be in radio contact with each other and with their leader, SI Nene, for procedural and tactical advice all through the weekend or till further notice. Honey Singh would only be referred to as the 'target'. The policemen and their jalopies were in their positions early in the morning by six. What if Honey Singh planned to leave his mommy's house early and take a short trip outside Mumbai?

They waited. They watched. An hour ticked away. As per the plan, Team One and Team Two cars that were parked in proximity of target residence dropped their passengers to keep vigil on foot, and swapped position. A car, however discreet, being parked at one place long enough always carried the risk of losing its anonymity.

Another hour and a half passed by. No sign of Mr Honey Singh, but 8:30 was still too early in the morning for a weekend. The cars rotated again: back to their original positions. Surveillance is a game played with gold chips of patience. Everyone in the police knew that; the four teams knew that. The fourth team, the one stationed at the airport, would possibly have to just endure the entire weekend without any real activity, but they were trained to watch, and wait for further orders, and they were trained to wait in comfortable and not-so-comfortable places. Stilling in the car at the airport was a lot easier than some other situations they had been in.

The ten o'clock call between all teams raised the question: what if Honey Singh didn't come home the night before the vigilance was set up? Just because his car was parked below his apartment didn't mean he couldn't have hitched a ride with some friend. Or his girlfriend. Nene ordered Team Three to drive into the complex, and circle Honey Singh's apartment block. Once they espied his white Honda Accord again, they were sent to Yari Road.

Even in the scanty weekend traffic, Team Three took almost an hour to get to Kitty Varghese's Yari Road apartment and return to base. The ASI who got down from the car made a rookie mistake. Although he didn't say who they were visiting, he flashed his card for the watchman to open the building gate. If Honey Singh was indeed Sishir Singh – and at this point in time the police had extremely meagre information to take that call, though they were following him without appropriate court order – the mere presence of police in his girlfriend's building might have raised an alarm if he came to know in some way. There wasn't any other activity reported by them after the visit. An ASI had gone up to her third-floor apartment and knocked lightly on the door. Kitty had opened the door with the security chain on. He had asked if she knew Mr Hari Prasad's apartment – a random name, and she declined and he apologized. There were no signs that there was anyone else in the apartment.

It was a little before eleven o'clock that Team One noticed another surveillance car. It was straightforward to identify. A blemished Maruti Alto, in white with enough dents and rust to be lost in the background and not be obvious. But for the trained eyes it strained too hard to be inconspicuous and hence gave away its purpose. The driver was alone, and he was as conspicuous as a polar bear in a desert: hardly a decoy. A man so large it would appear that he had been put into the car and then inflated to fill up the interior. Handlebar moustache, cigarette in hand that was attached to a thick hirsute arm in a Madras-check short-sleeved shirt. There were other cars around, parked with occupants in them, but almost all of them had pairs talking and most left after fifteen or twenty minutes. Handlebar appeared languorous, but then, given his size, it was difficult to imagine him being any other way. He hung around doing nothing for far too long but, it was when he took out his binoculars and keenly focussed on the incoming traffic from Takshila that one ASI in Team One started to keep vigil on him. It would have been simple to walk up to him and ask, but they decided to call in Nene and gave the registration details of the car. Team One checked if he had a backup. None. And they had no idea who he was waiting for. They agreed that one lone man on a stakeout was suboptimal effort. Maybe he wasn't being paid enough. Maybe the client merely wanted a cursory report. Maybe he had been trailing his quarry long enough to know something already, and had worked out where his target would go in or out from? Or simply feeling lucky: if you're alone you've got to work on probabilities. Maybe he wasn't in a rush; if he missed today he could catch his target tomorrow? Like slow-cooking on a simmer setting. There were a million plus one possibilities.

Nene came back in ten minutes.

The car was registered to Mr Joginder Raja. Handlebar was Mr Raja. He had a professional specialized certification in private investigation. A detective of some sort, he worked out of his office, which was in his residential apartment in Lokhandwala Complex in Andheri West. The police surveillance team knew that one of the most common patrons of detectives in India were spouses spying on cheating partners. The report and photographs from a certified investigator came in handy in divorce proceedings. So Handlebar Raja was, most probably, following some affluent philanderer who lived in the area, Nene summarized.

Noon. Team One spotted the white Honda Accord. The target was eventually on the move. They relayed it to the others. Honey Singh drove out of the block and turned right on Mahakali Caves Road. Tailing someone was simple. Tailing someone without being caught out needed a bit of caution. You needed to leave a few vehicles between yourself and the target if you didn't want to arouse suspicion, and if you think the target has spotted you, you abandon the stakeout right away. However, Handlebar Raja didn't follow the tenet. He spotted Honey Singh's Accord the same time as Team One did, but immediately turned and got on to the road. A car had slipped in between, which, if he had a choice, he wouldn't have let.

So, Mr Handlebar Raja – the private investigator – was following Honey Singh too.

The radio wave between Team One and Nene crackled.

But why?

Nene asked them to keep an eye on both. It could have been a coincidence: Mr Joginder Raja had left in a rush for something else that might have appeared to be following their target.

Certainly possible.

But Handlebar was positively tailing Honey Singh. He was only one vehicle behind Honey's car and two cars ahead of Team One. Honey Singh drove towards Kitty's apartment, no doubt. The convoy travelled at a steady speed. Honey Singh didn't seem in any kind of a rush to get to his girlfriend's apartment. He didn't change lanes to overtake anyone. He didn't accelerate to lose someone following him. Either he didn't detect two distinct cars following him or he didn't care.

Turning into Yari Road, Honey stopped outside Kitty's apartment complex. He got down and walked in rather than driving straight in. Perhaps there were no parking spaces for visitors. Handlebar kept going and overtook Honey Singh without evidently looking at his target and stopped at a vacant spot few cars down. He didn't get down. Team One kept moving and turned and left the location. Team Two rolled in and took over the post a few vacant spaces before Honey Singh's car. The watchman smiled when he saw Honey Singh. Apparently, the two knew each other, which was reasonable if Honey was a regular visitor.

Nene bristled. His first reflex was to drive down to Yari Road, pull Mr Handlebar out of his car and ask him questions. However, following Honey Singh, in and of itself, was hardly a crime. Handlebar could be following Honey Singh for any number of reasons. Maybe Honey's own girlfriend had put the tail on him. But it was quite a coincidence and police rule number one was to discount any and all coincidences. What was the bloody detective after? He thought about updating Rita but didn't. It was best to keep focus on Honey Singh for at least twenty-four hours, and if that detective featured in the surveillance, so be it. He decided to wait till Sunday morning till he had some logs to take to Rita.

Rita had slept for ten hours before waking up to the shrieking morning alarm. If she had her way she would have picked up and thrown the clock so hard that it shattered the windowpane and landed on the ground floor. She realized she had only been in Mumbai a few days. A part of her whispered she should pack her stuff, drive to the airport and board the next flight to Goa. *Sexy* could chase his tail. Or blame Joshi. Let the two of them manage the circus. Or whatever. But she couldn't. The rational mind reminded her she wasn't in this for a game. This is what she was made for. This was her calling. There had been a murder and the culprits had escaped the arms of the law. The wrong had to be righted.

The morning sun was mild. The overhyped cool Arabian Sea breeze was on strike again it seemed. Sishir Singh was still missing. You could run. You could also hide. But for how long? Could anyone escape forever? Statistics would suggest yes. However, statistics have a limitation; they only have the past for reference.

Nature is obstinate; it doesn't stand modifications. You cannot tame the wind. You cannot force a river to flow one way or the other. The stream flows in the path it finds depending on the slope, the grooves, the tide. If you asked snitches to dig up information for you, you should to be prepared for parting with something in return. What you do not know is where the information they gather for you might get passed on to. Informers worked for police out of fear, for protection. They had a stomach to feed. The other set of people who actually paid them for the information was the media and hence, it was unreasonable to assume that someone would not have whispered it to an enthusiastic media body. Not all snitches would do that, but all it requires is one poisoned arrow.

Rita woke up Sunday morning to the headlines in national dailies:

'Police Hunt for a Murderer.'
'Interpol after Killer in Mumbai.'

Nowhere was it mentioned that it was just one of the many possibilities they were exploring. The fact that the murderer was still in Mumbai or India was in itself unverified. But scribes have made press reporting an art, and why wouldn't they? The whole purpose was to sell paper or TRP or ad space on web. If truncating, a crucial part from the headline garnered higher revenue, so be it. Lack of knowledge or information never deflated the speculation or sales. The press, she knew with experience, would have a grand time with the story, and hence the time and effort put in.

From an angle it seemed pointless to tail the suspect anymore. If the suspect – Honey Singh or anyone else – had been presumptuous that he was safe, there was a chance he'd become reckless and err. Many criminals got apprehended only when they got comfortable and let the guard down. That opportunity had, indeed, perished. However, Honey Singh only looked like Sishir Singh, nothing more. She called Nene at seven and asked him to carry on with the surveillance. That's when Nene updated her about Raja.

'That's weird.'

'Yes ma'am.'

'We need to get to this quickly … get all details of Mr Raja. We need to pay him a visit. Find out a way to stop him from stepping out today, we want him at his office … say at eleven?'

'I'll make sure he is at his office-cum-residence today.'

'And no point in me getting to office, could you analyse all the logs and ask Vikram to pick me up from my residence please? I'll be ready.'

'Certainly, ma'am.'

NINE

Rita lived in Sheesh Mahal, a 1950's apartment block on St Andrews Road in Bandra, close to the posh Pali Hill. The building was hoisted on pillars to accommodate car park on the ground floor, the apartments were from first floor onwards. The monstrous concrete pillars – to counter the gradient in the plot of land – resembled kangaroo legs: short in front and long hind legs. The lopsided building only emphasized the quaintness that was Mumbai. Nothing was straight. Nothing was perfect. Everything was individualist yet charming in its own fashion.

Like any other apartment that was over half-a-century old, the façade was sad and dilapidated – Mumbai monsoon, the sea close by, the moisture in the air had all taken their toll, but interiors of most of the apartments, however, were totally in contrast with the exteriors. It wasn't Cuffe Parade, but it still was one of the most desired, most prosperous suburbs of Mumbai. Rita had bought a fourth-floor 2BHK apartment – a two bedroom-hall-kitchen – in the beginning of the new millennium; she had gladly sold two of her ancestral properties in Goa and invested the money in this. She hadn't spent a lot, like some others in the building, on the interiors. It was sparsely furnished, giving lots of room to her: minimalist was how she put it. No clutter. Everything was there for a purpose. Books. Turntable. Records. Lamps. Jim Beam. One photograph in the whole apartment: her parents' wedding picture at the St Michael Archangel Church near Benaulim Beach.

The only noticeable feature being that she had got one of the longer walls of the rectangular living room, the hall, painted in blue, which made it stand out from the other three walls that were in cream. It was a comfortable place. She kept most of the hall seating on the floor with lots of cushions thrown around to give it a cosy look.

Ten hours and thirty-three minutes after the observation teams saw Honey Singh return to his residence at Takshila, Vikram was at Rita's apartment to pick her up, as Nene wanted to run the stake out for another day. They were to drive to Lokhandwala to speak to Mr Handlebar Raja.

'Good morning, ma'am.'

'Good morning, Vikram,' Rita said as she climbed into Vikram's Gypsy. 'You still have a Maruti Gypsy?'

'I really like the vehicle, ma'am. It's just undergone a full rebuild, as I think the folks at Maruti aren't taking new orders. I have had to get a special permission for keeping it.'

'Good. If you really want something, you should go that extra mile to get it.'

'Why don't we just go and arrest Honey Singh, ma'am?

'We arrest him. He pleads innocent. His lawyer gets him bail, as we have no evidence. When we take him to court, his lawyer and the judge laugh at us. And if we're lucky he doesn't sue us for harassment or libel. You willing to bat with that?'

'Maybe.'

'Maybe. That's not considered an acceptable answer in any court across this country, when I last checked.'

'No.'

'Well, you have your answer then. Motive has to be evidenced, means has to be evidenced, and opportunity has to be evidenced. In short you almost need a picture of the killer in action to prove to a judge. Or the defence will slaughter us.'

Police work was like mathematics. You might know the answer to the question, but you needed to be able to walk the journey between the question and answer.

'Yes ma'am.'

'Also, the moment he knows we have his scent, he gets attentive, if he ever got complacent that is. So it is best to do some enquiries before we bring him in.'

The sun was now blinding. One needed sun visors the size of the windscreen to keep it out. Rita discussed her surmise – of Sishir Singh having an accomplice on ground – with Vikram as he drove.

'That's a very valid point. Sishir Singh or Honey Singh couldn't have carried a gun from India. And what about the heavy safe he replaced in the hotel room? He could have bought that there, but to buy, break in, arrange a Glock, all in a day, would be impossible.'

'So either he had an accomplice in Belgium or everything was immaculately planned in advance and delivered on time.'

'What's your gut feel, ma'am? Do you think he or they'll get away with this?'

'Devil is one lucky bastard, Vikram. If you took all the cases of significant crimes around the world into account, I'd bet the criminals would have escaped more times than the number of people police have ever caught. The statistics are always in favour of the Devil. Having said that, I think we have some good grasp now if we have identified Sishir Singh, and then a detective following him.'

The car turned left into the Lokhandwala complex. Rita noted that the place had developed an identity of its own. Nothing stark or discernibly different from other suburbs, but subtle changes in buildings and shops were evident. Lokhandwala, in Andheri West, looked like an adopted child of Bandra – the grandness was perceptible. Some shops were closed. Sunday. Shutters down. Dentist. Chemist. Dry cleaner. Hairdresser. Since when did hairdressers close on Sundays? The newsagent, the bakery, the grocery store and the *paan-wallah* were open. A bland array of grey shutters, some of them with colourful graffiti; mostly obscene but it still broke the insipidity. Funny how bad could, on occasions, be good.

Vikram explained to Rita that Nene had called in a favour from one of his buddies in Andheri Police who had notified Mr Joginder Raja that there might be some personal work from someone higher up the police tree which they needed carrying out surreptitiously, and they would visit him. 'He has been asked to wait at home for us.'

Always hungry for new business, and ever eager to oblige the police – life was always give and take, wasn't it? – Joginder Raja had cleared his office, bidden his wife to standby for coffees and samosas when the police-client arrived. He made additional effort to dress up in an ironed shirt and trousers rather than his usual unkempt field attire. So a senior police officer had a not-so honest spouse? he chuffed.

Joginder Raja lived in Trishul Apartments – a lot of Bollywood lived in Lokhandwala – so he wasn't doing too badly as a private investigator or he certainly had some other business to fund his lifestyle. Vikram showed his badge to the watchman who let them in without any questions. Rita took in the area. Sunday morning: there weren't many people outdoors, but the sound of the Gypsy engine did make a few people turn to see what seemed to be a couple in it. Nothing anyone should give a second thought to.

A chance thought hit Rita as she got down from the vehicle. Joginder Raja – a private investigator – shadowing Honey Singh meant someone knew something she and her team didn't. Not yet in any event. The predominant question was: who was that someone and what was that something?

Rita was already been apprised of the signature moustache, but the handlebar moustache Mr Joginder Raja carried on his extra-large frame was something no one could have prepared her enough for when he opened his apartment door on the fourth floor. It seemed the guy spent a lot of time and gel on the damn thing. Irrefutably, if one were to describe private investigator Joginder Raja in a word, it would be Handlebar. Funny, when a solitary feature dominates everything else. Wouldn't all the other features on his face feel deprived, Rita thought.

The guy beamed a wide smile, but it was scarcely visible from behind the hirsute curtain on his lips.

First impression: he looked like someone who had thrown the dice and the fucking dice itself had gone missing. And he waited for the dice to return. Talk about losers. *Should she, shouldn't she give her professional credentials to this man?*

'I'm private investigator Joginder Raja.' He stretched his fat arm forward to Rita.

'DCP Rita Ferreira.' No point in hiding it.

'Senior Inspector Vikram Patil.'

Raja acknowledged the hierarchy with a deep swallow. His Adam's apple jerked up and skated down. Rita could picture his mental cogs moving.

'I've heard about you, ma'am.' His voice betrayed the size.

Closet lush. Still single. Sleeps around. What had he heard?

'I don't acknowledge anything.'

Smile.

Rita had given up getting troubled by what people thought or said about her; what with an honorary degree in screwed up relationships?

'I followed the serial murder case in Mumbai. I never thought you'd need me.'

Rita just smiled.

'Oh, come in.' Raja realized his *clients* were still outside the house. 'I never had clients who were in the police, and to be honest, I'm a bit surprised ...' he stopped mid-sentence as he gestured them in.

Rita and Vikram sat in the living room. The room was large, with a television, stereo, leather sofas, and some vague prints on the walls. Nothing of note. In the background Rita could see a dimly lit hallway and more than a couple of doors on each side that, most probably, led to the kitchen and bedrooms. There was a door at the rear that opened into a small balcony that carried the potpourri of plants in pots. There was one family picture that showed a younger Mrs and Mr Raja and two boys. The quiet in the house probably suggested that the boys had moved out.

Good. Two smaller Handlebars were breathing and breeding somewhere else in the world.

'Would you want to come to office or is this comfortable enough?'

So one of the doors in the hallway was the office.

'Your house your rules. Whatever is fine with you, Mr Raja.'

'I think we should sit here, it's more spacious and, when I need to speak to one of you in solitude, I'll take you to my office one by one.'

Oh no, he must think we are cheating on our respective spouses? Or our spouses are cheating on us!

'That won't be required, Mr Raja. We can sit here.' Rita didn't want to ask why they would be required to speak to him in solitude.

'Tea or coffee?'

'We are in no rush. Please sit down, let's talk and we'll ask for coffee when we need.'

The three sat down. Raja pulled out a notepad and a pen. The poor guy still believed he was getting new business.

'How may I help you two?'

You are a private detective, Mr Raja?' Rita started the conversation.

'Yes.'

'What current cases are you working on?'

'Is that required DCP *Sahiba*?'

'I wouldn't have asked if it wasn't.'

'Nothing big, just a small enquiry.'

So Handlebar wasn't going to play easy.

'What was the last big case you had?'

'Mr Widhani's.'

'*The* Mr Widhani's of Widhani Industries?'

Widhani Industries were one of the big business houses that produced and sold tyres. A national brand.

'Yes, DCP Ferreira.'

'And what did he want done?'

'His daughter's husband, now ex-husband ... is that relevant?'

'Maybe. I can't say yes or no unless I hear what it was, can I?'

'It was the husband, I mean the ex-husband cheating on her and squandering Mr Widhani's money.'

'And you helped take pictures of him in compromising situations and facilitated the divorce.'

'So to speak.'

There were always a thousand distractions to digress from the case in hand. Discipline in a detective is mandatory.

'Are you sure you aren't working on any big case at the moment?'

'What is this? You want me to work on your case or not?' Raja sounded slightly agitated. 'I'm a private investigator. People trust me. I cannot tell you any cases I'm currently working on. That would be wrong on my part.'

'Let's not get too sanctimonious, Mr Raja.'

'How would you feel if I asked you about what cases you're currently working on?'

'We're currently investigating a murder. See, I told you.'

'Whose murder?'

'Mr Raja, I'm being polite. I could have called you to the Andheri Police Station and asked the same questions.'

The guy was somewhere between a mediocre and a moron.

'I know enough people here to be scared about being questioned by the police. And, the police aren't above the law. I know all about the police, their faults and I even know a lot about you. What does that tell you?'

'One, that you have a lot of time, second you have access to the Internet and third, you know about Google. This is a homicide investigation, and non-cooperation in a police investigation is a crime. Mr Raja, I hope you comprehend that I could make your life so miserable that you can forget about your business, forget you'll ever get another call from any client. I'll wipe you and your business out from the city, and wherever you go next. If that's clear, let's proceed.'

'You can't do that. You're just threatening for the sake of it.'

'You know, you disappoint me. I expected someone like you to have done his homework on me. I can do this. Did Google search not bring up how crazy I am?'

The hubris melted. Handlebar appeared a tad frightened, though he made a manly effort to not show it. A bit of hostility emerged but disappeared immediately. But it had lasted long enough to be perceptible. Masculinity swallowed. Being rapped by a female? He merely turned out to be a poodle dressed up as a pit bull despite his size and demeanour. The eyes were not miles away from welling up. Pure fear. He shut up rather than letting his voice give away his fear.

'So, I request you to calm down and relax. Let's have a coffee and begin again.'

Raja walked to the hallway and called out his wife, told her to get three coffees. His voice cracked a bit; a typical consequence when the trachea dries up due to anxiety or intimidation or some other unpleasant emotion. He returned to the living room and sat down once again.

Mrs Raja was like Joginder's identical twin, minus the moustache, of course. She came in with the tray, said hello, left the coffees and quickly went back into wherever she had come from.

'What is this regarding?'

'Do you know someone called Sishir Singh?' Rita took a sip and began all over again.

'No. Should I?'

Rita and Vikram were both trained investigators. Trained investigators only believed something when the words matched the countenance of the person voicing them. Raja wasn't meandering, he was telling the truth.

'Never heard that name before?'

'No. Should I have? What am I missing? What are you not telling me?'

'Mr Joginder Raja, I'm the one asking questions here. A simple *yes* or *no* will be sufficient. I promise I'll answer your questions if you answer mine honestly. "*Honestly*" is the operative word here, remember.'

Raja nodded and took a noisy slurp from his cup.

'Who is Honey Singh?'

Raja looked deflated.

'Do I—'

'Yes, Mr Raja you do …' Rita cut him in between before he could think of an annoying objection. 'Who is Honey Singh and why are your following him?'

'A client wants to know some things about him.'

'What kind of intelligence about Honey Singh have been passing to your client?'

'What the subject does, where he goes, who he meets.'

'You've snooped into his office too?'

'I couldn't give myself away by going there.'

'Not even under the cover of the night?'

'Wouldn't it be locked?'

'Are you saying you never picked a lock?' Rita smiled.

Handlebar looked away. He didn't want to answer. Didn't want to lie. Didn't want the truth out either. Rita recognized his dilemma.

'No, I've never been into Honey Singh's office.'

'Why not?'

'Wasn't part of the brief. I don't think my client wants me to go that far. He seems happy with daily logs on Honey Singh.'

'Who is your client?'

'I don't know.'

Rita and Vikram exchanged glances.

'You don't know who your client is?' It was Vikram.

'That's what I said. I don't know.'

'So there is a client who's asked you to follow Honey Singh, provide him with details, but you have no inkling who he is?'

'That's correct.'

'You just said, *"He seemed happy with daily logs ..."*, so how do you know the client is a *he* and not a *she* if you don't know the client?'

'The first call to me was from a man. Subsequently, all communication is from someone who uses Mister Singh in his sign-off.'

Another Mr Singh in the story.

'But that could be a fake signature.'

'It could well be, but I have no reason to doubt it.'

'When was that?'

'A little over three months ago.'

Rita mentally calculated that the spying on Honey Singh started around the same time Jogani was murdered. The date should confirm the same. Another coincidence?

'Fairly recent then. Do you remember the date?'

'Not of the top of my head, but I can give you the date from my records.'

'Could you check please?'

Raja walked into the hallways and disappeared. Rita and Vikram looked at each other in amazement.

Raja returned with the date. '4 April.'

Two days after Ron Jogani was murdered in Belgium someone had put surveillance on Honey Singh. A moment passed. A full moment of gaping mouths, wondering what they were against, but neither uttered a word. Neither, it appeared, knew what to say. How uncanny was this?

'You've been spying on him for over three months now and Honey Singh doesn't know about it? He hasn't spotted you?'

'I'm good, I blend in.'

You blend in with that handlebar moustache? Talk about gloating. Sexy would have called him a cockalorum: a self-important little man.

Rita stopped herself from commenting on his blending skills.

'How does the client communicate with you and how do you get paid?'

Raja explicated that he received all instructions via the email. The contract was also digitally signed. All reports that Raja gathered, including pictures, were to be uploaded to an email ID created by the client Mr Singh. Raja wrote the emails, attached what he had to and saved them in the Drafts folder. Mr Singh had the password, so he would read the draft or download the stuff and then delete it so Raja would know that the message had been read. No email had ever been transmitted. The client's instructions were very clear – he didn't want Raja to keep a copy of anything. No trail.

All under the radar in case someone was watching.

The initial lump sum payment was made in cash. No, Mr Singh didn't come to deliver it. The money was left in Raja's locked letterbox one night. No, Raja didn't know in advance which night he would receive the payment. Yes, he had tried keeping a watch but he had missed whoever had come to drop the payment.

'Do you know how long does Mr Singh want Honey Singh to be followed and reported back?'

'The initial contract is for six months, but extendable if I'm required for more time.'

'Bizarre, isn't it?' Rita looked at Vikram, like she was only making a side comment.'

'But I'm paid well for it.'

'Yes, I get that part. But don't you think it's a bit odd?'

'What is odd?'

'Is it too much to grasp that you don't know who your client is and why he's paying you?'

'No.'

'And that the said client might be a criminal and paying you blood money?' For some strange, unknown reason Rita believed Joginder Raja. There was no way Handlebar could have concocted this ludicrous yarn. It was someone else's brain. She shook her head in frustration. They were dealing with some real smart cookies here.

'Do you not believe me?'

'It hardly matters whether I believe you or not, but I can assure you that no one else will. Too neat and convenient.'

'I am not fibbing.'

'I didn't say that exactly but everything sounds a bit fishy, suspicious, doesn't it?'

'What?'

'This whole investigation for a mysterious client.'

'Why?'

Handlebar wasn't being difficult. He was plain thick.

'Reverse the roles and think. Do you even know how ridiculous it all sounds?'

'Certainly sounds ridiculous, but—' Raja blurted out.

'Like I said.'

Rita gesticulated to Vikram, who took over. He questioned Raja for about twenty minutes about Sishir Singh, cleverly asked circumventing questions about diamonds and burglary, but Handlebar didn't have a clue. Joginder Raja was stupid. Not crafty. Not goings-on.

Rita sat there, switched off from the conversation – she was confident Vikram would do a great job by himself – and reflected on the issue. All Raja was carrying on was an extramural investigation. Whoever his client was, he was definitely on to something. Something didn't make sense. But then everything didn't have to make sense to everyone and not every time. The client didn't want Raja to know who he was, and he was taking ample precautions not to reveal himself. Emails sent and received could be tracked. Emails left in Drafts folder are not transmitted, hence not traceable.

'We want you to carry on as usual, Mr Raja. Exactly as before. There should never be any mention of this visit to your client or anyone. However, anything you submit to your client from now on has to be approved by us.'

'You can't do this.' Raja uttered pleadingly. The voice didn't sound like he believed in his own statement.

'Yes I can'– Rita raised her hand to stop him from interrupting – 'and I'm asking you, requesting you to help us. We need to get to your client. We think he is paramount in our homicide enquiry.'

'But I am a very good investigator. I can find out who the client is if you want. I didn't do it because I didn't want to waste time and energy on it.'

Had this guy fallen on his head when he was a kid? Was he so dumb to not follow that compared to a case with the Interpol, he was not even enamel on a shark's tooth?

'Let me explain one last time, Mr Raja ... this is a homicide investigation. Besides it being classified information, it might also mean putting your life at risk. Please do as I say.'

Nod.

'How often do you submit your report?'

'Every Saturday.'

'So you submitted it last night?'

'Yes, and he had read and deleted it by the morning.'

'Did you notice anything unusual about Honey Singh's day yesterday?'

'Like?'

'Like someone else following him?'

'No. Was someone …?' Raja looked crestfallen.

'Nope. Just wanted to know if your client might have other sources too.'

'I don't think so.'

'OK. We'll be in touch. Meanwhile, as we said, carry on as this meeting never took place.'

They gave their phone numbers to Raja and told him to get in touch if he notices anything he thinks is worth reporting on Honey Singh or his client, Mr Singh.

It was 2:15 by the time they drove out of the building.

'Let's grab a bite, Vikram. My treat.'

'What would you like to eat, ma'am?'

'Some place that'll be quick.'

'OK. What do you think about the whole thing?'

'You can't believe in everything that surrounds you, or everything that you hear or see or feel but you can't ignore everything either because, they say, everything originates for some reason. No smoke without fire, right? So someone – and in this particular case, the mysterious Mr Singh – must have enough conviction about something to hire a third person to investigate Honey Singh. Agree?'

'And he started the surveillance two days after Jogani's murder.'

'Bingo. Someone knows something surely.'

Nod.

'So what is it about Honey Singh that a secretive man wants to know?'

They had a quick bite at McDonald's and started back. The conversation was strictly professional and to the point. Both minds were dominated by the case.

'Do you think the mysterious client has got what he is looking for?' Rita was surprised. She hadn't intended the words to come out aloud; she was only mentally calculating.

'It's safe to assume he hasn't. Why else would he still be prompt enough to download info that Handlebar is passing on?'

'What if it's some kind of a charade?'

'For whom?'

'Don't know.'

5 p.m. The Sunday was practically over by the time they got to Rita's apartment.

'Should we call on Honey Singh tomorrow?' Vikram asked.

'Let's see what others have got for us over the weekend and then take the call. I'll see you tomorrow. And thanks for the ride.'

'You're welcome. Somehow, I can't believe Honey Singh hasn't spotted a Mr Raja following him for months. There could only be two possibilities: he is either visually impaired or mentally vacant.'

'There's a third one too, Vikram.'

'What might that be?'

'Handlebar blends in so well.' Rita let out a laugh as she got down from the Gypsy.

Rita had an early dinner at seven-thirty.

The three-quarter ascending moon provided a nice glow, the breeze was still, not a sign of any cloud in the sky. The night was clear, dark, warm and silent – a total antipode of the night before. Rita sat on the rocking chair with her feet up on the footstool, in her bedroom, looking out of her window. Jim Beam sat beside her on a table along with some post-dinner cheese. The 13th Floor Elevators' psychedelic rock played on the turntable at moderate volume, giving Jim a warm boost; Rita's mind was engrossed in the case. All other thoughts, even amorous ones, gave a wide berth. What did they have till now? Sishir Singh resembled Honey Singh. A private eye, who was hired by an anonymous man, followed Honey Singh. It was like a chain of loose ends, didn't matter which link you held on to. It shouldn't be impossible to trace where the anonymous client was accessing the Drafts folder? Obviously, they wouldn't confiscate Joginder Raja's computer, they wanted to ensure Raja carried on regardless of this meeting or anything that happened in the background. The client – whoever he was – shouldn't get suspicious. Finishing her small and only drink of the evening, Rita retired for the day.

TEN

Monday, research has proved, is the dreariest day for the human brain. It's more psychological than physical. The brain processes all that looms in the next five or six days and sends nerve signals to tranquilize, causing a dull, depressing sentiment. But having forgone the break, albeit not in the office, Rita had the added mix of adrenaline rush that usually dominates police officers when in the midst of an active homicide investigation.

After breakfast – Rita never missed breakfast for two reasons: one, it kick-started her terrific metabolism and secondly, when in the midst of an open investigation, who knew when the next morsel would be served? – Rita was in office early to get paperwork out of the way before the rest of the team arrived and everyone got sucked into the investigation.

A new week. A fresh perspective.

The office was small. It had two visitor chairs, and one additional that had been pulled in previously on Friday. Vikram arrived first.

'Good morning, ma'am.'

Nene and Jatin followed him. They closed the door, pulled in an additional chair and sat down.

Pleasantries exchanged, small talk over, it was time to get back to some fresh thinking, time to improvize the plan. Last thing she wanted was to run a desultory investigation.

'Looking for Sishir Singh did anyone of you mention to snitches about the Interpol or homicide,' Rita started. She was still concerned how the media had picked up the information.

Everyone looked at each other. Nope.

'So someone's done some digging up after they got the gen. Try to find out who leaked the info to the newspaper.'

It was a known fact that media picked up morbid stories by looking at bodies delivered to the morgue. Postmortem equated to unnatural death, which equated to a police case, which equated to a story. Thus, it was difficult for a murder case to stay hidden from them. Of course, the status of the person dead or the potential suspect list could decide how significant the story could be, and for how much could it sell. However, in this case there was no body, ergo it was apparent that someone had leaked the story to the press.

'Anyone could have … it will be a futile exercise,' Jatin said. And he wasn't wrong. They could waste hours rounding up each snitch to ask. It could almost become a parallel investigation by itself. And why would anyone admit easily?

'Could we try to find out which reporter got it first and work backwards from his or her contact to some snitch please? Might be a long chain but it will help. We'll probably have to hold a press conference to calm down the media.'

Fortunately, the coverage didn't have much detail, it was a small column of news, but it would certainly invite attention of anyone who was looking. Sishir Singh, or whatever his name was, would be looking. No doubt about that.

'OK. What have we got? Nene, you go first.'

Nene detailed to the group the events of Saturday. They had tailed Honey Singh and found a guy already tailing him. A private eye, Joginder Raja.

'I know Joginder Raja!' Jatin interjected.

'You know him?'

'He helped us in an old case, years back. He must be forthcoming.'

'He wasn't initially, but he did comply.' Rita rolled her eyes; she remembered having to be a strict matron to get him to give out intelligence.

'Watch out guys, our boss is ruthless,' Vikram said, bowing his head towards Rita.

'She doesn't look it.'

'Deception is a bonus in investigation.'

'What is this guys? A college ragging session?'

The room went quiet.

'Ha-ha. That was just a phoney glimpse of my ruthlessness. No offence taken.'

As they had already broached upon the subject of Joginder Raja it was logical segue into their visit to his place, which Rita updated the team with.

'We need Raja's computer. Maybe we can trace where the other recipient is accessing emails? The IP address?'

'He'll obviously be using a VPN … Virtual Private Network that masks the IP.'

'Nevertheless, it's worth checking. Jatin, I shall leave that to you.'

'Yes, of course, ma'am.'

Nene didn't have anything to add. To be fair, nothing much was expected. The snitches weren't cops who could snoop around to find more details on Honey Singh. And what was the likelihood that they would have produced another Sishir Singh lookalike?

'We'll meet in the Operations Room after lunch.'

Bad news came in after lunch.

Jatin Singh had spent hours on Jogani's computer. Cracking the password, though challenging, hadn't been the deal breaker.

'It is something like I hadn't seen before, only read about it in fiction. The moment I got access into his computer I could see that everything – Jogani's files, cache, history, everything – started deleting itself like some weird virus had immediately taken over. The tech-whiz kids tried everything to halt but failed.'

Rita, Vikram and Nene looked at him, then at each other flitting their eyes, trying to grapple with what Jatin had just relayed. They understood computers. They understood viruses. But this was beyond the realm of an everyday computer user.

'What happened then?'

'Within minutes the entire computer was wiped clean, back to factory settings.'

'Hold on. Last time you said you had figured out that Jogani's computer hadn't been used since he left for Belgium, correct ...?

'Yes ma'am.'

'Why did this not happen then?'

'The IT folks hadn't connected it to the Internet then. They just used the machine offline. But to crack the password, we had to connect to use hacking software. The software worked, but as soon as the machine came to life, it died.'

'Did you try again?'

'Yes. But it started with the black and green screen asking me to load the operating system all over again.'

'Some form of malware, then?' Vikram asked.

'You know about them?' Rita asked Jatin.

'There are a few decent computer-cleaning software packages available, of course, but most of them normally require manual intervention.'

'Could someone not do it remotely?'

'Of course, it can be customized to operate remotely but the person who's installed it there in the first place needed to have had access to Jogani's computer at some point.'

'Which isn't impossible. There is every reason to believe that the murderer knew Jogani to have known his itinerary.'

'Or—' Jatin's eyes went up, he appeared to be consulting with his memory; something he'd heard somewhere.

'Or?'

'The person might not have had access to Jogani's computer physically. All the person needed to do is somehow get Jogani to open an attachment through an email, which if Jogani opened, could install whatever malware was sent across.'

'So how did it trigger just when you got access to it?'

'The malware was already on the computer, no doubt about that. I'm only hypothecating here so please bear with me, treat my words as if I'm thinking aloud, OK?' Jatin stopped.

'OK. What do you think happened?'

'I strongly believe that the person who had remotely installed this malware into Jogani's computer somehow knew Jogani wouldn't be accessing his own computer anymore, so all he needed was to activate something to activate the malware. However, that would not have been possible while the computer was switched off and disconnected from the Internet. But when I connected it to the web, the virus fired up instantaneously.'

'And the said virus can clean up everything, render a computer useless?'

'That depends on the virus used, which, as I mentioned, would be impossible to determine now as the machine is back to its factory settings.'

'Which also means Jogani's ex-wife hadn't even bothered to, as much as, switch on the computer after she moved into his house, which gives me a feeling that she's kosher. She's not involved in the murder. Or else she must certainly have looked up for details on diamonds, bank accounts, whatever. Let's still keep a vigil on her, but we should not burn too many resources there.'

'Some of it was beyond me. I kept wondering if I had something rather stupid to have got ourselves in this predicament.' Jatin unlocked his mouth again. He had appeared petrified when he had elucidated to the group on what could probably have occurred.

Rita applauded. 'I didn't realize you could be that good with computers. Thank you for the deduction of this entire sordid episode.' Rita stretched her hand out.

'Thanks, ma'am.' His voice filled with pride.

'Where does this get us?' Rita asked when they settled back after the brief bonhomie and handshakes.

'Dead-end. We're looking at someone who can hack into virtually anything, someone who can ruin a computer and network within minutes.'

For a few moments Rita pondered if there were nerds – real computer geeks and not those depicted on television – in the real world? And if there were, did they look different?

'How very optimistic of you, Jatin.' Vikram's words brought Rita back into the conversation.

'I'd prefer to be called a realist here, Vikram.'

'OK, let's go over some missing facts together.' Rita brought the conversation back to the investigation. More positivity was required than realism to solve the problem. 'We know there was a gun involved. A Glock 19, it's a small gun. Men call it ladies' gun. That small. It can do its job. Easy to fire. Easy to conceal, and super-efficient.'

'Why didn't the Belgian police find it?'

'Good question. It's been bothering me since the day I first read the report. My gut feel is that the gun wasn't brought to the scene to be fired. It was only intended to scare Jogani or be used in dire circumstances like it eventually was. If the burglar had intended to kill to rob the diamonds, it was easy to shoot Jogani and take the diamonds. Why arrange the whole charade of changing the safe in the hotel room, modifying the door lock, placing cameras.' Rita looked around; everyone seemed to be agreeing; or not disagreeing, at least.

'So what happened to the Glock after the murder? The perpetrator couldn't have flown back to Delhi with it in his pocket. He either returned it to someone in Brussels or simply dropped it somewhere. And he obviously didn't drop it negligently or the Belgian police should have found it. Unless it is now in the riverbed being admired by some fish.' Vikram chipped in.

'If he had a gun, he knew he had to return whether he fired it or not, right?' Rita didn't wait for a response. 'So it was definitely prearranged for the gun to be returned to whoever. Maybe he met someone at the airport or left it somewhere for collection before the Belgian police even commenced the search.'

'So there was more than one person involved.'

'A minimum of two – there had to be some collusion somewhere close to the location. Might be Brussels. Might be elsewhere. It could well be that the second person stayed out of the hotel the whole time, but collected and returned the gun and other items, and then flew back on some other flight after a few days. Or flew to somewhere else before returning to India. Anything's possible.'

'Wouldn't it have been impossible to enter and exit the hotel several times without being seen or heard? He should have left some kind of a trail behind.' Nene was surprised.

'He certainly moved like an invisible shadow. No one saw or heard the second or third person, no camera picked them up anywhere.'

'Or maybe the second person never returned. Maybe he was a local, given the local knowledge and sourcing of illegal stuff.'

'Indeed, that cannot be ruled out at this stage.' Rita shook her head like she was dislodging some idea that was forming. 'No. It seems unlikely to me that the murderer involved someone abroad. Too much risk, unless, of course, the supplier wasn't involved in the whole planning, but only supplied or rented out the gun. And, after the murder, he couldn't just walk into the police station and admit he supplied an unlicensed, illegal firearm to a foreigner and it was used in a homicide. Obviously, the gun was unregistered or Belgian police would have traced it back to the owner. However, we know the perpetrators carried out a lot of work in the premises, so that makes me certain the second and/or third person was actively involved.'

The three men nodded again. The hypothetical wasn't wrong.

The investigation reached another stalemate. Silence filled the room for a full two minutes.

Not a good sign.

'Someone in this whole operation is indeed a computer geek,' Rita started. 'They need to be to work the hotel's camera network.'

'And as much as I understand computers – and correct me if I'm wrong – the computer geek didn't even need to be physically present in Brussels to help.' Jatin looked at Rita to supplement his surmise.

'I think you're right. As long as the person had the detailed plan he could have sat at home and played with the hotel network, which again confirms there were more than two people: two on site, one playing with the computer network.'

'And how does one get a detailed plan of a hotel layout without being in Brussels?' Vikram asked.

'There are many ways. The hotel maybe on the Internet. More likely, someone was paid to survey the place without divulging the reason.'

'Hmm ...'

'Honey Singh is a computer programmer.' Nene smiled as he mentioned it. His countenance showed he knew that everyone else had also done the maths.

Everyone reflected on it for a few silent seconds.

'Which is worrying. It seems too obvious to find precisely what we're looking for. We find the guy who resembles the suspect, and who is also a geek and who shares the same family name. And an unknown person is having him followed.' Then Rita went quiet.

'Maybe someone is setting Honey Singh up.'

'Maybe you're right, Nene. If Honey Singh isn't the perpetrator we might have to get him out from under this too.'

Jatin split and called Mr Raja. He didn't have to do much for an introduction, as he already knew him from previous interaction, and Rita and Vikram having only met him the day before. He quickly got to the point that had been worrying him since Jogani's computer had buckled.

'Mr Raja, you said your mystery client had initially contacted you over the phone.'

'Yes correct.'

'And since then all you do is write an email, save as draft and he logs in to read it, and downloads and/or deletes the same?'

'Correct again.'

'So there has never been any real email exchange between the two of you?'

'Never.'

'Never downloaded anything he sent you?'

'No.' Jatin could visualize Mr Handlebar shaking a no.

'Not even once?'

'Not that I can think of at this moment, why do you want to know that?'

'How about the initial contract? How did they get exchanged?'

'Now I remember, he had sent it via email that I downloaded and signed, scanned and put in the Drafts folder.'

Downloaded an attachment. Job done.

The malware, in Jatin's opinion, already sat on Mr Raja's computer and the moment the mysterious client wanted, he could fire it and destroy everything on the machine. Disconnecting Mr Raja's computer could help only if the police got to it before the geek – whoever he was – came to know of police pursuing the investigation. And since they did not require cracking Raja's password, they didn't require plugging the same into online diagnostics to make the geek aware of a new IP address.'

'Mr Raja, is your computer switched on now?'

'No.'

'I'm coming right away. Please do not switch on your machine for anything till I get there.'

'Why? Tell me something.'

'I'll be there in as much time it takes me to get from Crawford Market to Lokhandwala. Just do not switch on the computer, is that clear?'

'OK, Mr Jatin, I won't only because you've been a long-term buddy, not because I'm afraid of the police or your DCP. I know my rights ...'

'Whatever. See you as soon as I can.' Jatin disconnected rather than listening to Handlebar's diatribe of being subjected to such inhuman torture as not letting him switch on his computer.

'I am confident the same malware is sitting on Mr Raja's computer,' Jatin informed Rita, who now sat in her office looking at the red Belgian investigation file again, 'I've spoken to him, and now rushing to his place with one of our IT guys to see what we can retrieve.' He gave a succinct account of his telephonic tête-à-tête with his old *buddy* Handlebar, and how he had surmised that the malware might have been installed on the machine.

'Good work, Jatin. Say my hello to your buddy, tell him I really love his moustache.' Jatin, she knew, would mine as much information from Mr Raja as possible in a friendly fashion. Perhaps more than Vikram and she did in their visit.

Rita sat thinking after Jatin left.

What if the killer knew about their visit to Handlebar the day before? Wouldn't a guy this wicked already know that? There seemed little point in getting the panties in the wad if the damage was already done. There will surely be other ways to get to these criminals. She closed the file. It was six in the evening. The sun was down, the dusk was up when the driver picked up and drove her home.

ELEVEN

There are times when you need to talk to someone, talk aloud and let the sound of your words resonate what you think. Rita had always believed that talking her thought aloud made her aware what she missed. But she didn't have anyone, which irked her. Gone were the days where she could come back home and discuss cases with Karan, he ex who dropped her for an opportunity in the US. To be fair, that was his calling like this was hers. They were only compatible to a point, but she missed him. He had a patient ear – he never provoked, solicited more info, questioned or answered her questions she posed to self.

It was August, the night was clammy. Rita had had her dinner and changed into her short nightshirt. She didn't see the need to wear anything else. There was no one who could have a view into her bedroom from the window where she sat with her feet up unless someone was watching her with binoculars and then, she smiled, the guy deserved to see her legs. What had she to hide anyway – her legs were shapely and shaved.

Jim Beam had been her only other friend. He, too, didn't answer, never interrupted the train of thought; just fuelled her imagination and kept her awake and kept her alert till she had had too many. But this evening she decided to give Jim a wide berth. It was time to think. Leave behind all that they had thought of, hypothesized so far. She wanted to concentrate on what might have happened. To add together whatever she knew, whatever she had heard from the Belgian detective, Victor and read in the file, and all that she and the team had seen and collected so far. Then re-add it. The trick was not to eliminate anything till she was absolutely certain that it was phoney or irrelevant, but all the while keeping in mind that she might know if something is irrelevant till they had all that she required. No rush. Haste makes waste – cliché, but factual. No conclusion was better than a false one. No conclusion would keep her running. False conclusion would halt the progress.

Think, Rita.

Albeit hypothetically, she adumbrated the sequence of events that could have led to the murder ...

She had a pen and writing pad to jot down what she could about the perpetrator:

1. Consummate planner
2. Improvization on the run. Sharp
3. Precise, almost perfect, execution
4. Careful, meticulous escape
5. He used computers and beat computers and networks

Think, Rita.

Every scene had layers. Someone didn't just walk in from the street on a hunch, shoot Jogani and walked away with the diamonds. Every plan had layers; the plan, the contingency, should something go wrong like it did horribly, the escape route, the getaway.

He's calm, she murmured. Even before the robbery he would have known that the whole incident could go wrong a hundred and one different ways due to a hundred and one unknown, unforeseen reasons. But he was confident that if crisis occurred, he could handle it, he wouldn't let the mission be compromised. And he handled it, didn't he? Certainly not from Jogani's perspective – turning the hotel room into the diamond merchant's sepulchre – but then crisis management hardly ever looked pretty anyway.

He had timed Jogani's travel from his room to the front desk and back, including the anticipated little fracas with the receptionist about the false alarm.

He certainly hadn't expected Jogani not putting the diamonds in the safe in the room – why else would a new safe be bought and installed? – but fastening the damn steel-reinforced briefcase to the water pipe with a bespoke handcuff instead that *maybe* couldn't be broken without a bullet.

Importantly, somehow Mr Sishir Singh was forewarned that Ron Jogani was on the way back because he wasn't the one caught in the en suite bathroom; star-crossed Jogani was the unfortunate one blind-sided. Therefore, indubitably, there was a second person on the ground, watching and communicating somehow. Which also connoted that the gun could easily have been passed back to the supplier through this second person despite Sishir Singh having left the country with the diamonds.

Given what she inferred now about the fastidious operation, she wasn't inordinately amazed that the team was astute enough that the second and/or third person never got caught on the lift camera; the only one that the team missed and that was in operation in the elevator.

And even if the other members of the group escaped all cameras, how was it possible that no one in the hotel saw them or spotted them either? Were they invisible? Yes they were. And how could someone be invisible unless he was part of the scenery? Like another ordinary car in a car park … who would spot it? That could only have happened if the other person or persons were a hotel staff but the Belgian police file said they had investigated and interviewed all staff, and cleared them all. No one had quit the job in the three months preceding or succeeding the incident. So … so there was only one possible explanation. Someone was a fake member of staff. A laundry man? Housekeeping personnel? Big establishments provided that safe haven of anonymity. Not all members of staff know each other, more so in a business like a hotel with three shifts. It would be virtually impossible to know all the other staff that worked here in rotating shifts. Then there could always be temporary staff, so why would an employee be concerned if they saw an unknown face in some sort of a hotel uniform in the corridors? They must see it every once in a while. Part of the scenery: inconspicuous, indistinguishable. How would they even remember it after the incident if they did not find anything out of ordinary in the first instance? And one of those individuals carried the gun out after the murder. Entirely possible.

Think, Rita.

No, it wasn't one person's job to manipulate the hotel security cameras, the safe vault in the room, install cameras in the room, and tamper with door lock. It needed help. Another pair of trusted hands and eyes, and lots more besides. But there was no evidence. Every definite, how much ever you believed it was, couldn't be proved. Not mathematically, and legally even less so. You couldn't go to court with *I think so and so happened …*

There were missing pieces, but it was always the missing pieces that made puzzles, she recognized that. Years of police training and experience had taught her that answers were never served on a platter, least of all in a homicide investigation. She needed more information. Unlike body weight, in a murder investigation it was better to have more than not enough. Trouble was discerning what fat to cut when you don't know what was profitable and what was unavailing. But because there weren't enough number of hours in the day, the detective had to make choices based on the preponderance or imbalance of evidence. Oh yes, of course, it could go wrong.

Welcome to the cynical world of a cop, she smiled.

Her mind segued into how all investigations began. All crimes could be unravelled with three dimensions: motive was always the starting point – why does someone do something so gruesome at all? Second came means – was the person equipped to do it? And third, did the person have the opportunity? If diamonds were the motive, then the motive stood solid for more than half the world's population: who wouldn't have wanted them? However, the cause-and-effect relationship between money and murder, she knew, worked both ways. Money could get you killed. Killing could make you money.

With Mumbai being the entrepôt of Jogani's stolen diamonds and one of them having turned up again in Belgium, it was fair to assume that, at least some of the diamonds had been sold and converted into cash. There was a mismatch was between the value of the diamonds and Honey Singh's lifestyle though – the only apparent suspect they had till date. It didn't add up. However, she reckoned, in today's time and day it didn't have to. For most of the people money was merely a number. On the computer or mobile. You didn't need to horde stacks of cash under or in the mattress. It could be stashed in an anonymous offshore account somewhere. Switzerland? Cayman Islands? How could they have access to accounts? The Swiss and Cayman Islands were from a different planet altogether. They wouldn't part with the details for Interpol even. Not for homicide. For acts of terrorism maybe but not in case of a lone dead Indian jeweller. Ergo, looking for someone with recent inheritance would be a complete waste of time. She considered it for a moment and then she struck it: that line of enquiry couldn't lead to the blooded hands.

Somewhere on the street below, a dog barked. It was followed by a series of barks by others. Maybe they were communicating something, maybe they were simply saying goodnight to each other. However, it broke Rita's deliberation. She had been sitting and reflecting on the case for over three hours now, and had only construed a possible sequence of events; she hadn't hatched any new eggs. The record player had stopped hours ago while she had been engrossed in her thoughts, she hadn't realized it.

Just as she planned to switch off for the day her phone rang. The caller ID displayed: Ash Mattel. Trouble these days was that there was no way to determine the geographical location where the caller was when the caller ID popped up on the screen of the recipient. Rita's Pavlovian conditioning compelled her to glance at the clock and calculate the time difference between India and UK, as Ash resided there. Midnight in Mumbai would be seven-thirty the prior evening in London. Why should he call her at midnight unless something was burning?

'What makes the great Dr Mattel call a lowly Indian police officer at this hour?'

'Ha-ha. It isn't a doctor calling a police officer. It's a patient calling a doctor. I'm the one in pain here, gorgeous.'

'What pain might that be?'

'Almost a heart attack.'

Despite all new mobile phones fitted with condenser microphones to cut down backdrop noise, the call highlighted that Ash was in some place that had more-than-average ground noise which spilled over. Rita's trained ears could pick up a fair number of voices, broken syllables and murmurs, and even some announcements over a loudspeaker in the milieu that conveyed to her that Ash was in a public place. The ground noise wasn't clear enough for her to discern what it was: maybe a hospital, maybe a railway station? Or an airport?

'Where has your flight landed?' she gambled.

'You are not just a pretty face, Rita. You're a smart cookie. How did you guess I was at an airport?'

Her gamble had paid off. And then she caught something in Hindi in the ambience and she knew he was somewhere in India, most likely Mumbai.

'Oh, I even know you're in Mumbai. Do you want me to recite your flight number now?'

'Oh my-my, someone's a Sherlock.'

'And what brings you to Mumbai? I thought you were scheduled for next month?'

'I couldn't wait to see you. What are you wearing? Feel free not to answer that, I'll just imagine.'

That was Ash Mattel: he was criminal psychologist by profession, master of cheesy chat-up lines. They had romped a few times, but there wasn't anything romantic between them, just two consenting adults. And even though Rita despised his tacky one-liners in the beginning, she had become accustomed to them later when she realized he only did the same to tease though one couldn't whisk away the licentious thoughts they kindled or the further conversations they provoked. Ash was quite unique. If you Googled images of criminal psychologists, Ash's persona would be the last to feature – if at all – after all the

Einstein lookalikes. Ash was tall, balding, and face like a deeply tanned Bill Murray. Not good looking but attractive to women nevertheless. Additionally, he was a charmer in person when it came to words that mattered; he could charm the feathers off a peacock in the mating season. He was recently divorced when he met Rita; the first time after a decade and Rita had still been licking her wounds since her break-up with her boyfriend a few years back. It was lust at first sight.

'Hold your imagination please. You admitted you only remembered me because you saw me in a bikini back in college.'

'Yes-o-yes! A small black one, if I remember correctly. Do you still have that?'

'What?'

'Just kidding. Anyway, you're right. I was scheduled to come for a conference in September, but that particular one got canned and they wanted me to join this one in lieu of another participant, so here I am. My flight has just landed in Mumbai. How're you doing? I hope I didn't wake you up at this unearthly hour?'

'I was about to switch off, just reading a case file.'

'Anything I can help with?'

'Maybe, though I might have to keep the names off, but two brains are better than one.'

'So are two bodies—' Ash effortlessly slipped into his amorous tone once again.

'Can you never be serious for the complete length of any conversation, Ash?' Rita sometimes wondered why she even bothered with him. It wasn't like there was a shortage of men. But, she knew well that there were insufficient interesting men; then the old camaraderie always worked well.

'Of course. We have a formal dinner tomorrow evening, but I should be free afterwards if you want to work late night.'

'OK, I'll keep the evening free. Why don't you give me a call tomorrow and we'll take it from there. Where are you staying?'

'The Oberoi at Marine Drive.'

'That's fine. Give me a call by lunchtime. Good night.'

'You too have a good night's sleep. I might not let you sleep at all tomorrow.'

The case slipped into oblivion as Rita switched off the light and passionate thoughts slipped into her consciousness unannounced. She had a warm feeling when she closed her eyes and, within seconds, she drifted into the abyss of sleep.

TWELVE

By late morning Rita's team, working with uniformed Mumbai Police in various locations, had run all the canvassing and came up empty. Anita Jogani and every single person she had been in touch with in the past one year had been checked out and cleared. The entire Jogani household staff – which alternated as his office staff – and their connections had been sussed and absolved. Ron Jogani's close social coterie had been examined, their alibis checked and their names struck off the suspect register. Rita and team had no doubt whatsoever that the killer had known Jogani; the question was how? How well had Jogani known the killer that he had divulged his plan?

'His travel agent must surely have known the detailed plan, maybe even the hotel Jogani was staying in?' Rita, coffee in hand, once again voiced the first new question in the Operations Room.

Vikram jotted it down.

'Anything from Mr Joginder Raja's computer, Jatin?' Rita asked, though Jatin's countenance displayed nothing of consequence was mined whatsoever.

'Obviously, we were careful to disconnect his PC before running the tests. As expected Joginder Raja's mysterious client uses VPN, and guess whose IP address came up when we dug in?'

It was a rhetorical question. Rita glanced at Vikram. Vikram glanced at Nene. No one asked or took a shot at answering. They waited Jatin out.

'His own.'

'Is that possible?'

'Well, the so-called client has masked his own ID and diverted the log in such a way that it bounced off somewhere in Hong Kong and then redirected such that it appeared that our Mr Raja is the only one who accesses that email account. We also tried to check where the email account was created, but the person masterminding the whole operation had been careful to mask the IP right from the beginning. A kind of dead-end.'

'Could it be that Mr Raja has prevaricated that he has some client when he's the one who follows Honey Singh, reports it and then reads it?' Nene wasn't serious, but nothing was ever impossible.

'You haven't met him, Nene. Or you wouldn't have given him so much credit. This is the same Mr Raja who missed that your team followed him following Honey Singh this Saturday,' Vikram explained.

'Really? He missed all three cars?'

'Vikram is being harsh on Mr Raja. I think the guys you sent on the task were real good.' Rita gestured a thumbs-up.

'Thank you, ma'am.'

'So, in effect, we are no better or worse with access into Mr Raja's computer?'

'No ma'am'

'Could our IT gurus not check what kind of malware this Mandrake uses?'

'They're at it, but it would be difficult to check without connecting it to online diagnostics.'

'OK. Ask them not to make that mistake again please. I am pretty sure that if we log in from another location, the change in Mr Raja's IP or whatever might send some kind of early warning sign to Mr Raja's client. They should do as much as they can without connecting it. Then return the PC ASAP, preferably today itself. We want Mr Raja to keep communicating with his mysterious client as usual.'

'Roger that, ma'am.'

Vikram noted Jatin's task, too, on his pad.

'At least we are clear on one thing,' Rita exhaled loudly to emphasize the effect. 'The guy who killed Ron Jogani's computer and the one who killed Mr Raja's mystery client are both computer-savvy. I can bet it's the same set of people. It's too much of a coincidence to swallow that two sets of computer geeks running two separate operations just happened to overlap, won't you say?'

Sure. No one could argue with that.

'And I can't believe why someone would do that unless they were to get the share of the diamonds? They might be in tandem or they might be the same set of people.'

'How can we know that?'

'That's what we'll find out.'

'Should we approach Honey Singh for help? He can assist us on tracing if he is any good?' Vikram floated a new idea.

Rita let that idea hang. It was like the proverbial catch-22. If Honey Singh knew – or could guess or conclude from what they tell him – why would someone be following him around, then there was a high probability he would also know who that person was or might be? And if Honey Singh didn't have the faintest of indication that he was being tailed, wouldn't he want to help the police to discover who it could be and why? Wouldn't anyone in that predicament? Conversely, if Honey Singh was even remotely involved in this entire Jogani case, the police would blow away any cover they thought they had by approaching him.

'No, let's exhaust all other possibilities before we approach Honey Singh. All we have till now are three ambiguous links between Sishir Singh and Honey Singh: they both live in Mumbai, share a common family name and both are well versed with computers – hardly any evidence that they are the same guy. There can be another five thousand men in this city with these three common attributes—'

'But they are carbon copies of each other. You've seen both pictures, ma'am,' Nene exclaimed.

'Yes, I have. You're the one who's done the entire search into his family. Any chance of an identical twin separated in *Kumbh-ka-Mela*?'

Nene smiled. 'Like some old Bollywood film, you mean?'

'Identical twin is a biological phenomenon, which we cannot ignore or deny, can we?'

'We can check with his mother, she would certainly know.' Nene concurred.

'But she might not certainly tell you the truth. Why should she if there is a tragic story behind? In any event, she is under no obligation to tell us the truth unless we subpoena her into a court, and we can't do any of that till we have a case against her or her son. How about we avoid the family and find out where

Honey Singh was born? We dig into hospital and municipal records and find it ourselves.'

Vikram jotted down that too. He was meticulous about every case.

Their tasks handed out, Nene and Jatin left for action.

'And Vikram, I want you to concentrate entirely on Honey Singh. I need all records of Honey Singh's travels – business or pleasure – from the beginning of the year. I doubt if they keep video recordings of passengers at airports for three months, but they should have printed records of travel from in and out of the country. Ask them to check if Honey Singh went abroad at all, not only to Belgium or Europe but also anywhere outside India. All the phones he owns or those listed as his company phones, their call records – especially in the week of Jogani's murder. And GPS co-ordinates, if any, of these mobiles; if any of the phones were taken abroad we should know. He runs a legitimate business so there should be no reason, at this point, for us to suppose he has any clandestine pay-as-you-go telephone connections. Any capture of his car on any Police camera in the city during the week of Jogani's murder in Belgium. Anything that can alibi him.'

Vikram scribbled on.

'Same for Kitty.'

'Who?' He looked up.

'Miss Kitty Varghese, his girlfriend who's a model – get her phone records too, and her whereabouts at the time.'

'Yes ma'am.'

'We find anything that places him near Belgium we have a case against him. If nothing comes up, we go see him. For all we know he might be in danger from whoever this Sishir Singh is or from Mr Raja's unidentified client, if they are not one and the same, but that's for after.'

Vikram left and Rita went back and prepared another cup of hot coffee – demitasse as she called it – for herself. It was nearing lunchtime now and Mr Hotness had not called yet. She checked her mobile, but there were no missed calls, no text either. She sat in her chair, reclined and ran her hand in her hair, only to realize again that they were shorter now than a year back. She smiled. What a case that had been, chasing a serial killer through Bhendi Bazaar and being taken captive herself. She still came out a winner. However, in this case she was working on hand-me-down information, which peeved her. But, she knew well that when the world, including *Sexy* and Joshi, put you at the top, you don't have a moral right to make excuses of any kind. She couldn't just go back now to *Sexy* and say she couldn't crack the case because ... that will be nonsense.

They say if you wanted to know about someone's private life you should ask their driver. The driver is the one who took them somewhere and brought them back. The driver overheard a lot of conversation since the invention of mobile phones. In some cases the driver also picked up and dropped their guests to local Mumbai stations or taxi stands. In some other cases the drivers in Mumbai also did miscellaneous shopping on their behalf. In short, the driver had access to information that some retail companies' CRM departments would be willing to pay to see add-ons and complimentary products they could bolt on to the original purchases. Not that Rita had any inhibitions or anything to conceal but there seemed little point in her police driver's knowledge augmentation by exposing him to the fact that Rita was to pick up Mr Ash Mattel after dinner and take him to her place. Worse still, DCP Ferreira stayed the night at The Oberoi.

Rita called Kuldeep and asked him to come up, hand over the car keys to her as she might get back late tonight.

'No problems, madam, I'll wait.'

'No, I will get back very late and there's no point in holding you back. You can carry on, you're relieved for the day.'

It's OK, madam.'

Why don't you understand my dilemma, you loyal soldier, she wanted to call out in frustration. It's not about you; it's about me.

'Please send the keys up. I'll call you tomorrow morning. No more discussion.' She asked him to hand over the keys to someone downstairs rather than come up to her office and reopen the same discussion.

'OK,' Kuldeep reluctantly agreed like his best toy had been snatched from him. Rita had barely concluded her conversation when her mobile rang: Ash Mattel.

'Apologies, I got withheld in some overheated discussion on one of the topics.'

'It's OK. And hello.'

'Hello, really tied up this afternoon, but I'll be free by seven as it's an early dinner.'

'Where's the dinner?'

'I haven't really checked, why? You want to join me?'

'As your ...'

'As my college friend, Hun-bun.'

'Will other people be bringing their college buddies too?'

'Why do you care?'

'Who said I do?' Rita laughed out.

'What's the plan? You said you wanted to discuss some case with me?' Ash suddenly sounded formal.

'Has someone just walked in your hearing distance then?'

'Kind of, yes.'

There was no way Rita was going to let the opportunity go.

'How about discussing the numerous techniques of sex?'

'Uh-huh, uh-hmm! Yes, certainly, we could do that.'

'Ha! You suddenly got a sore throat now?'

Ash didn't respond. He still seemed to be in someone's earshot.

'OK, I'll let you go now. I'll be in my office. Let me know when you leave for dinner so I'll time it such that I can pick you up after that.'

'That will be great.' Ash still sounded formal.

'I have a *"Bad case of loving you, Doctor, Doctor"*,' Rita recited Robert Palmer's lines before she cut the call.

Jatin and the IT team spent the full day on Handlebar's PC, but came up with nothing. If they could not connect the web-based diagnostics, there was not a chance in hell to trace any latent malware on the machine. Perhaps, it was hidden behind some files or ingrained into the hard disk or perhaps it wasn't there on Raja's machine in its entirety. One line of thought was that just a pixel must have been dropped, which, if and when activated, would be enough to scrape the data of the PC. Whatever it was, it was untraceable, and hence irremovable. You can't fight what you can't see.

A follow-up idea from the IT group was to replace Mr Raja's computer – like for like – with another machine without giving admin rights to Mr Raja so he couldn't download anything new sent from his mysterious client. However, after consulting Rita, Jatin vetoed it. The idea, when evaluated, had more holes than a colander. If the furtive client was so smart to erase Jogani's computer remotely, wouldn't he somehow tell that the machine that's been communicating with him for the past few months had changed? Plus they couldn't think of any upside of doing that. They had attempted discovering and unmasking the IP address of the client and failed; they had scanned Mr Raja's PC and found nothing that was of any import to the police, so changing the PC was saving exactly what? And the downside was that if the client discerned that the computer was changed he might break all contact with Mr Raja or worse still, go after Handlebar.

As agreed, Rita was still at work at seven when Ash Mattel called. Except a few random spotting of humans in the office, most of the others had left, as this wasn't one of the ninety-plus uniformed police stations; this was Mumbai Police Headquarters. The whole top brass was housed in Royal Alfred Sailors' Home, which was built in 1876. However, everything in the vicinity was dominated by one of the marvels of architectures called Crawford Market and all surrounding areas, too, were referred to as Crawford Market. Mumbai Police Commissioner and Additional Director General of Police for the state of Maharashtra, Mr Sanjay Saxena aka *Sexy* sat here, so did the several senior police officers that reported to him, and the Crime Squad of which Rita was a part: Deputy Commissioner of Police Rita Ferreira.

'We're going for dinner now, so my guess is I should be able to slip out by eight, eight-thirty,' Ash explained.

'I can pick you up, where is it?'

'There's a Japanese restaurant in this hotel that's been booked for us, so I don't think it makes any sense for you to pick me up and drive me all the way back to Bandra in Mumbai traffic. What do you think?

'You can always cab it after dinner—'

'Or you can sleep over at the hotel. I've got an ocean-view room.'

'Ocean view that looks over the Arabian Sea?'

'Well that's what they call it in the brochure.'

There was silence for a few seconds, as both of them mentally digested the repercussions, if any, of Rita staying over at the hotel, in Ash's room.

'You still there?'

'Yes.'

'Rita, if you're not comfortable, it's OK, I can understand. I can always cab it to your place.'

'Do I look like someone who gives a flying fuck what anyone thinks?' You know what Winston Churchill said?'

'He said a lot. What did he say about staying the night at a hotel?'

'Don't remember the exact words but it was something like "if you stopped and threw stones at every dog that barked you'd never get anywhere," something like that.'

'I only said that as you gave me a silent treatment when I mentioned staying over …'

'Oh that? I was only contemplating how it would feel making love with an ocean view.' Did he think she was some ingénue who couldn't render one-lines like him? She could almost picture Ash blushing at her retort.

'Okay, I'll see you around eight-thirty then?'

'Yep.'

Rita had an hour before she left. She always kept a spare set of clothing for this reason. One in police force never knew what emergency could land at your desk and how long one had to stay without visiting their residence to change. She closed her office door, lowered the blinds and quickly changed into a clean shirt and lingerie and put on the same jeans again. With her light cotton jacket on top to conceal the Smith and Wesson – she contemplated leaving the weapon behind, but decided against that. Who knew where she would be headed next or should some new emergency surface in the middle of the night? – she was ready for the evening. It was still seven-thirty and there was no rush to leave, she only had to drive a little over three kilometres. Maybe fifteen minutes.

Mr Handlebar Raja was livid; he was worried and he was scared.

His PC had been returned to him the same evening, but he was still furious. He collected all the papers scattered on his desk, tamped them and shoved them into one of the drawers below and kicked it shut. He had told his wife a million times not to leave her papers dispersed but she never listened. Wonder what women of today thought of themselves? This would not have been tolerated in his father's time indeed. That fucking DSP … DCP, whatever, the bloody police woman. What did she think of herself? He hated her guts, coming up to his place and rapping him like he was some spoiled schoolboy. He finally switched on his computer and logged in.

He was worried. If his client – and at this point in time he only had the one – discovered that he had been collaborating with the police, the client might take the business away. Handlebar didn't want to lose a client who paid in advance, didn't fuss too much on what information was passed on, no unnecessary face-to-face meetings, no nonsense, none whatsoever. All he had to do is write up Honey Singh's movements throughout the day and submit.

He logged in to the email account and it showed that there was an unopened message in the Drafts folder, which was odd because he hadn't put anything and his client hardly ever left messages for him; in fact after the initial exchange of contract, there had never been any message from the client. Only he left messages for the client and never heard back. Had some wiseass in the police put a message for his client? Oh God, no. He clicked on the message and his distress went up several notches.

Who was following you around when you followed Honey Singh on Saturday? And why was that not mentioned in your weekly report? Remember, I am not a fan of substandard work. As this is your first mistake I'm tolerating this, which is against my credo. Do not, I repeat, do not serve me any more lemons. And if I ever find out that you are being cute with me in any way – do not forget I know where you and your wife live, I also know where your sons and their wives and your grandchildren live – the consequences will be dire, to say the least. Let this be your first and last warning.

Handlebar felt sick to his stomach, his oesophagus pumped a gallon of acid upward, his heart burned, his mouth went dry like someone had soaked out the last drop of his saliva with a blotter. Involuntarily, his eyes welled with fright, and he could feel icy sweat racing down his thick spine. He was convinced he'd have a heart attack. He couldn't decide whether he should or should not respond to the note. There was no doubt in his mind that his client would know that he had read the note; there was little point in marking it as unread as he knew his client might have some way of finding out, and that might only further antagonize the enigmatic Mr Singh. And going by the terse warning he had just been served that was the last thing Handlebar wanted to do. Suddenly, everything he had so far deemed noble about his only client began to appear terrible. The guy's words expressed menace. He picked up his phone to dial DCP Ferreira, but stopped. What could she do? As a matter of fact, if he called her it was colluding with the police after he had been warned. What fucking mess had he got himself into? More importantly, what bothered him this minute was how could he get out of it?

Fifteen minutes passed, and when he was positive that the feeling of heart attack had also passed he *de novo* pondered what choices he had going forward. Supposing he made an excuse on medical grounds? But his client, he knew, was too sharp to let that go – he'd smell the sham straightaway. This wasn't some school where his truant could be corroborated with a medical certificate from a general practitioner. And if the client didn't buy his poor-health excuse, it was his family's life at risk. No, he couldn't get rid of the client, that much he was definite. He also didn't dare make a police complaint regarding this threat despite it being explicit. The police wouldn't – and couldn't even if they wanted to – provide twenty-four/seven security to him and his extended family; his sons and their wives lived in different cities, both had children who went to school. It wasn't possible. And what would they be guarding them against? The enemy here was unidentified.

If he had to explain the incident – though his client hadn't asked for any explanation, but if it ever occurred again – he had no choice but to admit to his client that he had completely missed the goons following him follow Honey Singh, and eat humble pie made of unadulterated dung; he was still sceptical if he would mention that the goons were policemen and that the police had paid him a visit too.

But how could he, the best private investigator in Mumbai, have failed to spot a car that was tailing him? – Handlebar had often preened at his genius, an effete self-professed best in business – and if *he* missed how did his client find that out? Was it a random check that his client had conducted or was there another team that followed him around when he was on the job? Nah, one sole incident of him missing the police car following him was only just about acceptable to his pride, missing another person or people every day for three months? No way. So the smartass police tailing him had also failed to notice that there was someone else stalking them? Well, police, in his mind, weren't immune to failures. It must have been a fucking convoy on Saturday then, he smiled for the first time since he had seen the email from his client.

Well, everyone made mistakes, he finally acknowledged. But he had to be exceptionally vigilant in future. A fresh frisson of fear passed through his body. This must be serious if his mystery client made him follow a target and then hire another team to follow the same target.

He decided he would not send his client any response, as it made no sense in explaining himself or apologizing at this point. He also decided he'll speak to DCP Rita Ferreira – or better still Jatin who was a little friendlier than that arrogant woman – and ask them not to follow Honey Singh, as that would jeopardize his business. Should he mention the threat? No, he decided, not for now. He didn't think it was needed, and that was Handlebar's first mistake. Had Rita Ferreira & Co. known there was another set of people following Honey Singh, perhaps they would have caught up with them and known who Sishir Singh or Mr Raja's elusive client was.

Handlebar's second and even bigger mistake was that he decided to play James Bond and call the shots from then on. He concluded he had to get into the game wholeheartedly and expose the identity of his mystery client, after all.

But when you are a textbook idiot and your IQ is the same as rpm of a long-playing gramophone record and you want to fight a nameless, faceless opponent who's wicked genius is so off the charts that it has baffled the Interpol think tank, such a resolution is not simply dangerous; it could be lethal. David and Goliath is a fable, and Santa Claus isn't real, but Mr Handlebar Joginder Raja was determined, overconfident and a lot unrealistic.

Pollyannaish is the word *Sexy* would have used to describe Mr Handlebar Joginder Raja: unrealistically optimistic.

THIRTEEN

It was past dusk when Rita left the office; even the shadows were long gone. The night was black, the breeze cool. Stars shone and the night sky over the Arabian Sea was clear, but the sea was anything but quiet. The waves splashed against the rocks and the promenade hard enough to be audible, even with windows rolled up, in her white Jetta 1.4 petrol. Surely, the Germans took the Indian small-engine-fuel-economy penchant very seriously. However, the small 1.4 litre engine was nippy.

Rita was lost in her thoughts – the case, for once, taking a back seat. From the moment she had *re-met* Ash Mattel – decades after college – she was cognisant that there could be no long-term-forever-me-and-you relationship. The awkward part was that the transience had outlived her anticipation and was now beginning to accord a sense of permanence. Both of them had to move on, and she was aware that it had to culminate at some point, hopefully with civility. Love on separate continents wasn't feasible or advisable. When she wasn't prepared to give up her career for her first love – the one that breathes in you, the one who you dream of, that love, unfortunately, only happens once in a lifetime, all else is a beautiful compromise; didn't they repetitively say that? Why would she sacrifice her career now? She had for long played the joker in the circus of love. She fitted everywhere and nowhere. A poster girl for failed romances. She sounded like a bad case of Mills & Boons. She shook herself out of the disheartening thought. There wasn't any purpose in keeping the past alive unless you were a masochist.

Nevertheless, she believed in love; as much as she could with a twice-broken heart. Frighteningly, though it wasn't love, it felt special. She couldn't pinpoint how or why, like sometimes you can't. Most men couldn't close their eyes and explain purely in words how to tie a good knot around their necks; that didn't mean those men couldn't wear ties. That meant they couldn't describe. It is a well-known fact that no one could really describe how it felt to have a sneeze or an orgasm; that didn't mean people didn't have, either.

The Oberoi is a legendary hotel. As she drove to it in the light traffic she wondered who were these conference organizers that had the wherewithal to spend that kind of moolah to fly guests from all over the world and then park their Armani-clad arses at The Oberoi? And if they, indeed, discussed criminal psychology stilling around the table with expensive pastries, sandwiches and coffees, why were the police never invited to these session? Maybe she could bring real-life experience into these. Or maybe she could learn some new theory that could be practised.

She arrived at the hotel at nine minutes past eight. As anywhere else in Mumbai there seemed a competition for parking space. She was quite pleased when the valet took her car and gave her the token. She smiled at the doorman and briskly faded into the hotel crowd. The hotel staff was either busy or uninterested in a lady walking into the lobby. Why should they?

It was a public place, albeit rights of admission reserved, but Rita didn't look like some street urchin or a hooker.

Ash was true to his word; he finished the dinner with other conference guests, said his byes and goodnights and rushed out of the restaurant. Eight-thirty-seven. He rushed to the hotel lobby to check if Rita was waiting for him. Nope. He walked to the reception to check if he had had any visitor, any messages. Nada. He wandered in the lobby for a few minutes, his eyes glued at the entrance to catch a glimpse of Rita before she saw him. He gave up after ten minutes and decided to go up and wait in his room.

Out of the elevator he slid his card-key into the slit and opened the dark door.

'Hands up.'

He felt the cold barrel of a gun on his back, but he smiled; he didn't freak out or pass out with fear.

'Wowo-wo! How did you get in here?'

Ash wore a natural linen suit open collared white shirt, and shiny tan shoes. He looked every bit ready to go out on a date. Or come to see her as it were.

'I turned on my charm, what do you think?' Rita lied. She had unscrupulously used her police badge, albeit not enforcing it but proving her credentials.

'Really? And they let you in?'

'Yes. I told them I'm your local Mumbai girlfriend.'

'Local Mumbai girlfriend?' Ash mused. 'As opposed to girlfriend from ...?'

'The one from England.'

'I have no girlfriend in England at this point in time.'

'Scotland then?'

'Nope.'

'Northern Ireland?'

'Nope.'

'The Netherlands.'

'That's not even in the United Kingdom.'

'But you have someone there?' Rita raised her eyebrows for effect.

'No. What's this now, an interrogation into life and times of Ash Mattel? I thought you had an important case you were working on.'

'I am a woman, I am programmed to multitasking.' Rita took off her linen jacket, the gun in holster showed.

Ash turned around and took her in his arms.

The kiss lasted several minutes. Tongues met, entwined, explored each other's mouth, performed a serpentine ballet while their hands explored the bodies till Ash's slid down and traced the gun in the holster.

'I always wanted to see an attractive woman carrying a gun in just her lingerie,' he said as the mouths detached after the oral probing.

'You've watched too many episodes of Xena, the warrior princess.'

'She didn't wear just lingerie.'

'She didn't wear much if I remember correctly.'

Rita unhooked her Smith and Wesson, pointed it towards the ceiling and carefully unloaded the cartridges while doing a mental count to ensure she didn't leave any inside the chamber. Ash hadn't used the safe locker provided in the room yet, so she placed the gun and cartridges inside the solid steel receptacle and locked it for the night.

'There I've just killed your dream.' Rita gestured towards the locked safe.

'Only part of the dream I hope.'

They kissed again.

The room was actually a suite. Rita always wondered why hotel rooms had such serious-looking furniture made of solid wood. She got the wear-and-tear part but wouldn't they want to change stuff every so many years? Ornate writing desk that no one used these days. A bed strong enough that elephants could make love on. The bed wasn't facing the window; the window with the view was on the left. And the view wasn't just another ocean view, it had the ocean as the only view unless one came really close to the windows and looked down at the street and the traffic. Both of them drifted towards the window and admired the seascape. Rita stood in front, Ash behind her with his arms around her trim waist. The sun having retreated, it was dark outside now. The famous Queen's Necklace was visible down below, the lights diffused in the slender mist that tended to envelop everything when it was adjacent to the sea. Mumbai slept late and got up early; it didn't sleep, it merely took power naps. There were still vehicles on the road below but the vertical distance between the traffic and them on the twentieth floor muted all unwanted sound. The iconic Gateway of India, which was roughly two kilometres east of them, was right behind them in a straight line. Till the far vista it was only dark waters with a few twinkling lights of patrol boats.

'So is it a sea or an ocean?' Ash asked. Rita could sense his fingers unfastening the top button of her shirt.

'It's rhetoric. It isn't like land that humans own and create boundaries. How can anyone really determine where the

Arabian Sea ends and where the Indian Ocean starts or draw a line between any two bodies of water for that matter? It's not like the colour changes as one crosses that imaginary line.'

Rita's shirt was totally unbuttoned now. She felt Ash's breath on her neck as he raised her arms and slipped her out of it. From there on it was a matter of minutes before he unbelted her and let her jeans drop like they were several sizes too big. She stepped out of them like a coy Barbie, still facing the sea or ocean despite him having unfolded his arms around her; the clang of the metal buckle and the rustle of clothes behind her back conveyed to her he was undone too.

'You look spectacular,' he softly murmured in her ear.

Rita closed her eyes.

'The Lord Almighty did a real major design fault,' Ash whispered when both were absolutely sans clothes with him still behind her.

'Do enlighten me.' For some strange reason both had dropped their voices to whispers. It wasn't like someone stood outside Ash's hotel room with one ear to the door to hear what they discussed. Or did.

'You see, he should have made a woman taller than the man.' He explicated, his hands now on her waist and moving upwards.

'I'm not sure I am following you.'

'With the woman being taller than man, the man wouldn't have to bend.' His tongue was in her ear like a viper lapping into a rabbit burrow. 'But, I guess man has improvized on God's design, that's why women wear high heels, isn't it?'

'What—' Rita was already in a pleasant delirium with Ash's hands and tongue all over her; her body was several degrees warmer now than the time she had arrived at the hotel. She had wanted to ask what he meant by bending, but his next action left no room for questioning. Ash had bent his knees to align his torso beneath her, pulled her closer with his right arm around her abdomen and with his free hand he steered himself into her. Rita let out an involuntary gasp, she stretched her arms, splayed her legs a little and rested on the reinforced windows to bend her torso forward and provide Ash the leverage. Within seconds, both were in a sort of symphony of moment.

The lovemaking was intense, feral. They came like teenagers. Like some fountain that had been abeyant for a while and then, unexpectedly, the main valve broke somewhere and passion pushed open the gates with the enormous pressure. A much-craved release for animalistic lust. Rita hadn't been with anyone since she had been with Ash last. Ash's breathing showed he hadn't been sleeping around either. She pressed her lower lip under her teeth to stifle the scream. His seed gushed in and, with her still vertical, navigated out and rolled down her thigh. Despite the air-conditioning, both of them were sweating. And spent. He finally withdrew and she pirouetted and came into his arms.

How long could this last? Rita got reminded of all she had pondered while driving to the hotel in the evening, in the throes of passion when Ash was moving in her she had almost cried out *love you* but Sinatra had warned of such circumstances for generations now: '*don't go and spoil it all by saying something stupid*'.

'It was amazing' is all she said.

'I'm off to New Delhi tomorrow, and will be back over the weekend,' Ash mentioned when they lay on the bed. Still sans clothes, but refreshed after the lovemaking.

'Is that an invitation for me to revisit you?'

'Why don't you stay with me over the weekend?'

'My boyfriend might not like that.' Rita yanked his chain again.

'You have a boyfriend?'

She burst out laughing. 'OK Ash Mattel, you have had your dinner, I haven't and I'm starving. Order something for your date till I have a shower please.'

'What'll you have?'

'Eggs, beans and toast.'

'And champagne?'

'I can be persuaded,' she smiled.

Ash picked up the room-service menu from the bedside table. Rita thought about covering herself with a sheet or walking in the nude. The clothes still lay commingled in a pile near the window where they had come off. She contemplated for a minute, then got up without covering herself and started walking towards the en suite bath.

'Has anyone told you you've got an ass to die for?' Ash had the room-service menu in hand still, but he was gazing at her rear.

'Thanks, that makes my day.'

'Thought it would be impolite not to compliment.'

'I wouldn't have minded at all.'

'Yes. I thought so but, your ass might.'

'Asshole.'

'Thank you. See that's how you take a compliment, girl.'

The bathroom was stocked with more soaps and shampoos and conditioners and moisturisers and lotions than Rita or Ash could possibly consume. What a waste of resources. Rita stepped into the shower and turned it on. As the first sprays hit her she reflected, once again, on her relationship with Ash. Sex with Ash Mattel was frighteningly good; it heightened her pathos of solitude further, the feeling for falling even deeper into the lonely crevasse. In her opinion, sex was much maligned when it was the purest of natural acts. But where was it headed? One day, she knew, she'd get a phone call from Ash telling her he'd found someone else in London. What then? She wasn't getting any younger, and she had no plans to die a spinster. And it was only as many times she could find an old college friend to romp with.

She stepped out of the shower. There was an overabundance of towels too. Possibly finest Egyptian cotton. White and thick. Thick enough that if one laid five of them on top of each other, it would become a mattress. She dried herself and looked in the full-length mirror. Smooth, toned and in shape. She could see her effulgent self looking back at her; she was happy and she looked it. What was wrong with that?

She walked out in the bathrobe.

'I ordered your dinner.'

'Thanks. Ash, let's make a pact …'

She could see Ash straighten up like he saw something serious in her eyes.

'What kind of pact?'

'If we're both single when we hit forty, one of us will quit and move to the other.'

'You mean if we do not find someone else by then?'

'Yes.'

'Don't know about you, but I have too many women chasing me all over the world.'

'You're such a bastard. I'm being serious here.'

'You know, I've always liked smart, strong women, not daft and delicate ones. I truly appreciate your candour, your straightforwardness, I like that you know what you want. And I concur. It's a deal. But remember what they say: be careful what you wish for.'

'But what happens if I still want to work?'

'I will quit. I can always sit at home, write papers, and travel as required.'

'That's the best thing someone's said to me in years. Thanks.' She kissed him, but before anything could happen, there was a knock on the door.

'Room service.' Ash got under the sheets. Rita wrapped the bathrobe tightly and opened the door.

The eggs and beans and toasts were over. The champagne was almost over too. Both sat in bed. Ash still hadn't bothered to get back into his clothes, and Rita still donned the bathrobe.

'So what's bothering you?' Ash began.

'The current case.'

'Care to tell me about it?'

Rita pondered a moment. Could she involve an outsider into a current investigation? She had in the past, but that had been with blessings from her then supervisor, Joshi. She couldn't just pick up her phone and call *Sexy* to check if she could consult a criminal psychologist without explaining. And what would she say she was doing with him at this hour? *'We're part-time lovers ... strangers by day, discussing criminal cases by night?'*

She decided to consult. Ash had been a great help then, Ash could be great help now. She trusted him. Hell with the textbook.

She summarized the case to Ash carefully: Sishir Singh, his murder in Brussels, and his doppelgänger Honey Singh. She also narrated about Handlebar following Honey Singh, and that Handlebar had no idea who was making him perform that task. She told him about the computer wizardry.

'And you were chosen to lead this case because ...? Ash asked when she finished.

'I'm told it was based on merit, but past success can be really scary sometimes. *Sexy* doesn't recognize that success is the coming together of skill and luck, and who would underwrite luck for me every time? I'm sure you know sometimes it's all about luck, and talent – or whatever you might want to call it – just gets a free ride. But, the downside of success is that it sometimes gives a false feeling to others about you being invincible. They think whatever goes up doesn't feel like it would ever come down. I haven't got a fucking clue how to crack this one. Seriously. Tell me what you think?'

Ash sat quiet for a few minutes like he was filing the information in his brain, shelving it in proper order to make sense. When he spoke, his voice was very measured, his countenance serious, business-like.

'I have a feeling something else is at work here.'

'Like what?'

Ash went quiet again. Rita waited him out.

'Something doesn't add up. Someone wants to know enough about Honey Singh, but we don't know who it is and why he is interested in him. And for the love of God, I can't think why the killer would want to know that. If the killer wanted to know more about Honey Singh, he would have studied the subject prior to the robbery, not after it. You with me?'

That is why she admired Ash; he made her think, he made her organize her thoughts better, word them, think the reverse and the obverse.

Ash nodded. 'As a matter of fact, the killer needn't be in the picture here. Think about it. The killer – for the time being, at least – has got away with the diamonds and the homicide. Why should he care if we arrest or hang Honey Singh? Him tracking Honey Singh might only lead us back to him if he makes some mistake. So the questions is why would someone keep tabs on Honey Singh at all?'

'Someone else who thinks Honey Singh is the killer. Someone who has vested interest in the diamonds that were stolen—'

'Hold on a minute,' Ash interjected. 'The surveillance was set up after the murder, and as you rightly pointed out in your summary, most probably, as a consequence of the murder.'

'But, how does the guy who hired Handlebar know that the guy who murdered the diamond merchant in Belgium looks like Honey Singh?'

'That is what you need to find out. I have a feeling that's the answer to most, if not, all of your questions. Want my hunch?'

'Go on, tell me.'

'The killer or killers knew about the existence of Honey Singh before the caper. Honey Singh wasn't discovered after the crime. Have you met Mr Honey Singh yet?'

'Not yet, but very soon. I wanted to know everything about him and around him before approaching him. We didn't want him to get alerted before we completed our searches. If he knew we are looking into him, we might get a tainted picture.'

'Makes sense.'

They talked till they ran out of possibilities, and also became mindful they were attempting to twist facts to fit their theories when some facts never fitted existing theories. Moreover they had incredibly little facts still.

'Could I have some coffee please?' Rita requested.

'At this hour? How would you sleep after caffeine?'

Coffee was her magic potion. Just how could the same coffee wake her up in the morning and help her relax enough to sleep was something she wondered at times too. But hey! If it worked, it worked.

'Don't worry about me.'

They switched off the lights at two in the morning. The silver moonlight flushed the room. The sky was clear; the stars were visible thought the glass. Smiling, twinkling, happy.

'You know why stars shine?'

Rita turned and gave him a befuddled look: *what the fuck is wrong with you?*' So are you just going to tell me some inutile facts at this hour of the day or are you going to make love to me?'

Ash looked dumbfounded.

'Why, what's wrong if I want you to? Hurts your male ego too much?'

'Nah—'

'Then take me.'

'That was great,' Ash said later.

'Thanks, Freud.'

'Eh …?'

'I love teasing you. It *was* great. Good night.' She put her head in the crook of his arm and closed her eyes.

FOURTEEN

Rita drove home early in the morning. She didn't wish to turn up to work in the same clothes as the day before. Not that someone would ask – maybe the men wouldn't even notice – but why tease the tongues?

She realized she walked sprightly when she got to Sheesh Mahal. She was happy. The body was clock-ticking, and she was always engaged in high-pressure cases like the one she had now. Criminal cases were hardly ever calm and relaxing. The subconscious was stressed, but today it seemed that some part of the private puzzle had been sorted. The mind was at ease.

She decided to do yoga. She was blessed with a great metabolism, but being slim did not necessarily mean being fit. She exercised for agility, for strength, for flexibility, for stamina, for body synergy. Later she showered, put on new work clothes – shirt and jeans, S&W, thin jacket to cover the gun – and left for work early. The team had been working around the clock, and she knew she would have loads to read. All that the team had ferreted out would have been summarized for her.

Irrespective of whatever anyone has ever told you, via various channels of media – television, movies or detective books – investigation is not an exact science. What works for one case does not necessarily work for another. Of course, all ground rules need to be followed: dig this, dig up that, but there are no sure-shot victories. The only method to increase the chances of success are to be thorough, to explore all possible avenues, spare no one, trust nothing till you've checked and cleared. Rita and her team were doing exactly that.

The records showed that one Mr Sishir Singh had cased Ron Jogani from Mumbai to Brussels. However, his image had not been captured by any of the million-plus security cameras at the airport. He was either in disguise or somehow keenly avoided every camera.

Out of the other 197 passengers that boarded Jet Airways 9W228 from Mumbai to Brussels at 0210 hours on the 2nd of April, no one was even tenuously associated with diamond trade. 144 of them were Indians or of Indian origin. Ruling out the fifty-three foreign nationals, as it was out of Indian Police's jurisdiction – even if they requested *Sexy* to intervene – to scrutinize. Nene and team eliminated women and families travelling with children. Not that it didn't have any precedent, but sheer common sense made them *assume* that people travelling to commit armed burglary did not travel with children. Disregarding them and the transiting passengers – those who had onward flight connections or took trains to other European locations – the total count of people in the latent suspect pool was reduced to seventy-three. Fifty-nine men, including Sishir

Singh, and fourteen women. Eleven were further jettisoned from the list, as they weren't Mumbai residents. It wasn't that only Mumbai denizens looted or murdered, but it was a process of elimination, and including someone from Valsad was regarded ludicrous, at least, in the first round. Nene's team visited each one of them, spoke to them but it was unavailing.

The police carried out a photo line-up. As some were NRIs who never returned, all the 110 people who were in India were independently shown a set of five photographs each – one of them being the honourable Mr Sishir Singh's – and probed if they could recognize anyone as a co-passenger on their flight to Brussels. Some recognized Sishir Singh, but then some others recognized other people from the same photo line-up when some other photographs were of police personnel. Even the two people, they knew from airline records who had sat on 29B and 29C – Sishir Singh occupied the window seat: 29A – failed to identify him

A similar exercise was performed on passengers who flew to Brussels from Mumbai on three consecutive days before the flight that carried Ron Jogani. Nothing conclusive could be derived. It was physically impossible to check on every flight that left for Belgium from India from various other airports. It was an exercise to check enough – if you were lucky, something might stick. There is nothing like too much information in an investigation.

The flight attendants, too, were scrutinized.

The report was condensed and provided to DCP Rita Ferreira who smiled at the fact how certain axioms were proved true every single time. Witness memories were acknowledged to be pathetic around the world. Most people couldn't have recognized Sishir Singh in a photo line-up two days after they had flown with him, forget identifying him after three months.

Rita was still unwavering that there was indisputably a second person, and probably a third, near or perhaps even at the scene of the crime. No doubt about that.

Oxymoron (noun): a figure of speech in which apparently contradictory terms appear in conjunction. Painfully delightful, chaotically structured are just as realistic examples as dissimilarly similar.

In the digging up of past burglaries, Rita and her team found a dissimilarly similar robbery at a jeweller in Mumbai only a couple of years back.

Dissimilar, because the modus operandi was starkly different.

Similar, as it was done at a jeweller where, at least, three crores worth of diamonds – and only diamonds – were robbed by someone not yet nabbed by the police, since even that burglary had been carried out with equal caution.

It appeared, the evening before the robbery was discovered, a lone man – it was all conjectural until someone was actually arrested, and convicted, and the case closed – had come to the jewellery store at Mumbai's affluent Pedder Road, impersonating a customer. Witness reports described him as someone who looked from a moneyed background, given his attire and mannerisms. Tall, pleasant looking, fair complexion, expensive clothes had all added to deliver that impression to the unsuspecting staff at that point. He was believed to be looking for a diamond ring to propose to his fiancée, and as such looked at quite a lot of expensive rings. He seemed acquainted with diamonds; he knew that seeing a diamond already set in a ring jaundiced its colour, and hence asked to see unset diamonds before he placed an order. He had finally selected an expensive diamond – with over 2.8 carat, a princess-cut solitaire – then decided on the design of the ring from a catalogue, paid a five per cent deposit in cash before his bladder made him enquire about customer toilets in the jewellery store. As he had completed all the sale formalities, the salesgirl who had attended him had moved on to assisting another customer and did not notice him leave. In fact, no one saw him leave the premises because, as the investigators later found out, he never did.

Given the plush nature of the clientele the customer toilets weren't simple urinals: the flooring was Italian marble, the taps were gold-plated, the towels were Egyptian cotton, and there was even a shower cubicle. Who has a shower at a jewellery store? However, over the shower enclosure was a false ceiling created to plumb the geyser and keep it out of sight. The expensively dressed customer – after placing the order for the engagement ring – walked into the luxurious toilet, apparently somehow climbed into the space above the shower and parked himself out of sight for the night. When the store closed for business that evening, the watchman had taken his usual round. Once convinced everybody had left, he switched on the night-lights, set the alarm and, lo and behold, the alarm's junction box was situated inside the toilet. He locked the store, handed the keys to the manager and took position as the night guard in a little hutch besides the main entrance outside the store, with another guy.

At some point in the night – again all conjecture till proven without reasonable doubt – the unseen customer climbed down, unalarmed the outlet and set about looting all the diamonds he could by breaking into the display cabinets. As the investigators by and by discovered, the customer-turned-filcher had attempted tampering with the big safe – its lock and arm were found damaged – but in some way fathomed that the safe was separately alarmed; he abandoned it at the last minute. A total of INR three crores of diamonds were reported missing, which, assuming that most jewellers never declared all their inventory and certainly not the correct value, meant, they were, at least, four or five or six crores' worth. The guy had then sliced the iron bars in the toilet window, using some kind of a mini hacksaw, and slipped away.

The robbery was discovered the minute the store reopened the next morning with broken glass cabinets and some merchandise trashed on the floor.

The offender was aware the premises was covered with security cameras and he had remembered to take the videotape along with him, ergo, no recording of him was ever found.

Sounded similar.

Sounded dissimilar.

The local police suspected insider foul play. It was deemed impossible for someone to just walk in from the street, know where to hide inside the shop at closing time, then set the alarm off in the premises and escape with the loot all by himself. There had to be some assistance provided from someone. That or someone had visited the store on more than a few occasions to recce the place and plan. As the recording cameras recycled every twenty-four hours, there was no way that could be conclusively ruled out either. Nonetheless, the police grilled all employees and what was common among witness statements was patchy at best.

Someone definitely assisted him; at least, in the escape at night. Some vehicle?

Everyone agreed that the guy who came to buy the diamond for the engagement ring was tall. Tall by Indian standard for a male was anyone over the height of five-ten.

Most agreed the man's age was about thirty.

There was disagreement about what he wore – shirt ranged from white to cream to faded pink. Most agreed on blue denim jeans. No one remembered the shoes.

Almost all remembered the Rolex on his left wrist. The guy had been sharp enough to be aware that all sales staff at a jeweller would recognize that watchmaker. But, the police couldn't trust whether anyone would have made out if it was genuine or fake. Probably fake to dupe people into thinking they were dealing with someone loaded.

After months of going around in circles, absolving everyone who worked in the store, the police came up with, well, nothing.

Similar.

Which meant the culprit or culprits were still at large, which meant the case was still open, which meant it could be the same group, bearing in mind their penchant for diamonds. And their kinship with someone in the local diamond trade to palm off their loot.

Similar.

The jewellery store caper wasn't an armed robbery.

Dissimilar.

But.

Perhaps, that was only because it wasn't required?

Indeed, nothing as abominable as murder occurred, but there was no reason to believe that the burglar was unarmed. No one intruded his game plan, ergo, he didn't have to use any weapon. Had Ron Jogani not intruded at the wrong moment, perhaps the robbery at the hotel at Brussels might have also featured as the unarmed robbery?

Similar.

No trace evidence, no biological evidence, no prints whatever.

Similar.

A burglary report only shines – slightly ironical to use *shine*, but – in the annals of police when either the robbery is of considerable amount (not too many people would delve too much into a bicycle robbery) or when the burglar has been successful – again, the paradox of using *successful* – in getting away with the loot. And in those archives of police files, Rita's team uncovered another burglary.

The Moghul emperor Shah Jahan, most noted for Taj Mahal, had a court jeweller of Gujarati descent: Shantidas Jhaveri. Shantidas Jhaveri exclusively catered to the royal line-up of queens the emperor had, but generations down the line and anglicized over the years, Zaveri Brothers was still one of the biggest names in diamonds in the country. One of their oldest and most iconic stores was located in Connaught Place, New Delhi, and had suffered the same fate as the Pedder Road jewellery store before it. The robbery in New Delhi was almost ten months after the Mumbai jeweller, which meant – conjecturally again, as no one was brought to book yet – someone had taken the time off after Mumbai larceny to let the proverbial dust settle and utilized that time thoroughly to plan the next one.

This heist was, again, dissimilarly similar to the one in Mumbai.

The lavish showroom had a spherical atrium that had rooms all around it on the ground floor and an elevator and staircase leading to the mezzanine floor. The mezzanine had a circular walkway overlooking the atrium that was double height with a stained-glass dome that was apparently from another era, and provided the coloured gleam into the already classy showroom in the day. The high-net customers who could afford to set foot in this palace of jewels were received at the reception in the atrium, then ushered into one of the requisite rooms after consultation. Some of the rooms on the upper deck were offices and vaults, and others – and one should award high marks to the creative genius here – were named as *gold-room*, *silver-room*, *ruby-room*, *emerald-room*, *diamond-room*, *you-have-too-much-cash-dumbo-room*.

A year ago, when the showroom opened for business on Saturday morning, someone had harvested the place. The diamond-room had been broken into, and several crores of diamonds had been filched. Now, unless one was to believe that the ghost of Marilyn Monroe was passing by and picked up her best friends, it was hard to argue that the gang had targeted diamonds and diamonds alone.

Sounded similar?

It didn't require Einstein to decipher why diamonds were being targeted: for one, diamonds yielded the best in size-to-value ratio; a handful of diamonds could translate into crores, while gold or other jewellery, albeit precious, would be much too much weight to transport. Furthermore, it more than appeared that the gang who carried out the capers had identified how and where to dispose them of clandestinely.

Similar.

The doors were protected, the windows airtight, the walls intact. With no visible sign of routine break-in or forced entry, what predominantly baffled the investigators, for the best part of four days, was how the person or persons got into the prestigious store in the first place. How, then, did someone penetrate into the heart of the store and carry out the robbery? Answers never travel in a straight line from west to east or vice versa, do they? This particular puzzle got its manna from north. The intruder had come from the top. When they investigated closely, they apprehended that the stained-glass dome had been removed and the intruder glided south from the ceiling on a suspended rope. The whole dome, which was set into the concrete of the roof, had been dug out, signifying it wasn't done in a day. Days of planning and effort must have gone into it. The police found a large metal hook fixed into the concrete nearby, which was apparently used to support the rope with a man's weight. Pure geometry at work. A pulley and cables were still there – wiped of all prints, naturally – that told the police a motor had been plugged in for the purpose and later taken away. An absolute *jhakaas* style, not some amateur stuff: strictly Bollywood. And like courteous citizens, the outlaws had, after exiting, put the dome back with strong glue so as to avoid it from displacement or damage by severe elements of nature. How considerate.

All security cameras had been drained of the tapes.

Similar.

The high-tech burglar alarm had not been deactivated. Nevertheless the expensive equipment didn't relay the break-in to the security guys like it was programmed to. That meant that the intruder had known the security system of the showroom well enough to somehow intercept the outgoing signal from the alarms. All security alarms worked on a generic principle: the sensors continuously scanned for movement or body heat or whatever they were encoded to. If any of the sensors picked up any unwanted motion, image or change in temperature, the signal was passed on to the main junction box located on site, which, using telephone lines or an inbuilt SIM, transmitted an SOS to the security office. Theoretically, all in real time. And the security personnel would attend the site within minutes. But every Tom, Dick, Harry and their cousins with a computer had been schooled that real time was never *real* time. There was always a time lag, albeit nanoseconds. But those very nanoseconds are the weakest link in the chain. And the intruder evidently knew that.

No security is ever foolproof. No technology is ever infallible. It is a common misbelief that all hi-tech gadgets were at the bequest of those who can afford them and deploy them when, in fact, they were at the mercy of those who can hack them. Computer passwords are cracked every day. They have even broken into Pentagon. By contrast, and with no disrespect to either, how difficult would it have been to crack the security of a jewellery showroom in New Delhi or of a hotel in Brussels? Must be like going for a picnic in a manicured park.

Dissimilar to the Mumbai heist. Shades of similarity with the heist at Brussels where the gang had shown considerable computer wizardry.

No human being was hurt. No evidence was left on the scene.

No one was arrested. Check that. The police did not have a single suspect after fourteen months: exculpatory explanations aside nothing further was found in the files. The case, like many others, was in the deep freezer getting colder by the day.

Long story short, even if one wanted to overlook the similarities it would positively be difficult to argue there weren't any, and if some ombudsman decided to go after your negligence or deliberate pretermit, you would have a harder time explaining than investigating the previous cases in the first place. Anyway, over a fifty per cent similarity in the two cases warranted an investigation and Rita opened both the past cases. In her mind there was a common element there even if the burglar wasn't the same guy, the brains behind the operations appeared to be; the person or the outfit being sold the stolen diamonds might be. She followed the age-old maxim in police: follow the money.

Though one couldn't help but marvel at the ingenuity of the Mumbai robbery, what with hiding inside the store while it was closed for business and getting away without leaving a trace, the New Delhi heist was definitely one notch up. It was something straight out of a textbook. The stakes had got higher and the loot had got bigger. And then the Brussels one. All dissimilarly similar. Nevertheless, some things were blatantly unique. Precision. Planning. Timing. Executing. Improvizing. Escape.

Three escapes.

The Australians call it *trifecta*: three victories in three.

Hat-trick is how any cricketer would have termed it.

There was no reason to suppose whatsoever why there wouldn't be a fourth one except for one hitch: Ron Jogani's murder. A murder might not have been accounted for in the original planning. The murder would, they must be aware, set the hounds and wolves chasing.

The passengers on Mumbai-Brussels flight had failed to recognize Sishir Singh in a photo line-up three months post the incident. Was there any point in subjecting the sales staff of a jeweller in New Delhi to the same drill after two years? Rita reluctantly approved the exercise.

However, no one recognized Sishir Singh.

FIFTEEN

Rita parsed all that she had till now. One person could not have reconnoitred any place more than once. You can only once or twice visit the place inconspicuously – though even the second time was a massive risk; you go there a third or fourth time and someone would notice you, someone would certainly remember you specially in a closed place like a shop, albeit however large.

An interesting thing in line with progression of robberies was that the group's daredevilry was also on the rise. They were getting adventurous. The first heist had been in Mumbai, which, evidently, was home turf. Furthermore, it didn't exhibit any technical proficiency either. The technical wizardry had skyrocketed after the first break-in, and so had the tenacity – taking several days to trench the stained-glass dome from the concrete. And success in Delhi must have prompted them to plan an even bigger robbery abroad, in a hotel. Given the loot, Rita wondered where all the cash was now. If the police could get access to accounts, tracing unusually sizeable transactions on certain dates wouldn't be impossible, but how could the police get access to accounts? But the money, in any event, might not even be in the killer's name. It could well be in an account of a shell company or false name.

Finding a clue in three robberies might be somewhat easier than one. Sheer probability. But, intuition, however infallible it might appear, could not be substituted for evidence. Rita needed evidence. She had some follow-up thoughts and ideas evolving in her mind but nothing concrete.

The search for the travel agent who booked Ron Jogani's ticket came up empty. Not that anyone had expected otherwise. Someone had to be dumber than dumb to leave an electronic trail if they wanted to do something as ominous as armed robbery. The least they could have done is wipe off all trails.

Nene had recapped the entire history of Honey Singh and family. His grandfather had been uprooted during Partition; he had arrived in Punjab and set up bicycle-parts manufacturing in Amritsar. The next generation – Honey Singh's father – expanded the business manifold. Honey Singh was born in Sri Guru Tegh Bahadur Hospital, and his birth was registered in the local municipal office. No, there was no twin, neither identical nor fraternal. And as Honey Singh's father passed away soon after, and suddenly, due to heart failure, there had never been any other sibling. Even if one hyperbolically assumed that his mother had copulated with someone clandestinely and delivered a baby somewhere, what were the chances that the baby would grow up looking identical to Honey? Identical stepbrothers? A biological impossibility. Unheard of.

End of story.

Rita pondered a bit. Could it be that someone had a fair resemblance to Honey Singh? Nah! Too many coincidences rendered that theory weak, even inutile. The first and the most extraordinary coincidence was that two guys were lookalikes. Second coincidence, they were in the same town. Mumbai was a megalopolis of 18 million people and thus, even if the two carbon copies were in the same city, it was more of a miracle than coincidence for one to find the other. Fourth coincidence: the evil guy – Sishir Singh or whoever – spots the simpleton and the simpleton didn't as much as have a clue about it. It was akin to pulling out four consecutive aces from a deck. The probability of first ace is one in fifty-two: greatly probable. However, the probability of pulling out three more cards and they, too, happen to have a single pip on their faces was twenty-four out of over 6.5 million. Impossible if one also took into account the time frame. The surveillance on Honey Singh had been put in place days after Jogani's murder. So the evil twin did not know about the simpleton before the murder and found him in two days post it? Impossible. It was likely that they knew about Honey Singh already.

Then there was prosthetics that couldn't be ruled out. All that needed was two guys that had the same height and similar body contours – merely a slight resemblance, a body double. And any good plastic surgeon worth his degree could perform some reconstructive surgery to make one look like the other. Challenge, in Rita's opinion, was could it be reversed? Would the guy be willing to look like someone else all his life? Or could there be a reversal – meaning the guy could undergo another facial reconstruction to not look like Honey Singh after all this was over. It sounded morose but, in Rita's experience, people had stretched way out on their limb for money. History was awash with instances of sons killing fathers for money and thrones and territories.

But where did that analysis lead her besides being just another fact of life? The police couldn't just go around snooping every plastic surgeon in Mumbai or India to check if someone looked like or was made to look like Honey Singh. And what if they even asked everyone that? There was no evidence to believe that the surgery was not done outside the country?

All details of Honey Singh's travels had now been gathered and condensed by Vikram.

Result: Zilch!

He did not even have a valid passport; consequently, he had never travelled outside India.

No international telephone calls made whatsoever from any of his listed telephones – mobiles or landlines.

The day Ron Jogani had been burgled and murdered, there was no record of Honey Singh being out of Mumbai. His mobile phone records showed he had called two of his employees, received three calls from another two of them. It was business as usual for him.

Kitty Varghese was another story. The file did not contain anything on her, which surprised Rita. Kitty was a model, a public figure. As such gen on her should have been a lot easier to gather than her boyfriend. Why had Vikram not put anything in the dossier?

The caucus of four was back around the round table in the Operations Room.

Case file – Ron Jogani murder file was already over two-inch thick – investigator reports, charts, witness statements, map, photographs, evidence collected, or received as in this case, was all in front now. Nothing gave.

'Brilliant work on Honey Singh, Vikram, but I didn't find anything in your report on Kitty Varghese? She being a public figure of sorts, I would have imagined data on her would be easier to get …,' Rita questioned.

'You're correct, ma'am. It was a lot easier to get and far too interesting to sum up in a report, so I thought I'd present to you all so we could evaluate it together.'

Rita could sense that Vikram had some proverbial ace up his sleeve. He had definitely stumbled upon something that could lead them somewhere. She glanced at the other two. Jatin and Nene had similar expressions of heightened expectation: eyebrows hiked up, pupils dilated, body involuntarily attentive.

'Go on then, give it to us.'

'During the Belgium escapade, Miss Kitty Varghese was in Germany, in Köln to be precise. She was part of a fashion show group which travelled there. The entire team was hosted in Hilton Köln that overlooks the famous Dom Cathedral. She flew out of India with the group on 29th March and returned with them on 7th April. I haven't dug up further to check if she went missing any night or nights because asking around will definitely get back to her. I thought it best to discuss among ourselves before going ahead.' Vikram paused.

'Go on … I can see you have more to tell us.' Rita could tell Vikram had some more update.

'Miss Kitty Varghese was in Mumbai when the burglary at Pedder Road occurred, but that, of course, isn't of much significance considering that she is a Mumbai domicile, but—'

'But she was in New Delhi when the heist at Zaveri happened,' Rita completed his line.

'How did you know?'

'I didn't know that, I just interpreted that. Am I correct?'

'Yes. She went for a fashion show to Delhi four days before the larceny and returned two days after that.'

'Couldn't it be a genuine coincidence,' said Jatin.

'Equally, it could be orchestrated.' Vikram opened the folder he was carrying and passed around Kitty Varghese's pictures.

Kitty Varghese was a model and she looked every bit like one. Sharp features, high cheekbones, light camel-coloured eyes, thick wavy hair with crimson highlights cut in layers and ran down below her shoulders. The body was fit and in great shape, and could give some of the cheerleaders at IPL matches a run for their money; her face, too, could shame some hot starlets in Bollywood. A head-turner surely. She was definitely younger and taller than Rita. Maybe five-nine in sneakers. Together Kitty and Honey made a gorgeous couple. If only they could do something about their collective names, Rita mused. Kitty-Honey.

Could she be the second person at the Brussels hotel? Rita made a mental note. She couldn't envisage why not? Likewise, she couldn't picture how she could have escaped to Belgium while she was on a tour with others in Germany without being conspicuous by absence.

'Vikram – follow it up with Victor in Belgium. They need to tell us if there is any way one could get from Köln to Brussels and back in a night?'

'Yes ma'am.'

'What else?'

'Kitty and Honey were introduced to each other at a party four years ago, which was hosted by Honey Singh's college friend from engineering, Veer Singh. He was some kind of an IT guru who had migrated to the United States a year later. And then he disappeared.'

'Disappeared?'

'From all the friends' radar. There is no known forwarding address for him; none of his supposed friends have any idea where he is now. It's like once Veer Singh went to the US, he just disappeared from the face of the earth. Various stories – mostly homemade – still circulate in the friends' circle: some believe he took to drugs and was no more, some are convinced he made it big in the Silicon Valley and is no longer interested in keeping in touch with old friends out of fear of being pestered that they might ask him to call them to the US too, still others believe he got married to some *gori* and has become a man of leisure.'

Rita figured that such tales rarely ever had any real foundation. It was actually lack of info that prompted friends to conclude some plausible explanation. Truth was that they might never know the truth.

'The story I got from a source is three or four months before Veer disappeared, he and Mr Honey Singh had a scrap over something. About what? No one knows. But, it was unquestionably something consequential. As these two were the main anchors, the whole coterie kind of disintegrated after the misunderstanding or fight – no one actually witnessed what happened, they just know that the friendship ended acrimoniously and two broke all ties with each other. The parties ended, the clique split because, perhaps, no one wanted to take sides. And later, by the time Veer migrated, everyone had moved on, I guess, so it was never the same again. They still meet once in a while, but are not so close to each other anymore.'

Vikram passed on an old photograph of the original group, he had wangled out of a friend, to Rita who looked at it closely. There were nine people in the picture: five men and four women including Honey Singh, Kitty Varghese and Veer Singh. She noticed that Veer Singh was only marginally shorter than Honey Singh, nothing that a good pair of shoes with some heals could not make up for. And since the photograph wasn't full-length who could argue that Honey Singh wasn't wearing heals in the photograph and that Veer Singh wasn't in flat shoes?

'Any more information on Mr Veer Singh?'

'Veer Singh was a *mona-Sikh* too: another tall *cut-surd* but besides that, nothing. His parents passed away in quick succession before he finished college. No siblings. Never married. No ex-girlfriend. He lived in a *barsaati* near Dadar station, but that was obviously vacated over three years ago, so as I said, I drew a complete blank.'

'So there was unquestionably bad blood between Honey and Veer?'

'As per my findings, yes.'

Rita's brain churned. Some clash between friends leading to animosity, vengeance? Or just plain lust, for money and good life, that couldn't care less for old friendship or friends specially after they split up? After all, betrayal wasn't a new word added to the English dictionary; it had been there since the 13th century. Betrayal had been a part of human history since the Advent, wasn't it?

Another variable had got instated in the already insolvable equation. It seemed like a litany of Singhs.

Sishir Singh.

Honey Singh.

Veer Singh.

'What do you think?' asked Rita, her gaze flitting from Jatin to Nene and back.

'Could it be that Veer Singh is the one getting Honey Singh followed?' Jatin spoke first.

'That does not make any sense to me … Veer Singh should already know more about Honey Singh than our dear Mr Handlebar Raja could ever dig out, don't you think?'

'And, as we discussed earlier, if he *were* involved in the robbery and murder why does he need to follow Honey Singh anymore.'

'Yes, but …' Rita collected her thoughts. '… If he – or whoever – is planning another heist, it would make sense to keep tabs on the guy they're planning to pin it on, wouldn't it?'

'You think they could be planning another one?' Nene.

'They might be, depending on what their endgame is. The pattern shows it has been one robbery a year in the last three years, which means they do some elaborate preparations. Of course, things did not go according to plan in Brussels or maybe it was always agreed upon that in case someone disrupted their plan that someone would have to be eliminated to continue with the scheme. Indeed, killing is vastly different from robbing, but these guys don't seem the ordinary souls to me who would go to a church for a confession before robbing again. My prognosis though is that they might need time to plan better to avoid a situation where they need to kill. But, never say never.'

'You make a good point, ma'am.' Vikram.

'We need to find Veer Singh. Let's talk to Interpol to see if they can dig up airline or immigration records in the US. They'll surely have them. Since 9/11 the US is more conscious of security and records than they ever were. Question is how much would the US be willing to share if it shares at all? I'll speak to Victor in Belgium, and also check if our Commissioner has any personal contacts.' The moment the word personal contacts slipped out of Rita's tongue she realized, maybe Ash Mattel had some contacts through his work with Scotland Yard who might in turn know someone in the Federal Government in the States? It was a long shot, but still worth a try. 'Anyone has anything else?'

'Mr Raja – Mr Handlebar Raja – had called to request if we could ask our guys not to tail him …' Jatin conveyed the private investigator's request. 'He promised that in case of any unusual incident or any change in pattern in Honey Singh's life, he shall report the irregularity to us immediately.'

'Do you trust him?'

'That he wouldn't do anything stupid?'

They exchanged glances. A much-needed smile passed their faces; they had been engrossed in the case for a few hours now.

'No. That he won't conceal any info?'

'I don't think he'll do that. We can always run random checks.'

'Then we don't follow Honey Singh from now on, but we still approve anything that goes to his client. That's the deal – he can take it or leave it.' There seemed little point in expending time, money and resources on tailing Honey Singh if someone was already doing the grunt work. 'But Nene,' Rita turned to him, 'ask your guys to keep a check on Mr Raja every once in a while.'

After an hour more of discussing what they had found so far they decided to focus on the next phase before splitting.

Rita was back in her office after the meeting.

When everything else fails you, they say, go back to the basics and start from the beginning. Nothing was unfathomable by the human mind. If you haven't caught it yet, it isn't because it wasn't there. It is most probably because you have missed some clue, some anomaly. Most cases are cracked open by anomalies. Someone, somewhere has seen an anomaly, but the thought might not have registered at the time. No anomaly was an anomaly in itself: it showed the genius of the group, their planning and meticulousness, Rita was aware. She brewed a fresh cup of coffee and sat down to deconstruct all that she had so far.

She knew the *why:* diamonds, money. Maybe it was speculation, but it was still a sensible one. Reasonable.

She knew the *when*: precise dates, approximate times. Accurate times might or might not have mattered. Hence speculation was not required, at least for now.

She knew the three *wheres* precisely: Mumbai, New Delhi, Brussels in that order.

She knew the *what*: burglary, and obviously, the murder of Ron Jogani.

She had constructed, from the files and her hypothesis, a loose *how* for all three robberies.

She needed to get to the *who*.

Or if only some of the *whos* could be linked, the chain would begin to come together. Like who bought the diamonds, who travelled to Belgium …

Then it was a question of intelligence and excavating the rest.

The pages were still far from coming together, but Rita could sense that the picture on the cover was starting to make some sense.

Veer Singh introduced Kitty Varghese to Honey Singh.

Veer Singh and Honey Singh had some conflict and split up.

Other friends didn't take sides, but Kitty Varghese stuck with Honey Singh.

Ruling out Mumbai, as she was a resident in the city, Kitty Varghese was evidently in the vicinity when New Delhi robbery occurred. Travel to Brussels was still a question mark.

She pursed her lips. What was she missing here?

Did Veer Singh have a soft corner for Kitty? Then Honey Singh came along and they hit it off? Veer Singh withdrew, but maybe couldn't forget Kitty? Maybe, the bitterness only got aggravated with time when he saw the two lovebirds together? Maybe Veer Singh never left India, never went to the US? Just sequestered himself and laid low and planned his moves?

Filmy, she recognized, but definitely possible, though everything that was possible wasn't likely.

A parallel thought hit her and she called Jatin.

'Why do you think someone only followed Honey Singh after the third robbery, and not after the first two?'

Jatin went quiet for a while. 'Maybe because someone got murdered?'

'Or maybe someone followed him after the previous two robberies and we do not know about it?'

'That is a possibility too, ma'am. But I'm sure if Mr Raja had done some tailing in the past he would have surely informed us.'

'How many licenced private investigators do we have in Mumbai?'

'I can check.'

'And ask Mr Raja too. He might not have been forthcoming, as we never asked. Best to check if he ever tailed Honey Singh before or has dealt with a similar stealth client on anything else?'

'Will do, ma'am.'

Rita kept the phone down.

Then she had another flutter in her synapse.

Maybe the killer knew he had been captured on camera. And that set the ball in motion. It wasn't impossible for someone to keep track of a murder and investigation in Belgium when they released the candid-shot from the concealed camera in the elevator.

She decided they needed to wait a few extra days to think and dig more before contacting Honey Singh.

But the media ruined her plan the next morning.

SIXTEEN

The fourth estate can make issues, make personalities, create success and define failures. When Rita woke up in the morning the news *du jour* was:

'Interpol Looking for a Killer in Mumbai.'

It wasn't in merely one newspaper; it was in all of them. Just why had they all decided that it was the best news of the day was beyond her ken immediately. But then as she showered and had breakfast, the rationale was evident. The elections were over, the monsoons had been on time, the fuel prices were in check, no VIP had died or eloped, it was a dull period for film releases, no film star was having an illicit affair, the IPL season had concluded, the Indian cricket team wasn't playing Pakistan or any other one-days for that matter, there wasn't any public unrest in the vicinity, India wasn't at war, and the Middle East wasn't burning either. But the media channels needed news, they needed a story, they needed the revenue to pay their salaries, to justify their existence. And she had to give it to them. What with the numerous underlying problems that besieged Mumbai and the country, they muckraked the forgotten murder – like World War III had started in Belgium and was racing to India. Talk about slow-news days. This was slow-news period; it was trivia's time to shine. The news channels covered it like the Pope had been caught kicking a dog on Marine Drive.

The turd had finally hit the proverbial fan.

Rita's search of *who* the initiator of the news was had been futile. No one had succeeded in ferreting out who had leaked it to the media in the first place; no one had yet figured out who the first journo to get their hands on it either. Nevertheless, because you couldn't find something it did not mean it wasn't there. Someone had excavated the whole case and laid it bare for public consumption. Mercifully, the details were sketchy, and no names were mentioned. The purported experts prattled nonstop nonsense only proving they had no clue about the issue. Their entire analysis had been picked up from Google: if-this-then-that kind of boilerplate.

However, the news that Mumbai Police was now involved would have surely touched the ears of the perpetrators. She had no misgiving about that.

The choice Rita had up till now was binary: either speak to Honey Singh or keep him thinking no one was snooping around. The media had snatched away the luxury of choice.

Rather than driving to the office – there weren't any new developments or promising leads since last evening when she had left work or someone would have certainly called her – she called Vikram to accompany her to Andheri East.

'But it's late, ma'am. Honey Singh would have left for work by now,' said Vikram.

'I know,' responded Rita. 'I'm not going to see him yet. I want to see his residence first. You said he lived with his mother. Let's go and meet her. We should take the picture of Sishir Singh to her. Let's see what she has to say. I have a feeling that if something's not right, it's best to see her before she is coached or coerced. But, we'll feign that we didn't know that Honey Singh wouldn't be at home at this hour. I'll think of some story till you get here.'

Mother knows best; Johnson & Johnson came a distant second, Rita remembered the line from the old J&J advertisement.

'Got that, ma'am. I'll see you in thirty minutes.'

Vikram arrived at Rita's place in forty minutes instead of thirty that he promised. Mumbai traffic. The two drove to Mahakali Caves Road. The traffic wasn't bad and Vikram skilfully threaded through the back routes. He took Linking Road, turned right into Khar Pali Road, swung left and passed Khar station on the right, crossed the subway, turned left and turned right on to JLN Road before turning left on to NH8.

'Funny, isn't it?' Rita commented when they got on to the highway.

'What?'

'Only a thoroughbred Mumbai-*wala* would take this route. I would have taken the highway as soon as I could get on it. It's so typical of Mumbai and its people, isn't it?'

'You are correct. I try to save every second I can by manoeuvring where I think I can avoid traffic.'

They drove the next fifteen minutes in silence. Looking at the traffic Rita got reminded of the crazy motorcyclist that Jatin and she had spotted. Jatin was supposed to speak to the local police station to give that joker a slap on the wrist. Had he? But with a murder investigation it was highly likely it had slipped down on his priority list, and who could blame him.

As they turned left towards Mahakali Caves Road, Rita got engrossed in the rich Indian history she had as one of the elected subjects in her graduation. Despite the name that sounded like the powerful Hindu Goddess of time and death, the Mahakali Caves were, in reality, historical remnants of Buddhist caves which had been their monasteries. The nineteen black caves were chiselled out of cooled volcanic lava between first century BC and 600 AD. The road that connected Andheri Kurla Road to these caves on the hill was called the Mahakali Caves Road. She always felt fortunate that during the course of her work, she got to see, or at least got in the proximity of, such historical testaments that most other folks simply read about in books. She made a mental note of visiting the caves when she was free some weekend. She also knew that given her workload and urgency that came with her profession, a hundred and one such plans and sites were already on the list. Wishful thinking.

The car drove into the Takshila complex and, like a wrench, the memory hit her on the head. She had been here investigating a previous case too. There had been a murder here earlier. The fetid stench of death she had whiffed then came back; they had found a putrid remains of a man who had been rotting for months before they had discovered his corpse. That wretched smell of death might have gone from her nostrils but it would forever stay in her mind.

What was this, some hotbed of crime and deception?

It didn't exactly look like the epicentre of criminality. Decent, law-abiding citizens resided here.

Honey Singh's apartment was in the third building on the left. On the first floor. Rita looked up as she climbed out of Vikram's Gypsy. There was a small balcony that had the usual plants in pots like many other balconies across Mumbai, and a clothes-stand that had some drying on. Unassuming lifestyle. Vikram locked his vehicle and they took the steps to the first floor. Rita noted there wasn't an elevator in the building either. Nothing indicated the man had several millions stashed somewhere.

The woman who opened the door wore a bubble-gum pink *salwar kameez*. She was scrawny and seemed devoid of vim and vigour; her wrinkled skin looked like someone had played origami with it one time too many. Almost cracked leather. She must have been seventy; Rita quickly calculated that Honey Singh had been a late child if he was still not thirty, which further reduced the probably of her delivering after Honey's father's demise. A woman in her forties would be far more careful when having casual sex, Rita presumed. She had a dour expression that passed a supercilious smile when she saw Rita and Vikram. 'Yes?' was all she said. She didn't appear like someone who was expecting guests or was in any mood to entertain any unannounced ones at this moment. Rita could take a calculated guess that Mrs Lucky Singh would have been considered quite a beauty when she was younger, a lot younger. Easy to assess where Honey Singh inherited his good looks from.

Then, almost abruptly, there was a change in her countenance as if Rita had just announced that she had won the lottery.

'Oh, it's you. I knew you would come. Come in … come in, why are you waiting at the door?' She seemed to have come alive.

Rita was baffled. She glanced at Vikram who appeared equally confused.

'Have we met before, Mrs Singh?' Rita politely asked as they followed their host into the living room that was at the end of a small foyer.

'No, but my instincts told me that you will come. Now tell me, what will you have, tea or coffee?'

'And why did you think I would come?'

'Because of my son, my Honey. He thinks he is some big shot, but I know everything. I am, after all, his mother, am I not?'

Rita nodded. There was certainly some confusion here. Mrs Lucky Singh had certainly taken her for someone else.

'I'm Lucky,' she said.

Wish I was too, Rita almost voiced, realizing just in time that her name was Lucky; she wasn't talking about being fortunate.

'Nice to meet you, ma'am, I'm Rita and this is Vikram.'

'Rita what?'

It took a minute for Rita to comprehend. 'Rita Ferreira, and he is Vikram Patil.' Rita deliberately left out the police ranks.

'You have separate surnames?'

This was getting nowhere.

'I'm terribly sorry, but Mrs Singh I can't follow what you mean?'

'I know you are the one he's been hiding from me for years now. I only came to know about you a few months back.'

What was Honey Singh concealing from her?

'Don't worry *beta*, I might be old, but I'm very broadminded. Someone from a different religion doesn't bother me one bit. My only religion is that my Honey should be happy.' Lucky Singh's eyes were cheerful now, the pupils dilated; she looked genuinely happy.

Jesus!

Rita's mind eked out the confusion the old lady had. *Rita Ferreira. Kitty Varghese.* Both Christian names. Someone had obviously relayed that her son was dating a Christian girl or maybe Honey Singh had dropped some hints, and Mrs Lucky Singh had misconstrued Rita to be Honey's girlfriend. *Hey presto! Mrs Rita Singh.* Lucky Singh was certainly unplugged from reality. Another sample of God's ingenuity.

'Oh no, Mrs Singh—'

'Come on now, *beta*, don't be shy. Is he your cousin?' Lucky gestured towards Vikram who, too, seemed to have unravelled the whole puzzle by this time and appeared like he was having a difficult time trying to control the snigger. Rita quickly looked away; last thing she wanted to do was to burst into laughter. She bit her cheek to avoid laughing. She realized that was the reason Lucky Singh had shown disbelief that Rita and Vikram had different surnames. Maybe Lucky Singh thought Rita had come with her brother. Or father? The thought of Vikram being her dad only magnified the humour.

'Mrs Singh, I am not who you think I am.'

'The only way you could know what I'm thinking is if you are who you say you are not.'

Save me, Jesus.

'Believe me, Mrs Singh. I'm DCP Rita Ferreira and this is my colleague ASP Vikram Patil.'

'Honey never told me you were in the police?' Lucky Singh almost exclaimed.

'That's because Honey Singh doesn't know me, Mrs Singh.'

'So how are you here if Honey doesn't know you?'

'That's what I'm trying to explain, Mrs Singh. What has Honey Singh told you?'

'That he had already chosen a beautiful daughter-in-law for me.'

'He might be right, but that daughter-in-law is not me.' Rita was aware that Honey Singh was right; Kitty was gorgeous, but she let the ambiguity linger in her response. She didn't want to spill out that they knew exactly what they knew. She wasn't here to give info, she was here to get as much as she could out of Honey's mother.

'OK, let me get tea and then we'll talk.' Lucky Singh did not wait for a response, didn't offer a choice of coffee or soft drink. She just got up and left the room.

Rita looked at Vikram and let out a silent laugh. She gesticulated to herself, then pointed downwards, then pointed at Vikram and gestured towards the living room entrance door: *I'll be here, you do the toilet run.*

Standard Operating Procedure.

Vikram would go to the bathroom and look for anything that could be of any use to the police. If he had time and opportunity he would also snoop into the bedroom for anything consequential to the case.

Vikram signalled with his thumb: *Message received.*

Lucky Singh paced back with a tray of teacups and cookies.

'Could I use the toilet, Mrs Singh?'

'Of course. Use the one in Honey's room.' She pointed towards the room on the right.

Rita took the time to convince Mrs Singh that she wasn't Honey Singh's girlfriend. She was a police officer who was looking for some information from him.

'What has he done? Eloped with someone's daughter?'

'No, Mrs Singh, he's done nothing wrong. This is just a routine investigation.'

'Tell me about it,' Lucky Singh poured her tea in the saucer and loudly slurped.

You asked for it.

Rita pulled out the photograph of Sishir Singh and passed it to her.

'This is my Honey. Where was this taken?'

The mother knows best.

'In an elevator at a hotel, nothing to worry about.'

If someone was playing Honey Singh, then that someone had done a damn good job of it. Good enough that the mother had been conned.

Vikram was back. There is an unstated limit on the time one can reasonably spend in the toilet without raising any suspicion. His headshake was extremely faint, but Rita grasped it; he had found nothing incriminating, which was frustrating, but what had they expected? Counterfoils of a boarding card?

'Do you know anyone called Veer Singh, Mrs—'

'Don't even take that thankless rascal's name in my home,' Lucky Singh barked; her face had gone bloodshot, she appeared furious.

And that told Rita what she sought from mentioning Veer. The animosity between Honey Singh and Veer Singh was genuine. And familial.

'Sorry Mrs Singh, my intention wasn't to bring up any unsavoury memories, but we need to find Veer Singh.'

'What does this have to do anything with my Honey? My Honey treated him like a brother. I treated him like my own son, never differentiated between him and Honey. He stayed with us for days, weekends, I did all his washing and cooking. And in the end, he just left us like we were some unwanted tramps? May he be consumed by worms.'

This was getting interesting. Not that Lucky Singh would know where Veer Singh was or if she knew she would tell Rita, but it still seconded what others had said about Honey and Veer: they were close, then they split.

'What happened?'

'I don't know. Honey never spoke about it except that they had a disagreement of dire proportions.' The fury she had exhibited in the past few minutes notwithstanding, deep down the woman was hurt; the optical waterworks were beginning to win. She wiped her moist eyes with the back of her pink sleeve.

'I'm sorry, Mrs Singh.'

'It's OK. But if it is Veer you're looking for, why do you have Honey's picture?' Lucky sounded sceptical now.

Smart question.

'Oh that? Our database showed Mr Honey Singh was the last one Veer Singh had any interaction with in a public place. As I said, it's a very old photograph.'

'I don't think Honey would want to talk about him.'

'We still have to ask.'

'I can understand.'

'Mrs Singh, do you know where Veer Singh is these days?'

'Nah. I don't know and I don't care. I saw him last …,' she looked into space like recalling something from an old album, '… three years ago, maybe even longer.'

'So no idea where he went, no correspondence?' Rita carried on.

'No, and I don't want to talk about him anymore. Is there anything else?'

'Not at the moment, Mrs Singh.' Rita got up.

Vikram took the cue.

The farewell wasn't as warm as the tea party. Rita heard the door slam behind them.

'What do you think, ma'am?' Vikram asked as they walked down the steps.

'You mean besides the part that you're my daddy?' Rita retorted.

'That was hilarious. I was about to burst out.'

'I could see.'

'The mention of Veer definitely embittered her,' Vikram said when they sat in the Gypsy. Rita looked around the apartment complex. She noted again that though it wasn't subfusc or rundown, it wasn't the poshest address in the city either.

'It's extremely important that we find Veer Singh, Vikram.'

SEVENTEEN

'Why this switcheroo?'

Switcheroo? Dealing with *Sexy* came with a cautionary; the perquisite was that the person already had the Webster's English dictionary app downloaded into their brains.

Sexy sat composed. Impeccably attired as usual, not a hair out of place. His long fingers in a steeple, manicured, his eyes behind the thin reading glasses that he took off before speaking. His question, though, wasn't unwarranted. His secretary got the weekly case reports on almost all current cases, and given that Ron Jogani's murder was an international incident, it was highly likely that he had asked for a summary on it and kept himself abreast. Hence, he knew the initial investigation had been to find the guy in the photograph given by the Belgians to Rita and her team. So why was Rita, then, here to seek help in tracing this other creature called Veer Singh? What had made the investigation switch tracks then?

Rita elucidated the recent developments, the discovery about other robberies in the last few days – since the last report had been sent – and the similarities that steered the team to consider other possibilities, and the revelation of an old friend-turned-adversary who had, since, gone missing.

'And he left India, did you say?' *Sexy* asked after ruminating on the details provided a minute ago.

'Yes sir.'

'Do you know where he has skedaddled to?'

We don't know if he has fled, Sexy; it could be only a concurrence, Rita wanted to say, but instead she responded: 'We're not sure if he deliberately disappeared or if it was purely a coincidence, but the info we have is that he had moved to the US.'

'US security wouldn't release any info – they are a bit solipsistic as you know … unless we have something to make some trade with them.'

He wasn't totally wrong. US had become a lot insular and self-focussed after 9/11 when it came to security, and rightly so. They had largely been successful in thwarting all acts of terrorism in their country since that event.

'We don't have anything to trade, except the fact that Veer Singh could possibly be a criminal, albeit we have no evidence against him, sir.'

'I'll see what I can do. Send me all details on this guy. When are you connecting with Mr Honey Singh?'

'Today itself, sir.' Having met his mother in the morning it is best to meet Honey Singh on the same day. Though Rita was positive that Mrs Lucky Singh would have already spoken to her son about the visit.

Rita took the opportunity to update the Commissioner that she had been in consultation with the criminal psychologist, her previous supervisor Joshi had introduced, without – not surprisingly – furnishing the minutiae that the discussions between Ash Mattel and her were held wearing only their underwear. Or maybe not even that.

Rita also mentioned that the media had been looking for an update after the news had been leaked somehow. She didn't think Sexy required the how.

'Media can be directed to me, I'll handle them all. Just ask my secretary to arrange one single press conference.'

Rita knew that *Sexy* was the master of ambiguity. The press would be none the wiser after he spoke to them; their lexicon would indeed by tested to the limits though. Good.

'Good luck. Anything else, Miss Ferreira?'

'No sir. Thank you, sir.'

The meeting got over, Rita walked out, her vocabulary increased.

Back in her room she called Victor in Brussels and put in the same request. She explained her hypothesis how Veer Singh could be connected and promised to send his only photograph for their experts to analyse. Victor and his government obviously had a vested interest in the case. He agreed to see what Interpol could swing out of the US though he, too, was sceptical about the US government releasing any info.

Rita wasn't terribly optimistic about getting any info on Veer Singh but you had to go through the hoops, you had to try everything. You couldn't know how the dice would fall unless you threw the dice. She had already thrown two dice. The third, she smiled, she would be thrown over the weekend when Ash was back in Mumbai.

Rita and Vikram drove to Honey Singh's office after lunch. They had confirmed he was at the location, but they didn't call ahead. His mother would have done that part already. There was congestion as they turned on to P D'Mello Road but the Eastern Freeway was thankfully clear all the way to BKC.

Bandra Kurla Complex is a string of intimidating glass buildings that look like prisons with finer cells and better facilities for those incarcerated inside for the proverbial nine to five. Tucked away among the overabundance of analogous glass penitentiaries was another insipid building – also glass fronted but dwarfed by other bigger, newer, flashier ones – that housed Mr Honey Singh's office. She looked around to spot Mr Handlebar but he was missing from the scenery. Shoddy work. Or maybe he was so well concealed even she didn't see him. Or perhaps he knew Honey Singh wouldn't be leaving the office till evening so why waste the hours on the watch.

The security on the ground floor was evidently non-existent. Rita looked at the placard on the sidewall that listed all the offices, found Honey Singh's office listed at the top floor, pressed the button for the elevator.

Security on the tenth floor was a different matter.

A runt man of five-foot-four sat at the front desk – diminutively built, middle-aged, with a bald head that brightly reflected the recessed halogen lights. A thin moustache like gents had in the sixties. Greasy jeans, old fake RL Polo blue T. He looked up when he saw two people approaching.

'We're here to see Mr Honey Singh, where is he?' Rita politely asked.

'Who wants to know?' Titu barked. He was loyal to the bone, but given his background and education, politeness hadn't touched him with a flagpole.

Rita looked at him, amused: a Chihuahua pretending to be a Doberman. She decided to play along.

'We both are.' She pointed towards Vikram and herself.

'And who you?' Titu, the street-side barber turned office administrator, asked in his street-side English. Besides the broken vernacular, the words came out scathing like there was a burnt steel blade in his mouth that made them abrasive. Rita wondered that when the short guy said *'you'* did he spell it as *'you'* or *'U'*?

Rita didn't respond. She looked at Vikram, who picked up the cue. Towering over the little man he took out his police badge and put it right in front of his face.

The hard demeanour cracked the moment the runt saw the badge.

'Now,' Rita spoke calmly. 'Tell me who are you?'

'I myself Titu, madam.' He stood in attention.

'And what do you do, Mr Titu ... besides trying to boss around here and scare people away?'

'I am office manager, madam.'

'So Mr Honey Singh is your boss?'

'Yes madam. Any tea, coffee madam?'

'Is your boss in today?' Rita asked even though the intelligence had confirmed that Honey Singh was on site.

'Boss in, but very busy today, madam. He tell me not allow visitors.'

'Tell him we are here now so he better see us.'

'Madam, he get very angry if I disturb.'

'OK, don't disturb. Tell me where his office is and we'll go there and see him ourselves.'

'No madam. You wait. I call him.' He picked up the phone at his desk and punched some numbers.

EIGHTEEN

When the foul-mouthed administrator made the call to his master, his tone had *volte-faced* into a rather benevolent one. 'Some people from police want to see you, sir.'

Rita could hear the loud crackling from the other side that suggested that Honey Singh wasn't pleased to be disturbed. The intrusion wasn't welcomed. Titu nodded in acquiescence and apologized for bothering. 'I told you, sir is busy,' he conveyed as he kept the receiver on the cradle.

Rita didn't bother speaking to him. She picked up the receiver he had just put down and pressed redial.

'What is it now? Didn't I just tell you I'm in the middle of an important conference—'

'And I'm in the middle of a police investigation, Mr Honey Singh. It's my duty to let you know that there is a very bleak line between not cooperating and perverting an ongoing police investigation and both instances are criminal offences in themselves.'

'But I am actually in the middle of a client conference ...'

'Ever heard of the word *emergency*?'

'Yes?'

'It is now. Finish the call because we're coming in.' Rita put the phone down before Honey could utter another word.'

She looked at Titu who instantly, without her having to ask, pointed towards the door at the rear-left of the reception desk.

Rita took a few deep breaths. She was a bit agitated that she had let the words 'police investigation' slip into the conversation; she should have mentioned that when she could seen Honey Singh to gauge his reaction. The rulebook was explicit on this. Listen. Listen to each word very carefully. Read between all the lines. Read the punctuation marks. Read the face. Any unusual or frequent scratching of the limbs, notice the eyes for any false foibles. Analyse the speech, the tone, the everything. Observe the subject.

Before opening the office door she reminded herself that everything was benign, everyone was innocent, and that's the way it should be: innocent till proven guilty. She looked at Vikram to check if he was ready; he nodded.

They walked in.

The office resembled a bouillabaisse; a fish stew might be good to taste but the sight of an assortment of fishes floating in the liquid is anything but pleasant. The office, too, might have worked efficiently for Honey Singh with everything spread all over, but the place had scatterings of papers and computer chips and parts and cables and whatnot just about everywhere including the only visitor chair.

Honey Singh passed an impish smile, said hello and got up behind his desk that had four laptops working simultaneously. He stuck out his muscled arm for a handshake.

It wasn't anything less than a vice when Rita shook it, and then made the introductions after the perfunctory hellos.

Rita looked at the only chair there, which was covered with papers too. Honey Singh looked embarrassed. He walked out from behind his desk, picked up the papers and put them on the already full window.

'I'm sorry I don't normally get any visitors. I'll arrange for another chair, just give me a minute.' He walked out and came back within a minute rolling an office chair on castors.

Two minutes later, Rita and Vikram settled into the chairs.

'How may I be of any assistance in a police enquiry?' There were no exaggerated gasps, no stammer. Only pathological or practiced liars could lie while making eye contact. Was Honey Singh either of those or was he an honest bystander in a game that had included him without his consent or knowledge? Either he had prepared well for this day and enquiry or he was a consummate liar or he was speaking the truth. It was difficult to tell.

Rita wanted to play down to check if he knew anything.

'Do you know Veer Singh?'

'You already know that I know him. You met my mother this morning.' Honey looked annoyed at Veer Singh's mention. It hardly surprised Rita after what she had known about his relationship with Veer and because she had seen his mother raging like an injured bull facing a matador when Rita had cited Veer. If anything, it tied in; the hostility was beyond one-to-one.

'You have any idea where he is now?'

'No. Would you mind telling me what this is about? It's been three years since I last met Veer, so what has he done now that the police is looking for him? And how am I concerned?'

'Mr Singh, please answer my questions and I promise I'll answer most, if not all, of your queries.'

'How long would this take?' Honey looked at his wrist showing off his Omega.

'If you answer without wasting time, I'd say an hour.'

'OK DCP Ferreira.' He snapped shut all four laptops at his desk.

'So tell us more about Veer Singh, how and why did you two break up?'

'It's embarrassing, and maybe you'll think I am evil. Veer introduced me to my current girlfriend, Kitty. We started dating, but we didn't know he had the hots for her. Needless to say, things didn't work out for all of us so we parted ways.'

Rita realized she had worked that out as one of the scenarios already.

'And you guys never met up again?'

'Nope.'

'And you have no idea where he is?'

'I came to know he had left for the Silicon Valley after he was gone from India.'

Rita looked at Vikram who, too, noted that the geographical co-ordinates had been somewhat narrowed down from all fifty states to just Silicon Valley. But would that little piece of info help in any way, who knew?

Rita pulled out the candid-shot she had shown to Lucky Singh in the morning; the one taken in the elevator in Brussels, and passed it to Honey.

He looked at the picture for a few seconds, then looked up at Rita, then Vikram but uttered nothing for a full minute.

Rita couldn't discern if he was worried because he knew where it had been taken or concerned that someone and clicked it without him being aware and that someone was then following him? He maintained the bewildered look on his face. If he was faking, it he was succeeding.

'Where did you get this from?'

'Is that you?'

'Looks like me.'

'Then you should be the one telling me where this was taken.'

'Is this the person you're looking for?'

'Mr Singh, that's not the answer to my question.'

'I don't know. It looks like someone's taken this photograph without my knowledge from somewhere over my head. I can't imagine where and why.'

'Take your time …' Rita couldn't see any signs of any prevarication yet.

Honey Singh appeared confused.

Confused because he was surprised? Or confused about how did the police get this far?

'Honestly, I couldn't tell you,' he said and looked up from the photograph he had been staring at. 'Could you tell me how this is connected to Veer please?'

'It's taken inside an elevator.' Rita ignored his question.

'Where?'

'That's what we would want to know.'

'No idea where and no idea why someone would snap my picture in an elevator.'

'Before you answer my next questions, Mr Singh, I want you to think very carefully—'

'Oh, there's more?' Honey Singh interjected, his anxiety exposed, he appeared fretful.

'Lots more. Do you know anyone by the name of Sishir Singh?'

'No.'

'Who is he?'

'Never mind. Now listen carefully and don't interrupt me please. Have you in the past few weeks or months noticed someone following you around?'

'Follow me? Why? Who's following me?' His voice was aggravated, his face flushed red with fury or frustration. Maybe both.

'Calm down, Mr Singh, there's no threat to you.'

'But why would someone follow me? Is someone planning to whack me?'

'Again, that's what we would want to find out. But ... coming back to my question, are you absolutely certain you haven't spotted some unknown person or persons or some cars more than usual?'

'Not at all.'

Up until now Honey Singh did not even blink an eyelid or show any usual tell-tale signs of insincerity – no involuntary gulps, no loss of words. Rita had held that he had been speaking the truth. But his response to the last question–that he had missed spotting Handlebar Raja totally – put Rita in a quandary. She had been around in this job long enough to read that although he had dispensed the '*not at all*' with all sincerity, Honey Singh was lying. Definitely. Handlebar Raja might not have been obvious at first, but if he tailed Honey Singh repeatedly, the guy would positively register, at least in your subconscious. There was no way someone like Honey Singh could have missed Mr Handlebar and his noticeably derelict car tailing him daily – maybe even twice/thrice a day – for almost over three months. A near impossibility. Question was, why was Honey giving a false statement? Why was he misguiding the police? And as it always happened, if you trapped one white lie, you became sceptical of all that was said earlier or what will be spoken thereafter. If Honey Singh's mien did not reveal signs of dishonesty in the one answer Rita was confident he was fudging, she lost all credence in all the previous ones too. Honey was denying the simple fact of having spotted someone tailing him.

Why? Did he plan to settle it himself? Rita's follow-up thought was if it was even worth Handlebar tailing Honey Singh after she had just told the target that he was being followed. If Honey Singh genuinely didn't spot a tail before, he would now.

What if the secret client's other option was to dispatch a gunslinger?

'Are you absolutely sure?'

'Yes. I haven't spotted anyone.'

'Make no mistake, Mr Singh – if you're on board the train to Bhopal, sooner or later you will get to Bhopal. There is little point in blaming the train later.' The sarcasm in Rita's voice could corrode steel. She could see Vikram look agape at her.

'I'm not sure what you mean?'

'If you don't tell us the truth now, we cannot help you is what I'm saying,'

'I am telling you the truth.'

Rita kept a calm façade but she was annoyed with Honey's repeated lies. 'Let me repeat: you've got a little window here to tell me the truth. I don't know what you know about me but I don't believe in giving anyone a second chance to tell me the truth.'

'Are you threatening me, DCP Ferreira?'

'If I were you I'd take it as a warning. At this moment neither of us knows who's out there or how threatening that person is. All I can tell you is that someone's following you around. For what purpose, I have no idea, but I will find out. So, if you know or suspect anyone, now is the time to tell me.'

Honey went quiet like he was contemplating pros and cons of something in his mind.

'Why me?'

'Why you what?'

'Why is someone following me?'

'Let me ask you a question from an old fable – have you ever seen people fishing, Mr Singh?'

'Yes, just once with some friends. Why?'

'Did you or any of your friends manage to catch a fish?'

'Yes.' Honey looked perplexed.

'With so many other fish in the sea, did the fish you guys had at the end of the line ask *"why me"*?'

Honey did not respond, just passed a crooked smile.

'You have our sympathies but don't ask me self-pitying questions please. We will, of course, find out why you've been targeted, but in the meantime let's assume someone must have a strong motive.'

'You may be right. Is this guy, who's supposedly following me, in some dilapidated car? I think I've spotted the vehicle a few times, but I did not realize someone was actually following me like in the movies. Now that you asked I think I've seen him at more than once place ... but why?'

Out comes the truth.

'Like I said, I don't know for now but we'll find out soon.' Rita didn't think it was advisable to let Honey Singh know that she would have her guys follow him around once again, just in case. 'Don't worry too much. If someone wanted to get you whacked, they had a few months. If they haven't done it yet, it means they don't want to hurt you. However, I have to ask you to be extra careful.' Rita looked at Vikram who still sat silently scribbling in his notebook; she raised her eyebrows to ask if he had any further questions for Honey. He creased his brow and shook his head slightly to decline.

Rita asked about where all had Honey spotted the familiar car and Honey told them it was somewhere between his residence and office.

'Has anything like that had ever happened before?'

'No.'

There was a slight pause in the conversation. Then:

'You said you would tell me what this is about? I can't believe that someone looking for Veer Singh is tailing me after three or four years since I've seen him last or even spoken to him. I don't even know where in the world he is or if he is even alive.'

'This is a murder investigation, Mr Singh.' Rita decided it was time to drop the other shoe now.

If he was aware of what Rita was actually looking for, he did not let it slip. But Rita was now aware that it was difficult to redline what was true and what wasn't with Honey Singh. He was crooked, but he didn't appear to be the guy they had been looking for; doubts were indeed denting the initial euphoria of finding someone who looked like Sishir Singh.

'Who ... Veer?'

'No. You must have read it in the papers that there was a murder in Brussels in April. One Mr Ron Jogani got shot in his hotel room and the killer or killers got away with diamonds worth millions.'

'Yeah ...' Honey said seemingly without having to think. I read about that and my question still remains, what does it all have to do with me?'

'The suspect fleeing the murder scene was caught on camera.'

Rita paused, half expecting Honey Singh to utter something. But nothing except cold stare came from him for full sixty seconds.

'So if you have the photo of the killer why don't you just arrest the suspect?'

Rita was mindful he will comprehend the dilemma in a second. She waited him out.

'You're not saying the photograph you showed me—'

'I'm saying exactly that. The photograph I showed you ...' – she pushed the photograph that still lay at his desk towards him once again – '... is this. And this was taken inside the elevator in the hotel in Brussels, and which your mother and you have identified positively as you.'

Confusion. Apprehension. Exasperation. Grimace. All expressions passed Honey's face in quick succession. Then Rita saw fear in his eyes, which could mean anything or nothing. The dichotomy was that if he had been involved in the crime either directly or indirectly, he'd be afraid, but in case he wasn't aware about the Brussels' murder till he had read it in the newspapers, he'd still be fucking shitting.

'There has to be a mix-up. I've never been to Brussels.'

'We know that.'

'How d—.' He stopped halfway through. 'So I don't need to even ask you the exact date and time of the murder to provide an alibi. You should know that this couldn't be me in this picture. It may be some kind of a coincidence—'

'It's seems like one hell of a coincidence, doesn't it?'

'What do you mean?' Honey looked pale.

Rita was certain Honey Singh had attempted to lie, but eventually gave up and admitted. She was equally concerned that if Honey Singh wasn't involved, Vikram and she coming to his office might get reported to the killers and that could trigger events that might not have been in their agenda presently. A thought pushed through that if there was some real threat to Honey Singh's life, she had to do something about it. She had to divulge a bit more. If she were to err, it would rather be on the side of caution, she couldn't just let someone's life be at risk ... she waited till some colour had returned to Honey Singh's face.

'We think it's orchestrated, not coincidental.' She gesticulated to halt his questions. 'We also think it *might* be someone who knows you or knew you well enough—'

'Veer Singh?'

'Maybe, maybe not. So now what more can you tell us about him?'

'As I said, we were close friends. Very close friends.' Honey detailed their long friendship from engineering-college days till when they both started their careers in Mumbai, running their respective businesses. Veer was also an information-technology expert. As Veer had no family, he used to hang at Honey's apartment on most weekends. And Veer had met Kitty through one of his business contacts and later introduced her to Honey, and things just went down from there.

'So how tall was Veer?'

'An inch shorter than me.'

'Weight, colour, built?'

'Almost the same as me, we used to be in the college basketball team together, visited the same gym, exercised almost the same amount, so our builds were obviously comparable, unless he's changed in the last three years or so.'

'And face?'

'Obviously, we weren't a replica of each other. We have … or rather had – as I don't know what he looks like now – common features like skin colour, sharp-*ish* jawline, but that was because our roots were similar; our forefathers came from the same region in Punjab.'

'Were you ever misidentified for Veer Singh or him for you by someone? Anyone? Ever?'

'No.'

'Not even in the dark?'

'Nope, never, at least not me. If he was even mistaken for me, he never told me. But I cannot believe this. Why would he do this … sure, I mean we split up, but he was still a very close friend, we loved each other like siblings. Why would he do something that would hurt me, why would he let me down?'

'By definition only people whom you love or have loved can let you down. Think about it. How can someone you don't know or never trusted let you down? And as far as betrayal of an old friend goes, worse things happen, Mr Singh.'

'You can call me Honey.'

'No,' Rita smiled. 'Believe me, I'm fine calling you Mr Singh.'

I wouldn't have minded if you were Sonny, but I won't be going around calling someone Honey. Sheesh!

'So you think he framed me or he is framing me?'

'Again … maybe, maybe not. We do not have sufficient evidence to conclude that.'

'Why would he get me followed then? If he wanted to frame me, he's accomplished the burglary and the diamonds and got away with it so far. What is in it for him to get me followed now?'

Rita knew she had to draw a line here. Perceived threat to Honey Singh's life may have prompted her to give him more details than she had originally set out to provide, but outlining her entire theory and conjecture wasn't in her agenda. She had no desire to spill the proverbial beans of the past burglaries, and her hypothesis on the future ones even if Honey Singh was the priest in the confession box.

'That's precisely what we are trying to establish, Mr Singh.'

Rita pondered asking Honey Singh about Kitty Varghese, but in the end dropped the idea. She had not intentions of cautioning the model. She didn't want Honey or Kitty to know that the police had uncovered a potential link between the murder in Brussels and other burglaries in India. There wasn't any evidence yet, just conjecture. Rita checked if Honey had ever been mistaken for anyone else, not just for Veer Singh. Nada. Was his identity even stolen? No. Had he ever been a victim of something as simple as credit card fraud? Nope. She spent another hour combing for, well, anything but failed to get anything that could implicate Honey Singh or give her some kind of a clue to progress.

She looked at Vikram with eyebrows raised a bit: *have I missed anything?* Vikram only shook his head a millimetre: *No.*

'OK, Mr Singh,' Rita stood up. 'We'll leave you to your work now. If you think of anything that might help us or anything unusual, please give us a call.' She gave her card to him. Vikram handed Honey Singh his card too. 'And what is the best number to get you on in case we need to speak?'

Honey opened the top drawer, took out two cards and handed them to both detectives. 'I always carry my mobile.' He pointed towards the iPhone at his desk.

Not Blackberry, Rita observed.

Rita and Vikram took the elevator down and walked up to the Gypsy. There was only a pedestrian exit in the back of the building that led to the next office block, so Vikram needed all his driving skills to reverse the vehicle all the way out because people rushing into the voluntary prison didn't seem keen on extending any courtesies to those exiting.

'I find it hard to believe that Honey Singh does not know about being followed. He lied at first, and then he vaguely remembered sighting someone. If it were me someone was following for so long, I would have even found out who, why, where, what? Wouldn't you be curious, ma'am?'

'*If* I knew someone was following me, I would be … quite worried, actually. But he says he didn't even notice till we prompted him to think hard.'

The evening rush hour had started and it took Vikram over an hour to cross over from Bandra East to Bandra West to drop Rita off at her residence.

'Each day on the wrong track is also a day away from the right track,' Rita murmured before she said bye to Vikram.

NINETEEN

Mr Joginder Raja aka Handlebar, the best intergalactic private investigator you could find, ladies and gentlemen, did not succeed in the challenge he had set himself up for. The gauntlet he had thrown up of ferreting out his mystery client who had set him up to tail Honey Singh had only steered him into a spot of frustration. He realized that the technology his client used was far more secure than he had anticipated. The VPN walls showed every sign of being impenetrable. Moreover, the fear factor played with his nerves. The client had already warned him once. And that DCP woman had mentioned in the conversation that there was a murder investigation that was associated with this, in some way. What if the client decided to carry out the threat against his family if, in some way, the client established that Handlebar was taking shots at scrapping the VPN wall? And what for? Did he care who the client was in the end? The client had reprimanded him for not being diligent on the job that had been assigned to him, which, in itself, wasn't overstepping. Like most people, after having vented his frustration on his own incompetence, he justified his client's transgression and carried on. It was Friday and his next report was due the next day. Thankfully, the cops had left him alone so the client would have no more nuisances from someone tailing Handlebar tailing Honey Singh.

He had set out early this Friday morning to take his position but the front driver-side tyre had a puncture just outside Lokhandwala. Cursing his luck, he tried calling for help, but eventually gave up the doomed pursuit and changed the wheel himself. Conscious that he had lost the crucial forty-five minutes, and Honey Singh would have left his home for office by now, he decided to drive straight to BKC. When he got to Bandra Kurla Complex he spotted Honey's car in the parking. Assured that he had only missed the first leg of the chase, he drove further down into a private bank's car park and left the car. He sauntered back a few metres and placed his considerable haunches on a small plastic chair provided by a makeshift tea stall. He was careful to move his seat behind the vast trunk of a tree, ostensibly looking for shade but in reality looking for a spot where he had visibility of Honey Singh's building exit while he stayed concealed; he ordered a masala chai and a packet of Gold Flake Kings and sat down. It was his typical routine for the last few months now. The tea vendor had a surplus of newspapers that kept him occupied for a few hours till lunch. His cover had not been blown so far and there was no cause of worry that it would be now. The quarry was too posh to visit this little outfit. Unless someone actually walked past the stall looking for him, he wouldn't be spotted. Even that smartass DCP with her police guy were there the day before and he noticed her looking out for someone, most probably him, but she had missed. She might have expected him in his car, but with him and his car separated even her hawk-eyed inspection had failed to detect him. He might have slipped once, but he was still the best investigator, wasn't he? See how he blended in with the crowd here?

However, he was concerned what that DCP Ferreira woman had visited Honey Singh for? He had thought about calling Jatin Singh to check but didn't follow through with his own plan, and now sitting here again, that troubled him. He made a mental note to check later when he would be in touch with them regarding this week's report to his client.

Boisterously slurping his tea and patting his vast moustache with his kerchief after every sip, he settled down by 11:15 to read the news. He hadn't even finished his first cup of the day when he saw Honey Singh arrive wearing a powder blue T and dark denims – he was roughly six to seven hundred metres away but Handlebar was certain it was his target. The distance didn't compromise his vision or his ability to recognize his subject; he had tailed only one person in the last hundred days. Honey Singh was difficult to miss or mistake: there was not even in iota of doubt there. Heck, he even knew what temple Mrs Lucky Singh regularly went to. He even recognized the milkman who visited their apartment every morning. He could rattle Kitty Varghese's figure statistics or her swimsuit size without blinking an eyelid. Not recognizing the target was out of question. 700 metres? He could have recognized Honey Singh by his body odour now.

Seeing Honey Singh stealthily sneaking into his own building got Handlebar a second wind. He upended his cup finishing the remaining tea and got up. Though he had a lighter in his pocket, he walked to the vendor under the pretext of asking for matches. He got a little over two metres closer but when standing, he had an even clearer sight to the coast. It was indeed Honey Singh, but he had arrived in a taxi, which meant he had left his car in the office parking and then gone somewhere and was returning now. He had got dropped a few paces before the gate, which surprised Handlebar. That was only first of the firsts: Honey Singh had never taken a taxi previously – since he had been watching. This was also the first instance when Honey Singh left the office and ventured out soon after arriving there. He normally stayed in office all day; in all the time Handlebar had been watching him, Honey Singh had left the office in the day only five times. On emergency client visits when, Handlebar guessed, something critical broke and there were no personnel to be sent immediately. However, to get to some place right away why would Honey Singh take a taxi and not drive? Maybe his car had broken down, too, today?

He twisted the ends of his handlebar moustache in succession: right first, left next: always in that order. Taking out his Samsung phone he zoomed and snapped a picture.

And as if all that irregular activity wasn't enough, Handlebar saw Honey Singh stop at the gate and surreptitiously glance around like he was looking for someone, something. Had he been warned of someone following him? That fuckin' DCP woman. Intestinal cramps ensued. What if Honey Singh wandered down to the tea stall and questioned him? More importantly, if his client even got a whiff of this, he would be fired instantaneously – no question about that. The greater problem would be if the client got to know that the police were in touch with Handlebar and the same police-fuckin'-woman was the one who had apprised Honey Singh of the surveillance, he better be prepared for a severe repercussion. The client might not carry out what he had threatened to do to his extended family, but Handlebar didn't want an encounter with some rogues and a few broken bones in his body either. Who knew?

His thoughts returned to Honey. Where had he arrived from and what was he secreting or ensconcing himself from?

Had Handlebar missed the police car that might already be in the building? Had the police come again today? He might have missed it in the three minutes he had gone into the bank building to park his own car? Fuckety-fuck, he cursed under the breath. He had buried the fact that the police had visited him at home, and gotten away with it, and his client, presumably, was still ignorant of that. He had seen that DCP and her police-boy the day before, but he could easily mask that feigning ignorance: he didn't know the unmarked vehicle that arrived yesterday was the police's. And even if he knew, how was he to know that with so many businesses in the building, who did the police actually visit? But if that DCP woman was around again today, the client might get to know somehow.

Handlebar Raja's mind was going through the hurdles, his thoughts jumping all over. What should he do if Honey came down to the tea stall? It wasn't proscribed to be at a roadside tea stall, was it? Still, he couldn't think coherently for a few minutes till he was convinced Honey Singh had no plans to walk to the tea stall. He exhaled in relief when he saw Honey Singh walk into the building and disappear. He smiled at the vendor to diffuse his own stress. If the tea vendor didn't ask him '*what's wrong*', then everything in his visage should be right.

However, the relief was short-lived.

Less than five minutes later he saw Honey Singh drive out in his car with Kitty Varghese. They turned left as he exited the building and sped in Handlebar's direction and passed him seemingly unaware of his existence at the tea stall. Handlebar had no chance of following, as he knew by the time he would have got to his car, the couple would be out of sight. And then something occurred to him after Honey Singh's car was out of his vision. Honey Singh wasn't wearing the blue T. He couldn't see the jeans from the car window, but Honey Singh was now wearing a check shirt in red. Why did he change? Handlebar quickly snapped another picture and sat down to think. This was bizarre. Honey Singh was up to something. What? Why did he leave his office twice today? Earlier by taxi, this time driving his car. And changed his shirt? If Honey and/or Kitty had known they were being watched, they didn't show it. The two young birds had blithely passed the tea vendor without slowing or looking. Having missed tailing the car carrying Honey and Kitty, he ordered his second tea, lit up another Gold Flake and sat down. Handlebar had spent months at this location, another few hours couldn't hurt. He was certain Honey Singh hadn't left for the day, and would be back. It gave him time to ponder.

But ponder he couldn't.

The glug of first sip from the second cup of tea he had in his mouth whooshed out without a warning. He shook his head. He blinked, closed his eyes tightly till it hurt for a good five seconds before reopening them to focus. Was he in some trance? Was the tea vendor mixing some other leaves into his tea? His brain couldn't register or process what his optics signalled. Standing a few hundred metres from where Handlebar Raja sat was Honey Singh in the blue T. Honey came out of the building as cautiously as he had entered only some minutes back; he didn't seem comfortable, which was a surprise as this was his own office building. He appeared scared, nervous like he didn't want to be where he was. But how could he be here when Handlebar had seen him drive away merely minutes ago wearing a red shirt? Handlebar had been watching the building gate and Honey Singh's car hadn't returned. Neither had Handlebar seen his target walk back, which would have been equally impossible to miss.

How could ...?

Handlebar quickly took out his phone again, zoomed in as best as he could and took a picture before he saw the blue

T-donning Honey Singh flag down a taxi and sit down. The car took a U turn and sped in the opposite direction.

How could … and then his brain warmed up a bit.

He acknowledged why he had been hired months back. His client suspected it all along, but required a confirmation. It wasn't puzzling after what he had witnessed.

Honey Singh had a double.

The surprise was that Handlebar had been watching Honey Singh for months now and he hadn't spotted the dead ringer earlier. And he would not have spotted the other guy even today if the other guy hadn't visited Honey's office.

Wrong.

He wouldn't have spotted him even today if he hadn't seen the two together. One taxiing in, the other driving out; both wearing different coloured tops. Did that mean he had seen both of them before? It could well be. It was a case of him not knowing that he had. Fuck! The guy in blue could be … but how could Handlebar or anyone distinguish who was the other guy among the two? What if the other guy visited Kitty at night? Would she be able to discern the right guy between the sheets? However lucidly he could visualize the raunchy thought – Kitty sleeping with Honey Singh one or Honey Singh two or both – he was aware it couldn't pay his bills. There would always be time for them later.

He realized, in his anxiety, he had put his half-smoked cigarette in the remaining tea in his cup and trashed both. He ordered another tea. Lit up a new stick and sat down without camouflaging himself behind a newspaper. He needed full visibility of events as they occurred. It struck him that this had to be a significant development for his client. His client had paid him advance and what had he tendered till now that could be of as much importance as this? Hitherto, he had sometimes wondered why his client was even paying to keep a tab on Honey Singh. He reckoned his client's motive had always been to confirm there was a Honey Singh two. He couldn't and wouldn't keep his client in the dark regarding this even if that policewoman asked him to. Did he even need to disclose this little secret to her? He knew he had to, in light of the promise he had made in bargain when he had asked the police not to follow him following Honey. If he screened this, the police – if and when they came to know – would come down heavily on him, won't they? He had to get his weekly report checked and censured by the police before he left it for his client in the Drafts folder. The only way further for him was to come up with a convincing argument that the police would suck up and let him send the info forward. How, he did not know.

His concern – who was Honey Singh two? – did not live long. He assumed his client, too, would want to know that, and that could translate in extension of his initial contract. More money. Perhaps, that dumbass policewoman might also get this in her thick head that private investigator Joginder Raja was, after all, the best person to flush out who Honey Singh two was. Yes, that is how he will have to convince her.

He was still going up and down the meandering lanes of his mind when he saw the car in the distance. White Honda Accord. He saw the registration plate before he caught a glimpse of the driver. Honey Singh – the one in the red check shirt – was returning to his office. Kitty was with him. Translation: If Kitty was in the car, this was Honey Singh one. He zoomed and clicked again. The time was 3:14 p.m. Handlebar noted that too.

Kitty left Honey Singh at office and drove out at 4:03 p.m. in the Accord.

Nothing eventful happened for the rest of the day. Handlebar had had eight teas, two packets of cigarettes and noshed two sandwiches through the day. Kitty returned to pick her beau up at 6:54. Handlebar followed the two to Kitty's place and left for the day. He had been long enough on the job to know that it being Friday night, Honey Singh, in all probability, would stay over. The raunchy omnibus he had left imagining midway in the afternoon boomeranged. He wished his client had asked for watching them in close quarters. The first camera he would have installed would have been in Kitty's bedroom. His voyeur thoughts, his soliloquy of cheesy Bollywood-movie dialogues and item-number humming only concluded when he had plied from Versova to Lokhandwala and turned into his own building.

Later that night, at dinner, Mr Raja animatedly discussed his despair with Mrs Raja. He explicated the discovery of two Honey Singhs and his dilemma of what to conceal and what to relay to his client and the police. Without illuminating the graveness of the threat his covert client had issued, he told her that the client had already warned him of missing the other surveillance that the crafty policewoman had placed. Another mistake and the best case was that he'd be fired; worst case wasn't a pleasant thought. On the contrary, if he let the cat out for the client, the police would also have to know.

'You should tell the police about the threat, Joginder-*jee* …'

'Why?'

'The police need to know everything to help you. Actually, if you ask me, you should not hide anything from either one because there is a possibility that your client might come to know this at some point, in some way. I cannot let you take the risk of upsetting the client. And to be fair to him, if he's been burning our kitchen fire for so long, you should report what you've learnt. I think if you explained this to DCP Ferreira she will understand your position. She seemed a smart woman.'

'She's a dumb woman. What if she does not follow what we tell her?'

'Ask her, don't tell her.'

'*Ask her* …' he snorted. 'What if I make amends to the client's report after I show it to the police? How would the police know?'

'What is the point of hiding it from the police?'

'Because if I am loyal to my client we can get more business, my sweet darling.'

'But what if the other Honey Singh is the suspect who your client and the police are both looking for?'

'So?'

'So how is it beneficial to give him away to your client who you do not even know and not to the police?'

Handlebar remained silent.

'What if you ignore what you saw today?' Mrs Raja asked.

'The risk is that if the client had another team somewhere and they tell him, we're doomed. We can't do that.'

'When do you have to decide on this?' Mrs Raja chimed another question.

'Well, we don't have to take a decision right now. It's not like I have to write the report tonight. Let me sleep over it. I'm sure I'll get some more ideas by morning.' Handlebar happily concluded the verbal exchange knowing his wife had another two hundred possible questions. He was also well aware that the demons wouldn't let him sleep a single wink tonight. If the nausea of threat from his client, the damned policewoman and her schmuck, and the two Honey Singhs even excused him for a few moments, the spicy Kitty Varghese would definitely keep him up in more ways than one.

TWENTY

Saturday. 15th August: Happy Birthday, India.

Rita was cheerful when she woke up. Ash was travelling back from Delhi tonight. Unlike his last visit to Mumbai, he planned to stay with Rita over the weekend and leave for London on Monday afternoon. Not that her house was dirty or disorderly, but she still did a round around to check if all was in order. She took out a set of towels and smiled thinking if she should put them in the guest bathroom but decided against that. Despite his subtle lewd one-liners at times – *Sexy* would have certainly used the opposite of euphemism: *dysphemism*, she mused – Ash was a great friend. Rita liked him because his company was good, the sex was amazing and the relationship was totally unconditional. No expectations. No jealousy. He never once asked if she had seen somebody in his absence. That didn't mean he didn't care but such trivial things didn't seem to bother him like some other guys.

She took extra time in the shower conscious that she would still collect soot through the day before she met Ash, but what the heck! She spritzed more than normal Clinique Happy on herself, then dressed into her usual jeans and shirt with Smith and Wesson on the holster and a *bundi* on top to cover the gun. Before she left the house, she had decided on a black dress for the evening, took it out and said 'hello' to it as if not having worn it for a while might have upset the poor thing. And she didn't forget the stilettos: wasn't their sole purpose to complement God's design of making Eve a smidgen shorter than Adam? She beamed.

Vikram had called ahead, and was already waiting outside the building gate when Rita walked out.

The team had decided the day before that it was time to pay a visit to Miss Kitty Varghese. Köln to Brussels was around 225 kilometres. Taking into consideration the good motorways in Europe and high-speed cars available in Germany, the distance could be comfortably covered in a little over three hours if one drove nonstop. Back and forth, say seven hours. Certainly feasible, but they didn't have to deliberate long, as Jatin had checked that Kitty Varghese hadn't gone AWOL on any of the days she had been in Köln. Obviously, she didn't share a room with someone – not that someone in her capacity would, she was a model not some junior make-up assistant – but she was with someone or the other throughout the day during rehearsals and fashion shows. No one recollected Kitty getting away for seven hours at a stretch. To corroborate, Jatin had liaised with Victor in Brussels who, in turn, checked all car rentals in and around the city. No car had been rented to any person called Kitty Varghese or any single Indian lady. He had checked if any hotel taxi was hired for an unusual out-of-country trip and back but nothing turned up. Trains and buses plying on the route had been asked to submit passenger records for the period. They drew a blank there too.

With nothing new uncovered, meeting Kitty Varghese, if only to get her side of the story on Veer Singh, was necessary as some loose ends needed lacing up.

The lookout at the gate didn't contest when Vikram flashed the police badge as they walked in after parking the car outside the apartment building in Versova.

Kitty Varghese was even better in the flesh than in her pictures. Her glowing skin, a shade of bronze, big eyes like limpid pools, long lashes and a slight but near-natural pout. Hair carelessly coiffured in a French bun held together with a barrette. Long toned legs. She wore a light pink silky-satiny shirt – epaulets on shoulders, patched pockets with buttons – that was some inches higher than her knees and she was absolutely comfortable in it. The woman exuded inimitable sexuality. And this was without any make-up. Yes, Kitty Varghese was a model: a catwalk and a close-up model.

'Hello, how may I help you?' she asked opening the door when she saw Rita and Vikram who had come unannounced. She had a husky voice. Check that. Kitty Varghese had a sultry voice. If some poor guy managed to escape her looks and body the voice would get him. In God's kingdom even the visually impaired weren't devoid of the femme fatale.

Poor Vikram.

Rita introduced Vikram before self. Explained there wasn't any reason to be alarmed as it was a routine enquiry.

'Are you the one who met Honey yesterday?'

Rita had fully expected that she would have been spoken to about their visit to Honey Singh the day before. Thankfully, Kitty had the brains to not feign ignorance.

'Come in,' she said and held the door open for them to walk in.

It seemed like Kitty had done a lot of clothes shopping recently. That, or some show organizers had sent her loads of clothes to try on. They were strewn about everywhere. Dresses. Lingerie. Shoes. Stockings. Garters. Scarves. Some of it was as fetching as Kitty herself.

Kitty was barefoot. She slumped on the sofa and folded her legs beneath her in one swift motion – lithe and flexible– showing off a bit more of her flawless model skin while Rita and Vikram sat on the sofa opposite.

'We are here merely to ask some questions, Miss Varghese ... is it OK if I call you Kitty?'

'Of course, that's what everyone calls me. Could I get you two something to drink? Tea, coffee or a Coke?'

'Only if you're having,' Rita responded looking at Vikram in case he had any objections. None showed. His face revealed that he would happily consume potassium cyanide if Kitty offered him that.

'I was about to have a coffee. The kettle had just boiled. Give me a minute.' She got up and almost catwalked out of the living room. Feline grace. Years of walking the ramp had inured to make it second nature, Rita figured. She looked around. The apartment was luxurious. Italian marble flooring in the living room; the walls were covered with Kitty's blown-up pictures from her various modelling assignments. You didn't need Mona Lisa to adorn your walls if you were Kitty Varghese. There was a credenza in one corner that had a framed picture of Kitty with Honey. They would produce startling kids indeed.

The coffee was really good. Hot and dark. Only Vikram added milk and sugar.

'How may I be of any help?' Kitty asked again.

Rita took out and presented the candid-shot from the elevator and passed it to Kitty who looked at it for barely a minute.

'What about it?'

'Do you recognize the man in the photograph?'

'It's Honey.'

'Sure?'

'Of course, a million per cent. How can *I* make a mistake?'

'Could you identify where it has been taken?'

Kitty glanced at the picture again, but shook her head in a negative. 'Not sure.'

'Have a look at it again, Kitty. Is there any chance this could be your old friend, Veer Singh?

The mention of Veer Singh caused an ever-so-slight quiver in Kitty's pupils: a sign of fear or uneasiness. Again that could be because Kitty reckoned Rita knew something or it could just a simple concern as Honey Singh must have told her about police's questions the day before. There was no exact science of comprehending. But it was there and it was noted. From the corner of her eye she stole a glance at Vikram who scribbled the incident too. Kitty looked shifty.

'Is there anything you would like to tell us Kitty?'

'What are you looking for from me?'

'Anything. We need to find Veer Singh to eliminate him from our investigation.'

'Murder investigation?'

It was evident Honey Singh had spoken to her. And why wouldn't he? Maybe he expected the police to quiz Kitty or maybe it was a simple conversation with his girlfriend: police did not come around asking questions every day. And Veer Singh having been a common friend it would have been suspicious if he hadn't actually. Moreover, Rita or Vikram hadn't told Honey Singh not to talk to his girlfriend or anyone.

'Yes,' Rita replied. 'Would you know where could we find Veer Singh?'

'As far as I am aware he moved to America years back.'

'How well did you know him?'

'What do you mean?'

Something wasn't what it seemed at the surface.

Kitty looked and sounded guilty, like a kitten caught with milk in her whiskers.

'Well, weren't Veer Singh and you friends before he introduced you and Honey, am I right?'

'You're correct. I got to know Veer through an advertising agency I was working with at the time. He was around for something about the website – he was extremely good, probably as good as Honey when it came to computers and software. Yes, Veer introduced me to Honey a few months later.'

'And then the guys, Honey and Veer had a misunderstanding and for obvious reasons you sided with Honey, and in time all of you friends lost track of Veer after he moved abroad,' Rita filled in.

'Precisely.'

'So what are you not telling me, Kitty?' Rita was now getting frustrated with going around in circles with the same story she had, now, heard initially in the investigation by Vikram and then rephrased by Mrs Lucky Singh and Honey Singh before Kitty.

'What does that mean?'

'There is something more to it that you're not telling me. What's that?'

'I had a short fling with Veer. Is that what you're after? But we quickly realized we weren't compatible and we agreed to stay friends. As I told you he was the one who introduced me to Honey …'

So this wasn't purely a tangential relationship. Kitty Varghese actually had a fling with a person who was supposedly missing.

They certainly need to speak to Veer Singh now, police, if only to clear him.

'What was the incompatibility, if you don't mind telling me.'

'He wasn't comfortable with my career choice. He didn't think modelling was a "decent" enough line with all the travel and skimpy outfits for audience and camera. And I didn't want to give up. Specially as I don't think I can do anything else.'

Fair enough. Easy to infer why they broke up quickly. Though, with Veer Singh missing from the picture, there was no way of checking her story. And if they located him, there seemed to be a pile of questions before asking him about his opinions on women's career choices. Typical chauvinist male. Bastions of women's moralities. No issues with seeing other girls flash skin but want to keep their women in covers. Veer's loss indeed. Kitty Varghese was an iPhone: there wasn't any dearth of admirers.

'Did Honey Singh know you had a fling with Veer?'

'No.'

'Does he know that now?'

'No. Would you be telling him?' Kitty asked with a straight face.

'Where were you in the first week of April this year?' Rita ignored the question. She wasn't wont to promising anything to anyone and certainly not before she knew the whole truth.

'That's easy. I was abroad, in Köln, for a fashion show. Why?'

'Just for records.'

'Now what are *you* not telling me?'

'Lots. Kitty, you have to understand that I have no personal agenda to know about your life. I'm running an investigation into more than one offence at the moment and I cannot – even if I wanted to – tell you everything. So it's better if you answer my questions. I promise to answer yours to the extent I can. Do we have a deal?'

'OK.'

'Do you travel quite a bit on work?' Rita knew the answer to that.

'Quite a bit.'

'Is it always abroad to exotic locations?' Rita knew the answer to this one too.

'No. Mostly within India actually.'

'So, would you have travel records of all official travels in the last, say, one or two years?' Rita wanted the Delhi travel details from Kitty specifically, but she didn't want to ask for it.'

'What's that for?'

'As I said we are investigating more than one incident at the moment, so this is just for a routine enquiry.'

'Should I be concerned?'

'Not if you haven't done anything wrong.'

'Are you … hold on a minute.' Kitty straightened up, became a bit animated. 'Are you trying to check if I'm still dating Veer Singh and travelling around only to see him and hiding my trysts with him?'

'It's none of my concerns who you date. I want to meet Veer Singh but your travel records aren't required to check on your love life.'

'Do I need a lawyer?'

'You've been watching too many American legal dramas on television, Kitty. If I want to question you, I can come up here with lights and siren and no lawyer can help you. This is Mumbai and I'm not a constable. I'm a DCP in the crime branch.' Rita didn't raise her voice but it was menacing enough to deliver the message.

'I have rights.'

'This meeting is over. Vikram, let's go.'

Vikram closed his pad and got up immediately.

'Wait. What do you mean?'

'I'll send the police van to pick you up and we'll talk at the police station. Thanks for the coffee.'

'You don't really mean that.'

'Try me. I've been unusually patient and polite, but I want the truth without any further complications. You think you have rights, I'll show you what all rights *I* have.'

'OK, OK … I'm sorry I overreacted. Please calm down, Rita. I'll dig out and send all the travel records over to you as soon as I can.' Kitty looked appalled by the sudden eruption of Rita who, at first, had been extremely polite but now she was nothing short of a raging tigress. Not many people had the fortitude to challenge that.

'I want all the records at my desk on Monday morning. Please don't test my patience anymore.'

'But you have to promise you won't tell Honey I had a fling with Veer once.'

'As long as it isn't part of my investigation, and you don't know where Veer Singh is at present, then no, I'm not going to spill unnecessary beans.'

'I swear I haven't seen him since Honey and Veer broke up.' Kitty was almost pleading now.

'Don't tell me. I don't care. I only want to know where Veer Singh is now, and if you honestly don't know that you shouldn't be worried at all.'

'You really think Veer could be responsible for murder?'

'I didn't say that. As far as my suspect list goes, everyone is a suspect till this case isn't closed.'

'Why would Veer do anything like that?'

'To seek revenge? Or to implicate Honey to get back at him while pocketing millions on the way. Or maybe he doesn't care ...'

'He won't do that.'

'We'll exculpate him after we find him and speak to him. Much as I would like to take your word for it I'm not halting my search for Veer.'

Kitty was part scared, part restless, but Rita knew, with what hard treatment she had meted out, Kitty's travel records would be available by Monday. Not desirous of spending any more time than required, Rita and Vikram said their byes and left.

Was Kitty complicit? How could she be involved? She might not be involved, at least not directly, but Rita's gut feel was she wasn't entirely hapless either.

Not finding the whereabouts of Veer Singh was a concern.

Maybe he went to the US and never looked back.

Maybe he never even visited the US embassy.

'We have approximate dates, Vikram,' Rita said as they drove to the HQ at Crawford Market. 'Could you ask the Commissioner's PA to make a call to the immigration officials please? There should be a record of Veer Singh flying out of the country.'

'Yes ma'am.'

TWENTY-ONE

Jatin tried his best, but could not unearth if anyone had followed Honey Singh before the previous two burglaries in Mumbai and Delhi. Handlebar certainly hadn't. How many private investigators could he contact? Asking around wasn't much help too; too much time had elapsed for any bystander to have any memory of anyone following someone. Honey Singh, of course, had denied it. There were no other avenues to check.

Anyway, at the very best, Rita and team had an extrinsic line connecting the three incidents; they didn't have any circumstantial evidence, not even an oblique one. It was well within the scope of possible that they were three disparate, unrelated capers. Or any two were related while the third one stood on its own legs. They knew Kitty Varghese was in Delhi at the time of Delhi theft, and in Mumbai at the time of Mumbai theft, which would be corroborated by her travel records that she would send on Monday. And she was 200-plus kilometres from Brussels – not in Brussels – when Ron Jogani was whacked. So even if she was complicit in some way, how did it incriminate

Honey Singh? If she was an accomplice, who was the master of ceremonies then?

'If Honey Singh has never been out of country how did his picture get captured by the elevator in the hotel at Brussels?' Rita sounded frustrated.

The four – Rita, Vikram, Jatin and Nene – had weaved and hashed theories since Rita and Vikram returned from the morning meeting with Kitty. Nene could always be trusted for provisions – he knew the best local street-side food places. The *vada pav* with the red garlic chutney that he had brought in for the team was such comfort food, and ounce for ounce it could beat coffee in keeping the brain awake.

'We're missing something crucial here, guys,'

'Is it at all possible …?' Jatin stopped, like he was still contemplating.

'Out with it whatever it is.'

'I'm wondering if the whole *missing-the-camera-in-the-elevator-thing* was fake.'

Rita got it instantly. 'You mean the alleged Mr Sishir Singh knew about the obscured camera and planted the picture they wanted, and made it look like they missed it?'

'Yes. Think about it, ma'am. If they could freeze all other cameras, misdirect the entire hotel security to believe they were watching live feed across the property while those schmuks watched the replay of the day before, how challenging would it be for that brain to feed a chosen picture into a still camera?'

'Brilliant. Bloody brilliant, Jatin,' Rita clapped.

'You mean this picture was taken in some elevator locally?' Nene asked.

Everyone looked at the XL candid-shot of Sishir Singh or Honey Singh plastered on one of the walls in the room. There was nothing that revealed where it was clicked. The angle from where it was shot warranted it had no background of any consequential value to determine where in the world it was. Not a chance.

'But why was Honey Singh's picture chosen?' Nene questioned after a few minutes.

'Maybe it was random ...' Jatin hadn't thought of that.

'Nope. It can't be random. Someone knew Honey Singh, at least cursorily, to plant his picture. How else would they find him to follow him?' Rita said.

'So if it was merely a picture-plant why follow Honey Singh and spend cash on that?' Nene quizzed further.

'It could be that following Honey Singh was the only logical way to keep track if and when the police got involved and, if that was the motive, we sucked it in. They might only be following Honey Singh to follow us. On the two previous occasions – and my gut feel says they are connected – there was only robbery, no murder, and because it was domestic they would have known exactly which police station would investigate. They didn't need to leave phoney breadcrumbs and trick us to follow. That picture brought Victor to Mumbai and led us to Honey Singh. If that was the intention, it worked,' Rita reasoned on the fly.

'But the hotel and airline staff did recognize Sishir Singh when they were shown the picture?'

'Well, we know recognition across diverse human races is never absolute. If the guy who carried out the theft and murder even remotely resembled Honey Singh in shape, size, skin colour and hairstyle it could very well be an error. And therefore Honey Singh wasn't a random choice. You need to know the original to fake it. They knew that if anything went wrong they'll make Honey Singh their fall guy.' Rita thought about Veer Singh's description as she spoke.

'So how does Kitty fit into all this?'

'That, like so many other things, is a mystery—'

Jatin's mobile phone rang before Rita could finish.

'Joginder Raja,' Jatin saw the caller and announced and moved out of his chair to take the call. 'What?' he almost screamed, 'Wait a minute, Joginder … let me put you on the speakerphone so we can all hear this.' He muted the call for a minute and said: 'Joginder Raja is on the line, says he saw Honey Singh's double yesterday.'

'What?'

'Joginder, you're on speakerphone now. I have DCP Rita Ferreira and Senior Inspectors Patil and Nene in the room with me. Tell us what you saw.'

The police quartet in the room was stunned as Handlebar Raja narrated the events of the previous day. He had seen two Honey Singhs – one nervously lurking around the office complex, the other driving out and then driving in with Kitty – in different outfits. No, there was no confusion, he was absolutely clear on that; he even had pictures of both on his phone. No, he couldn't follow either of them as it happened quite suddenly. Yes, it was the first time he had encountered the two of them together.

Handlebar sounded nervous but he also told them about the threat he had received from his mysterious client the week before for missing the police following him and Honey Singh.

'Are you saying your client spotted the police surveillance teams?' Rita asked. Not because she hadn't comprehended what Raja had just reported, but she expectantly looked at Nene: how had his competent police teams overlooked a tail?

'Yes madam, he said he has more than one person following Honey Singh—'

'You mean the other team has also been following Honey Singh for the past few months?'

'I don't know that, madam.'

'But you didn't see anyone following you ever?'

Handlebar remained silent.

Nene, reddened with embarrassment, got up and walked out of the room. The other three didn't ask. They knew Nene would blast the surveillance teams that had covered the patch the other weekend for overlooking a critical incident. With what Handlebar had just conveyed it seemed the tail was there for pretty much all day. It was unacceptable, even laughable, to miss such things after years of police training.

'Why didn't you tell this to anyone of us for a week, Mr Raja?' Rita growled after Nene had left.

Handlebar justified his actions by referring to the threat to his family. He was frightened, and irrespective of how hollow the threat was, he wasn't willing to take the risk. He sounded high-strung and justifiably so.

Rita's temper calmed, albeit Handlebar had wasted a week of theirs. Had the police known that they had missed being followed once they would have been extra cautious the next day. They couldn't have missed the other person or people the second time around, certainly not if they had known about them. Talk about a wasted opportunity.

'I wanted to ask you what should I put in my weekly report today?'

'What do you mean?'

'Should I report that I spotted Honey Singh's duplicate?'

'No way.'

'But what if someone else saw it and they report it to my client? He would be all over me again, madam.'

'Let us think. We'll come back to you in a couple of hours. Meanwhile, send us the pictures you took of the two Honey Singhs.'

'OK, madam.'

'Thank you, Mr Raja.' Rita pressed the red button on Jatin's phone.

Jatin's phone beeped. Handlebar had texted the two pictures. Jatin opened them, had a close look at them and shook his head in disbelief before passing on his phone to Rita. She did the same and passed it to Vikram. The three sat dumfounded.

Doppelgänger: a ghostly double of a living person. Honey Singh had a doppelgänger, and that changed everything. Their entire search, their analysis, their conjectures, their theories, all seemed redundant. When a paradigm shifts everything goes back to zero, isn't that what they say?

'He can't be real,' Rita finally broke the silence.

'You think Handlebar has made up a story?'

'I wouldn't award him such high marks on ingenuity. One possibility could be that someone coached him, which should be simple to figure out though. Jatin, call Mr Raja and ask him not to delete the photographs, then I want you to go over to his apartment immediately and see the date and time stamp on the photographs he's just sent. Take someone along who's good with technology, who can determine if the photographs were actually taken when and where he says, and not imported into his phone or photoshopped. That should be enough to corroborate his story.'

Jatin nodded.

'And before you leave give these pictures to the print lab, they should be able to clean and enlarge these. Thanks.'

'What is the other possibility, ma'am?' Vikram asked after Jatin left the room. 'You said, one possibility could be that Handlebar Raja was faking it ...'

'I can't believe it's possible to have an indistinguishable double from two different sets of parents. Isn't it a biological impossibility? I doubt if history has any such recorded occurrence. If Handlebar truly saw two Honey Singhs as he described, then someone's used a lot of plastic to make himself look like Honey Singh.'

'There aren't many plastic surgeons in Mumbai. We can check.'

'I thought about it before but I am pretty sure the surgery wasn't done here in Mumbai, Vikram. Or if it was, then it's not on the registers.'

Vikram acquiesced with a nod. 'What do you think we let Mr Raja write to his client?'

'I think we should not mention the double, at least not this week. Ask Nene to put his best guys on surveillance on Honey Singh and Handlebar. Our guys shouldn't miss anything this time. I want to know if any fucking leaf is red or orange when it should be green or yellow. And I need one plainclothes team to watch Handlebar and his wife – twenty-four/seven security, without letting them know or anyone spotting our guys. Let there be no mistake this time.'

Rita sat ruminating long after everyone else had left. Would Honey Singh number two reveal himself if he was Handlebar's client? That didn't make sense because he would know he'd be discovered and, being in vicinity of the real Honey Singh, he'd be distinguished too. However, what could be the worst consequence of him being espied by Handlebar – Handlebar will write a report and tell him about it? And if the second set of comedians to spy on Honey Singh were also on his payroll they would, too, report the same sighting to him. At best they will report that Handlebar saw him too. Big fucking deal that. So the second Honey Singh didn't have anything to lose by revealing himself if he was certain that no one but the people he remunerated were on the lookout. Most investigative puzzles were perplexing because they had missing pieces; this one was mystifying with an additional piece. How did that fit in? In her mind, Rita went through the whole story Handlebar Raja had relayed. Step by step.

Honey Singh number two had arrived at the scene when Honey Singh number one was still in office, and he went in. Where did he go? He must have hid somewhere outside in the complex till he saw the other one leave? But how did he know that the real Honey Singh would leave the office at the time and day he went there? That didn't need too much explanation: if Honey Singh number two was actually Handlebar's mystery client then Rita and the police department were already aware of his technical capability. All appointments these days were in people's online diaries. If Honey Singh's diary was kept *au courant* the info could not have stayed veiled, not for someone who could penetrate a hotel's security networks and manipulate surveillance cameras. The thing that baffled Rita was what was so important that the duplicate Honey Singh required from the real one's office? Couldn't he have sent someone else? Or did he trust no one? Whatever it was it must be important and urgent. Like, maybe, planting a bug in the office, which only he was adept at? And how did the duplicate Honey Singh enter into the office? Wasn't Titu, the guard dog-cum-receptionist there? If he was he must have surely noticed Honey Singh return earlier than expected and in changed clothing? Indeed, that would have been a giveaway. It was worth checking Titu's schedule for the day too.

And if Honey Singh number two wasn't Handlebar's mystery client who was? And how would he react to this new dimension. That is, if this was a new dimension for him. Maybe, he already knew about the existence of the doppelgänger, and the whole thing was only set up for evidentiary purpose and, maybe, the surveillance on Honey Singh will now be terminated. Rita wasn't pleased. There were too many *maybes* here. Moreover, they had stopped Handlebar from reporting the existence of the duplicate. If the second surveillance guys hadn't spotted the doppelgänger, the client would still not be in the know. And if they had seen the duplicate and reported what repercussions could that have on Handlebar for censoring that info? Maybe dire?

She was contented she had placed Mrs and Mr Handlebar under security. Nevertheless the thorn that still hurt was who was the anonymous client? And what did he want?

She segued back to Handlebar's story. Didn't he say that the duplicate Honey Singh was there before the real one left? Where was he hiding? That was easy. One could find a million-plus places to lose oneself in a crowd of people. What if – a thought jumped out with a start and came right upfront into her mind – what the fuck if Honey Singh knew about his replica and Honey Singh number two, instead of hiding, had gone to the office to meet him?

The phone rang and axed the thought. She looked at the display. The call had been routed through the switchboard. 'DCP Rita Ferreira.'

'Hello, DCP Ferreira,' said the male voice. 'Finally, after going through the whole series of checks, I did get connected to you.'

'And why are you looking for me, if I may ask?'

'It's you who are looking for me, DCP Ferreira, not me. One of my friends called up to say they had been contacted by one of your people asking about me.'

'And you are ...?'

'Veer Singh.'

Rita looked at the display again. The call routed through switchboard should have been clocked there. The whereabouts shouldn't be impossible to trace. 'Yes, Mr Singh, we are. Who told you?'

'Doesn't matter, does it? You wanted to speak to me and I called. Why bother the person who made your task easier? How may I be of any help?'

'Fair enough. Mr Singh, we need to speak to you, meet you as soon as possible.'

'What for? Am I in any kind of trouble?'

'Not at all, it's an enquiry and it's best we meet. I'll explain.'

'I'm not in town, DCP Ferreira, could I not answer your questions on the phone?'

I need to see you.

'Where are you, Mr Singh?'

'Away, but you are in luck. I was planning to visit Mumbai so why don't I come and see you on Monday? That's the best I can do.'

'That's great. I didn't know you were in India.'

'I've been back for quite some time now.'

'Should we say Monday morning at my office?'

'My flight only gets there around lunch. I'll give you a call as soon as I land if you give me your direct line – it will save me the bother of going through the whole hoopla again.'

Rita gave him the number.

And that pushed her mind into hitherto unknown conjectures. The man they had been looking for since almost the beginning of this investigation had called up to say he wanted to come down to see her. On his own. There was some catch here, had to be. She immediately called the switchboard to check where the call had come from. It seemed Veer Singh had called from a mobile with a concealed caller ID. No sweat, there were other ways, she knew. Mobile calls are anonymous for ordinary citizens. The police, working with any mobile operator, could find the true caller ID using the nearest mobile tower. It wasn't instantaneous; it was difficult, it wasn't impossible. She called Nene, briefed him on the call and asked him to find the number and even triangulate the location of Veer Singh, if he was, as he said, in India. It was a matter of hours. She decided that she wouldn't wait for Veer Singh to turn up on Monday, she'd get him picked up as soon as they knew where he was.

It was a little over seven in the evening now. Ash's flight was scheduled to land in Mumbai at 8:55. There seemed little point in hanging around in the office till late. She decided she'd rather go home and relax.

TWENTY-TWO

Sheila was not her real name. No one knew her real name except her and her parents who had named her. But they were long dead. She changed her name and looks with every assignment. It was past midnight and she was past her quota of drinks when her mobile phone rang: Caller ID 'Unknown'. She had a good idea who it would most likely be at this godforsaken hour. It was her handler who she had met merely once in her life and who lived somewhere in Ranchi or Patna or somewhere between the two cities in Bihar, and who vetted all the jobs and collected all the cash. Ten lacs were enough to bump someone off. Considering there weren't too many hired women assassins available, Sheila pocketed eighty per cent of the earnings plus reasonable expenses.

Terms were simple: all payment in advance, no evidence or clue or even a trace left, nothing that could lead to anyone, no questions asked and no contact post the deal till the task was accomplished.

Sheila jotted down the target's name and co-ordinates. It would be an early-morning drive for a late-morning flight, she calculated after the call. Nothing to worry.

Kovalam Beach Resort, Kerala

The guy with his back towards her was tall – maybe six-feet-one or two, shaved head, built like a tree trunk and there was a humungous multicolour tattoo that covered his entire back: some kind of a dragon or something alien just as her handler had described. He sat on the stool at the beach bar wearing his trunks, barefoot. She knew it was him she had been sent for. She didn't need any further verification, but still it was best to check. She clandestinely clicked a picture with her mobile phone and texted it and waited sixty seconds. Her mobile vibrated. The sender was 'Unknown', but she knew who it would be. Most people couldn't send SMS as anonymous; calls yes, but not texts. But her handler knew people who knew the technical wizardry to keep his identity concealed. The message was short and to the point: 'Yes, it's him.' Meaning, he was the target.

Sheila wasn't checked-in. She went to the shower rooms and changed into a bikini to display her own large tattoo on her back, and came out like she was just another hotel guest walking out to the beach. She walked unbridled to the bar, asked for a strawberry margarita and sat down three barstools away from the guy, well aware that he had spotted her. She wasn't someone men missed usually – not least, when she was in a bikini. The bartender got busy preparing her drink as she looked ahead at the vast expanse of the sea, avoiding all eye contact with the guy who sat a few barstools apart.

Psychologists have statistically proven that the human brain processes and retains absolutes over relatives. People are inclined to remember or relate to an absolute distinguishable feature. A man six feet from the ground is tall. But put him next to Big Show or Khali of WWE and suddenly he is relatively 'the shorter one'. Same for dark, fair, fat, slim. Brown hair colour? Dark brown? Light brown? Coffee brown? Chocolate brown? L'Oreal could actually run a course with a degree on fifty odd shades of brown.

Bald is a near absolute.

The target here was bald.

Moustaches aren't absolute or distinguishable. Handlebar moustache was a near absolute.

If you sent someone to pick up a beautiful woman from an airport and you had Cindy Crawford, Sushmita Sen and Jennifer Aniston arriving by the same flight, it made the choice relative. If you told the same guy to pick up the girl with a mole on her upper lip, he'd surely come back with Cindy.

Pockmarks are absolute. Visible moles are absolute.

A larger than usual, unmissable tattoo of Linda Goodman's sun signs on Shelia's back that was visible, because she wore a bikini, would be the only thing remembered long after by people who merely got a glance. They would forget her face, hair, skin colour and body contours. Save for the bartender, Satish Menon, who had seen up close for a longer duration, which wasn't good. It wasn't good at all for Satish.

She waited.

Let him come to you. He will, she knew. She knew the game. Heck! She made the rules of the game.

'Your drink, ma'am.' Satish, the bartender, brought back her pink drink.

'Oh, that looks great, thank you.'

'Would you want to sign it to your room?'

Sheila looked around as if she was sceptical of letting anyone around know which room she was in. 'No, I'll pay cash before I go back if that's OK?'

'Sure, ma'am.'

Sheila took a sip, kept her glass down and walked towards the water, which was barely ten metres away from the bar. It was late evening but the sun still lent warmth to the cool water. There were only a few people on the beach, two families with kids that were in the distance, and what seemed like a honeymooning couple that was totally engrossed in each other. If they saw her from this distance, they would indeed only remember the tattoo. She took a dip, played with the water and returned to her drink ten minutes later. The bald guy was still there, sipping his beer, mesmerized by the sea or her or both.

'You here alone?' he finally asked.

'Yes. How about you?'

'Yep, alone.' He got up and moved to the stool next to her. He was not a bad-looking guy. Chiselled face, high cheekbones, just as she was told. No fat. In fact, he looked like someone who visited the gym pretty often. The abs were a testament to that. 'What, if I may ask, is someone like you doing alone on this beach resort?'

'I could ask you the same question.'

'I'm on a vacation.'

'All by yourself?'

'Yes. You see, if I wasn't alone, I would miss all that is beautiful in this world. Like you,' he said.

'Talk about a back-handed compliment.'

'I'm sure you have no dearth of admirers—'

'And yet, I'm vacationing alone.'

'Perhaps, you don't want to be tied down too. Like me.'

'So what's your story?'

'Born in Mumbai, well, it was Bombay back then. Finished schooling there, then went for engineering to Delhi, returned and set up my own business. It didn't do too well, so I moved to the US and tried my luck there and set up a company with a few other brains. We wrote an algorithm that got bought – lock, stock and barrel, as they say – by a much bigger fish so all of us cashed out.'

'Loaded then?'

'Sadly not as much as I made.'

'Why? Spent it on women and booze?'

'Wish I had, but I got married, got divorced, remarried, re-divorced …'

'You seem to be a serial divorcee.'

'You could say that, and I could justify that both times it wasn't my fault but, what's the point? I still lost a lot of money particularly in the first divorce. I was careful and, thankfully, had a pre-nup or else I would have been wiped out twice.' He let out a gruff laugh for effect.

'So what are you doing in this property in Kovalam? I mean it is beautiful but it is back of bloody beyond.'

'I find it very peaceful here, don't you?'

'So you live at this resort?'

'No. I live on a houseboat in the backwaters near Cochin, but I come here once in a while looking for good company.'

'And do you always get company?'

'Not necessarily, but I must say I have been luckier than many,' he said.

'Would I be correct in assuming that you're not looking for permanent relationship?'

'Yes, you would be absolutely correct in assuming that.'

'So you're looking for sex?' She looked into his eyes.

'I wouldn't reduce *seeking companionship* to merely some kind of a carnal rendezvous.'

'I have to admit, I like the way you play with words, camouflaging your promiscuity under companionship.'

'Can I buy you a drink?' He ignored her observation and asked.

'Depends …'

'On?'

'What do I have to do to return that favour?'

'You can buy the next round, what did you have in mind?'

'I was wondering if you were buying a drink for companionship—'

'I am already in your company.'

'Oh, if this is the boundary of companionship, I am in, absolutely. A margarita for me, I think I'll take a lemon one this time.'

He waved to the bartender who came immediately and took the order.

'I'm sorry I didn't get your name.'

'Sheila,' she said, and put her hand forward for a shake.

'Nice meeting you, Sheila, I'm Veer Singh.'

The two had a few more drinks and spent another hour exploring and teasing each other before, finally, agreeing to hook up for the night.

'What's your room number?' Veer asked.

'What's yours?'

'1104.'

'Why don't you carry on, and I'll change and see you in your room later?'

'Suits me. I have a call to make that I'll do on the way and then see you in my room.' He paid cash for all the drinks and left.

The Sig P238 is only 5.5 inches long and weighs about 430 grams, and one could be forgiven to think this diminutive handgun doesn't pack the same accuracy and as much firepower as any big Sig Sauer. But it does. And in any event any gun was great at close range, and so was the P238. Sheila had taken her handbag into the bathroom while Veer Singh lay on the bed in anticipation of a steamy session. It took her longer than she had expected to attach the Poseidon silencer – minutes seemed like hours, but she wasn't some novice, she had done this before numerous times – but came out when she was set. Veer Singh's brain was still processing the randy desires when the 9 mm bullet caught him unguarded and killed him along with all prurience on his mind. The bullet tore through his right eye and lodged itself inside the brain, destroying his face beyond recognition in the course. Just as instructed.

So much for seeking random companionship, thank you very much for the drinks. She looked at him cavalierly once and walked out of the hotel room.

The police would discover two bodies in the hotel complex the next morning. Veer Singh's and Satish Menon's. Satish was collateral damage, he had seen Sheila chat and get cosy with Veer Singh, and though the couple had not left the bar together, anyone with half a brain would have guessed they would regroup for a rendezvous. Sheila wasn't wont to leaving loose ends.

Sheila left under the darkness of the night – long before the corpses were discovered – walked five kilometres, keeping away from the main road, walking in the sides, till she found an old Ambassador car that she could open and jump start. She drove the rest of the way to Thiruvananthapuram airport and took a flight to Kolkata. She made a quick call from the airport to convey to her handler that the task had been accomplished. She used the railway station retiring room to wash, peel off the tattoo sheath from her back and flushed it down the toilet, changed from femme fatale into a *salwar kameez*-wearing plain Jane and boarded the Rajdhani Express from Howrah to Delhi the same evening and got off somewhere before the train arrived in Delhi. Sheila was now dead. The next assignment she would be someone else for someone else.

TWENTY-THREE

Rita zapped a fish patty in the microwave, put it between a bread roll with mayonnaise, mustard and lettuce and made herself a DIY burger. She saw no point in waiting for Ash, as he would have had his dinner before the flight and some further snacks on board if he wanted. She thought about having a drink but decided against it. If Ash was coming over, it was best to wait than lose sanity to alcohol before that. As it is, the case had put her in a spot of bother. After weeks on merry-go-round what did the team have? Clues? None. Leads? Hardly anything noteworthy. Evidence? Zilch. Theories? Galore. The case now seemed like a multi-starrer flop film of the 80s: one where even the director had lost the plot halfway through.

Thankfully, to take her mind away from the problem, she saw the dress she had kept ready for the evening: the little black number and the stilettos. She had a quick shower and got ready for the evening. Besides it being an amorous weekend with a friend, she recognized that her excitement to see Ash was also fuelled by the fact that Ash would have thought about the case.

With her past experience of working with him she was familiar that he did not need to see the evidence per se to come up with his analysis. And being a trained criminal psychologist he had been in practice long enough to have seen so many strange cases that didn't make sense on the surface, but had underlying connections that led the police to the perpetrators. Or, at least, he could help work out some new suspects or a pointer.

The sun was gone, the moon looked tired. To make up for the dark night, she lit some candles and opened the window only a bit, as it had been particularly windy since morning. The gusts came in spurts, flickered the candles and carried the vanilla scent all over the apartment.

Ash was at the door at a few minutes past ten.

'Oh my, my ... someone's out to seduce me tonight.'

'You're so vain, why do you think I'm dressed for you.' Rita kissed him on his mouth.

'You're correct. You should be undressed for me. Except for those stilettos.'

They lay spent in bed after a while.

'Can I get you a drink?' he asked.

'I've never been served a drink in my own apartment; come on, go for it. You know where everything is kept.'

He had been here before but it was the first time he browsed through her music collection. She came behind him and sat on the settee in the living room.

'You've got a lot of jazz and rock,' he said, returning with two tumblers and the bottle of Jim Beam.

'My dad always said there are only two genres of music – besides the classic of course, which are the roots for all music – jazz and rock. The rest, in his opinion, was all bastardization.'

'And what's your opinion?'

'Like father like daughter. I hold that view too, I'm afraid. What about you?'

'I listen to the radio, mainly classic rock. I have occasionally ventured into jazz but I don't know where to begin. Why don't you put on something while I make the drinks?'

Fastidious as she was, Rita knew where each of her records was in the collection. She walked over, pulled out 'Black Saint and Sinner Lady' and put it in the disc.

Despite a few crackles, Charles Mingus' 'Solo Dancer' sharply rose and fell in the otherwise still room.

'Did you get some time to think about my case?'

'Oh yes, of course. You had any new developments while I was away that I need to be aware of?'

Rita told Ash everything. Interviews with Honey Singh, his mum, his girlfriend. That Veer Singh and Kitty once dated. The brace of Honey Singhs: the spotting of Honey Singh's doppelgänger. The unexpected call she received from Veer Singh, and that he was coming to Mumbai to see her.

'You see, if the murderer isn't a relative or business associate, if an old vendetta isn't revealed, if the person who informed the authorities about the murder isn't actually the doer of the misdeed and, like in your current case, if the victim and killer are not connected in any way and, again like in your present case, if the killer hasn't left clues or a picture of him behind, even Sherlock Holmes would have a hard time finding the murderer. You have to find the connection. Of course, you've got a motive: diamonds. You have no DNA, no fingerprints, no clue, not even the dead body.'

Rita nodded, not wanting to break the rhythm of his analysis.

'Then you've got links to previous equally efficient burglaries. You have one instance of suspect's girlfriend in the area where the burglary was committed. One in three occasions could merely be a coincidence. Totally random. And as if it wasn't complicated enough already, you've found a dead ringer of the suspect, and an old animosity that you think might be working at the heart of it.'

'You mean I'll fail?'

'I didn't say impossible, I said hard time, which is what you're having. Anyone can win when they have aces; the art is in winning when you are dealt a lousy hand, Miss Ferreira.'

Smartass.

But correct.

'You have the classical investigation dilemma. How far can you go searching for the suspect? You can't cover every person in the world because, quite simply, in this particular situation anyone could be the murderer. And the reverse is also challenging. If you contact only the people who knew Jogani you might leave out the actual murderer who, I now think, wasn't Jogani's acquaintance,' Ash carried on.

'Why do you say that?'

'Firstly, if it were, you and your team would have certainly found them by now. No one can bury all the clues, some link would have steered you to them. Secondly, how do you explain the other two previous burglaries that occurred at non-Jogani places then? Ergo, this guy or group has no tenable connection to Jogani. You with me on that?'

Rita nodded.

'Now here's the thing, no matter how smart you are, a jigsaw cannot be completed till you have every piece. An important piece is either missing or you have overlooked it.'

'Like what?'

'Are you sure you haven't eliminated someone from the investigation a bit too early?'

'You mean his wife and business associates?'

'Could be, but as I said if anything linked back to someone acquainted or connected to Jogani, it would have been a lot simpler. Who else have you eliminated so far?'

'No one. If anything, more people are getting added to the list. This duplicate Honey Singh is the latest one. All along, our premise was that Veer Singh could be working behind the scenes—'

'You mean with Kitty Varghese?'

'Yes. I had a strong hunch they were still in the game together, somehow. But, if there is a second Honey Singh, and if that isn't Veer Singh, who is he and how is he connected?'

'Why do you think that the duplicate Honey Singh isn't Veer Singh?'

'Because if he was, he wouldn't have called me and agreed to see me.'

'But he hasn't turned up yet.'

'Oh, he will. Or we will find him if he's in India. And if he isn't in India then he's obviously not in the frame. We should check with the immigration authorities, and if we are assured that he hasn't visited India in the time frame, we should eliminate him from the investigation in any case.'

'That is if the guy who called you was indeed Veer Singh.'

Rita's eyes rolled. That was something she had totally missed with a million other things running in her brain simultaneously.

'Don't get me wrong, I'm not saying he's not who he says he is, but it is a possibility, don't you think?'

'Of course. But, when we trace the call we'll also know who was at the other end of the phone, so I'm not so distraught for missing that.'

'You know what I find most amusing in all this?'

'Amusing? What?'

'I thought about what you had told me last time. Do I understand this correctly that Mr Honey Singh missed being followed by Mr Raja who in turn missed being followed by your police guys and who in turn missed being followed by another party? That's three groups of people fail to spot a tail. It's ridiculous, how is that even possible? Particularly the police guys – they are trained to keep looking over their shoulders for any kind of surveillance?'

'So what do you think happened?'

'I have no answer, I just find it odd. I wish I knew. So what's your view about Honey Singh's lookalike?'

'I can't decide if the original knows about his twin or not? The duplicate went into the building while the original was still there. He either hid, waited – risking someone else might spot him – or went straight in to see the original Honey Singh.'

'In which case, there is something even more suspicious.'

'What is?'

'Why wasn't the duplicate spotted for over three months? This can't be the first time they met if they are hand in glove. So how was he missed in Mr Raja's surveillance all this while?'

They debated till well past midnight. The candles were sleepy now, almost nearing the end of their life. The bottle of Jim had been cherished to a good level. They went to sleep.

The phone ring woke up both a little before six in the morning. The sun had come up, spreading its light and with the trees standing still it didn't appear to be a windy morning like the day before.

'DCP Ferreira,' Rita voiced.

'This is SI Nene, ma'am. Sorry to bother you so early, we've just received a message from Kovalam at the office, so called me.'

'Kovalam ... in Kerala?'

'Yes ma'am, Veer Singh had called you from Kovalam last night.'

'Are you sure about this location supplied by the mobile company?'

'This wasn't worked upon by any mobile company, ma'am. The Kovalam Police called us. Veer Singh was there when he called you.'

'So where is he now?'

'Nowhere. He was killed last night at the beach resort, where he was vacationing. The local constabulary dug into his mobile and because the last call he had made was to our office, they called us to know who he spoke with and what.'

'What? Killed how?'

'Shot at close range. I don't have other details, but I'm leaving for office now.'

'Shit. I'll meet you in office in an hour.'

Rita had coffee, showered, dressed, had another coffee, kissed Ash bye and was out of the apartment in nineteen minutes. Her driver wasn't available so she chose to drive. The tyres screeched, the rubber peeled as she took off. With minimal Saturday morning traffic at this hour she was parked in Crawford Market in less than twenty-five minutes.

TWENTY-FOUR

SI Rajesh Nene was already in office. He had already called in for Vikram and Jatin who were on their way when Rita walked into the Operations Room.

'Good morning, ma'am.'

'Good morning, Nene, tell me everything you know so far, from the start.'

Nene outlined whatever info he had received from the Kerala Police in Thiruvananthapuram. Veer Singh and Satish Menon were two guys whose bodies the police had recovered from the beach resort in Kovalam. Both the bodies were in for autopsy though the first impressions were that both targets had been shot point blank by a 9 mm gun, which suggested that the victims knew their assailant and did not suspect him or her. The police were treating it as a double homicide, not two separate cases, but they had no suspects at the moment. The beach resort being one of those joints where a lot of amorous rendezvous happened between consenting adults, the place was devoid of any surveillance cameras to capture guests coming or going.

No one questioned so far – other guests and hotel staff – knew anything consequential. No one even remembered seeing Veer Singh except some staff but they had no vivid memory to give anything to the police. Satish Menon, however, was obviously a known face among the colleagues and even some guests as he was the bartender by the pool. There were no other records of any other phone calls that Veer Singh and made or received – except the one to Mumbai Police – that could lead them anywhere. The only local calls made were for taxis or to travel agents to book flights. He was booked to fly out of Thiruvananthapuram airport for Mumbai on Monday morning just as he had told Rita. The police couldn't access his emails on the phone right away, but the unit was working on it. That was all they had so far.

'What do you think happened?' Nene asked after he finished his spiel.

'My hunch is,' Rita thought as she surmised, 'that we've somehow let the cat between the pigeons. Trouble is, we don't know which pigeons or what caused the panic, but it definitely has all the bearings of it. Someone got unnerved that we were getting too close. Someone knew Veer Singh was at that beach resort near Thiruvananthapuram, and that he had been in communication about the case and he might take some action that might not have suited them—'

'Or maybe they informed Veer Singh themselves via some means to ferret him out if they didn't know where he was.'

Rita kept silent, thinking for a minute.

'Which makes me think that there is indeed something dubious about Honey Singh and/or Kitty Varghese, since Veer Singh was connected to them … so either whoever is framing Honey Singh didn't want Veer Singh to appear and we kept looking for him. The plan must be to frame Veer Singh in absentia, but that warranted Veer Singh to still be abroad for them to be safe. But Veer Singh in India could have blown their cover and that was obviously not acceptable to them.'

'What about the duplicate Honey Singh. Who is he then?'

Vikram and Jatin arrived together, exchanged quick salutes and took the vacant seats. Nene updated them of the events of the previous night and the discussion Rita and he were having.

'What have we missed, guys?' Rita asked herself as much as she voiced it for the three men.

There was a hush in the room for a while. The cogs in the four brains were roiling mutely.

'Nene, how soon can we get confirmation that the corpse found in the beach resort is Veer Singh?'

'I'll check. Though I don't know how they can confirm that except for the papers they found on him. There is no DNA to compare it with, and as he had no living family it would be impossible to prove that anyway.'

'You're correct, but see as much evidence as we can get. Photographs on his passport, driving licence, whatever – if that can be authenticated then, at least, we have some verification.'

Nene left the room to make the calls.

'Vikram, have we ensured safety for Mr Raja? Ron Jogani might have been an unpremeditated murder, but this one surely isn't, and I don't think these guys will stop at anything that can blow in their face. I ponder if we should ask Mr Raja to send a special report to his mystery client telling him about two Honey Singhs. What do you think, guys?'

'I have a feeling that the two Honey Singhs are arm-in-arm, ma'am,' Jatin said.

'Walk us through that conjecture, Jatin.'

'I don't know how he has a double, but Honey Singh knows he has an evil double. I can't tell you who found the other one, as we have found no familial connection—'

'So far,' Vikram interjected.

'Yes so far. And I think it is impossible for two people to look identical without being from the same embryo. They can look similar, but not identical. So one of them is evidently plastic, he has to be. If they are identical we actually don't know which one is the real one, right? So how do we know which Honey Singh was captured on the camera in Brussels? Whichever one *we* followed would have been the one who never travelled to Brussels. Right?'

'Wait a minute. If there are two Honey Singhs why didn't the police informers find the other one too?' Vikram made his point.

'Maybe they did, but did not realize it. We don't know where the other one lives. Maybe they live under the same roof, which only confirms my hypothesis that they're colluding.'

'So you think Mrs Lucky Singh knows this?'

'Kitty Varghese would definitely know that, I am certain.' Rita could also feel the theory leading somewhere.

'All this while we had assumed that the Honey Singh lookalike was actually Veer Singh; his murder, obviously, eliminates him from that theory totally. But she can't be living with two identical men. That's not possible. It would be too confusing,' Vikram said.

'Remember what Sherlock Holmes said,' Rita reminded them, "*once you eliminate the impossible, whatever remains, no matter how improbable, must be the truth.*" Two identical men residing in one apartment is not impossible – neither in Kitty's apartment nor Mrs Lucky Singh's. How else could the informers miss? However, what I cannot bring my mind around is if they live in one place what was the need for Honey Singh number two to visit Honey Singh number one's office and giving himself away?'

The triumvirate was silent again. The moments passed like years, slowly, ominously. Nothing in the case seemed to give. All their theories so far had been fractured.

'Jatin, did you get the pictures from Mr Handlebar Raja's phone?' Rita cracked the stillness.

'Yes ma'am.' Jatin got up and picked a folder where he had put the blown-up photographs he had recovered from Handlebar's phone.

Handlebar's zoom was admirable. It had captured the face of both Honey Singhs pretty well. Identical faces. The apparently fake one was standing so his height-weight-built looked the same as the one Rita had met. For the one who sat in the moving car, they could only see the face and that was a hundred per cent match too. So was Kitty in the many frames. Jatin had taken the time from Handlebar's phone and stamped it on the reverse of the photographs. The two were spotted moments apart, it suggested. First the alleged fake snooping around and then the original one leaving with Kitty. Then the *supposed* fake one leaving the office building and once again the real one returning to his office, in that order. The only reason attributed to the original one being the original was that he was with Kitty Varghese.

'They know each other, ma'am,' Jatin voiced again.

Nene was back after the calls and updated that he had asked the Kerala Police to establish and authenticate Veer Singh's ID as soon as possible. Rita in turn updated him on what the three had conversed in his absence.

There were still too many unknowns in the case. Who was Handlebar's client and how was he connected or what was his motive of getting Honey Singh followed for months? It must be significant for the client to pay Handlebar and on top of that then compensate another set of eyes to keep tabs on Handlebar. Why ... and then Ash's words echoed in her brain. '*Mr Honey*

Singh missed being followed by Mr Raja who in turn missed being followed by your police guys and who in turn missed being followed by another party? That's three groups of people fail to spot a tail …'

'You know what we missed, guys? The guys following our undercover guys when they were following Honey Singh and Handlebar might be none other than Honey Singh number two.' Nene left it there to see how the others reacted.

It was undeniably a new conjecture that they hadn't thought of before. The room was so silent they could have heard a leaf drop on the ground floor.

'Which is even more worrying, if you ask me …' Rita started and left it mid-sentence. 'Does any one of you have a cigarette?'

The three guys looked bewildered. Aghast, actually. Like they had inadvertently walked into their parents' bedroom and seen them make out. Check that. Like they had seen their mother bumming their dad with a strap on.

'What? I'm an adult.'

'But you don't smoke,' Vikram responded.

'I did till about five years ago. And in moments like these … you know what they say, once an addict—'

'Bullsh ...' Vikram realized his *faux pas* after the word had already slipped out of his mouth.

'What?'

'I'm extremely sorry, ma'am.'

Stopping your boss from doing something stupid or harmful is one thing, saying bullshit to her in any informal corporate office may be, perhaps, acceptable too, but in police and armed forces where a commanding officer is never questioned on their authority or requests? Really?

'I'm really, really sorry, ma'am,' he apologized again.

'It's OK. I know your intentions were right, *da'ddy*.' Rita stretched out the daddy for effect.

A paroxysm of hysterical laughter ensued.

'Is there something we should know?' Jatin asked, looking at Nene.

'Yes.' Rita gestured to Vikram to share the episode at Mrs Lucky Singh's apartment when she had presumed that Vikram was her brother or father.

Humour at such times, when nothing seemed to be going your way, was a relief. A segue from the usual, routine morose life the police officers live and face every day.

Jatin and Nene looked at Vikram and said in unison: '*Daddy*.'

'OK, so where were we?'

'You were looking for a cigarette.'

'No. Before that.'

'Nene said that Honey Singh number two was the tail that our undercover guys missed.'

'Thanks, yes. What's even weirder is how could our guys miss a tail that resembles their target? It should have been spotted from a mile; the face should have registered as familiar.'

'Maybe he was disguised.'

'Wow. So first he gets plastic all over his face to look like Honey Singh and then he disguises it to not look the same?'

'Only to follow Handlebar so that Handlebar doesn't know.'

'That is possible, of course. But that, kind of, proves that Honey Singh number two has to be Handlebar's mystery client, which also means he knew Handlebar would see the double when the double appeared.'

'So how is Veer Singh connected? He had to be, why else would he be murdered?'

'Let's build on this hypothesis: our premise here is Honey Singh knows about his doppelgänger. They've managed to, somehow, carry out the burglaries; it's Jogani's murder that puts them under the lens. As one of you mentioned earlier, they get one of the Honey Singhs followed to see if the local police have picked up the scent. They further encourage the missing Veer Singh theory and that has worked to their advantage, because, let's admit it, we succumbed. By letting the doppelgänger sighted by Handlebar in the hope that we'll think that it is definitely Veer Singh because that's who we thought was the duplicate – *plastic-ed* enough to look like his adversary Honey Singh, snooping around for something? Presto! All is worked out till they find out that the real Veer Singh is back in the country, and that could be disastrous to their plan. They couldn't let him meet us to be ruled out as the suspect? Once we saw him we'd know he wasn't a doppelgänger, right? Hence, they had to get him whacked. The timing wasn't the best because, regrettably for them, he had already made the call to us before his death, which they might or might not be aware of at this moment. So, first things first, Nene please ask – whoever is heading the investigation in Kerala – to stop the police there from letting the names of the victims out to the media. If required, we'll ask Commissioner Saxena to make the call.'

'But if they are the ones who got Veer Singh killed, they would have already received the confirmation that the job has been done, wouldn't they?'

'But they don't know that we know that. It's more about them believing that we are still in the dark, which might make them live in the false confidence that we're still chasing him. If Veer Singh's name is all over in the papers, they'd know that we have that info and we'll dig afresh. We have to act like we don't know about Veer Singh's murder – this is perhaps the only chance for us to be ahead in their game.'

'Got it.' Nene walked out again to make the calls.

He was back in five minutes to say that Kerala Police wasn't agreeable to keeping the double murder under wraps merely because Mumbai Police had requested it; there had been some bumpy incident in the past between the two constabularies.

It so happened that five years earlier – a full *quinquennium* previously, if you let *Sexy* voice half a decade in his words – Mumbai Police had declined some insignificant request that had come from down south. And five years, albeit a long time, wasn't so back in the past to have been forgotten by the police machinery. There was no reason for them to decline Rita's request but it was tit-for-tat politics.

Those on the outside frequently call it a dirty game, but if you observed closely, hard politics is an extremely funny game. Friends in the daylight are vicious foes by night; foes today are friends tomorrow; bed partners change faster than the bed sheets; adversaries by day, lovers by night. Embittered today, mellowed tomorrow. Pawn guarded the queen, queen sacrificed the pawn. It was a relational kaleidoscope. However, all that could only work till you did not come between the lion had his cub. Commissioner of Mumbai Police, Sanjay Saxena, was furious when he was told that someone down south actually refused a request that had gone from his office. That too, on a case he was overseeing and which had an international agency involved. It took two calls and eleven minutes to the chief of Kerala Police and the local police superintendent called back Nene to apologize and retreat from the previous position. The local police there would only talk about the double murder but not disclose the identity of the victims to the media for now.

'OK, here's the plan,' Rita started when they reconvened after an hour. 'I want all the trees shaken, forests brought down if need be but I want the whereabouts of this second Honey Singh. Ideally,' she stalled for a minute, organized her thoughts and continued, 'we should put a totally different set of informants on the ground ... ones we didn't use last time around. Give them the same candid-shot from the elevator we originally received from Victor – not the ones of Honey Singh number one that we've collected from various sources – and let them go hunting. Let's see where the second search leads us. We might get lucky.'

Nene and Jatin nodded. Vikram, in his usual manner, noted it down.

'Nene, I want you to handle that please.'

'Yes ma'am.'

'Please ensure to pick up the guys who wouldn't speak to any media bodies. We don't want this to leak to them. If they find out we are searching for the same person the second time, it will cause more damage than last time.'

'Got that, ma'am. It won't happen again.'

'Thanks you, Nene. And Jatin, I want the entire buildings in the vicinity – at least the apartment complexes Lucky Singh and Kitty Varghese live in – canvassed. Our guys should meet every single male personally before eliminating him from the enquiry. The duplicate has to be somewhere close enough to be undetectable for so long. We have to find him.'

'Yes ma'am.'

As Ash had elucidated, murder investigations were never simple, Rita sat evaluating after the guys had left – unless the killer was caught in the act or it was witnessed by someone or the killer had left his calling card behind in way of clues or a piece of him: hair, blood, semen, prints, skin residue or some DNA that could be decoded – this case rattled her in an altogether dissimilar manner. She wasn't still getting that feeling that she was on the right track. The Ron Jogani murder case dossier had gotten even heavier now. The Kerala Police Department could run their enquiry into Veer Singh's murder however they deemed appropriate and deduce whatever inference they regarded as pertinent, Rita couldn't care less. She was all but convinced that it was linked to her case.

Nevertheless, there was still a smidgen of apprehension, which was expected given that there were still so many unknowns. Was Ron Jogani's murder indeed a burglary-related homicide and then Veer Singh's assassination was carried out only to cover up the tracks? Or was it something else altogether, something a lot more sinister that she and the team had overlooked or disregarded and that might come back to bite them? Whatever it was it now looked unlikely that it was some vendetta-avenger-picking-a-bone thing as they had previously thought after meeting Kitty Varghese and discovering that Miss Kitty had had a short fling with Veer Singh.

Thankfully, the news of Interpol and Mumbai Police looking for a killer locally had slid from front pages, first into the local pages consuming far less column centimetres than it had threatened to initially, then completely disappearing to make any news whatsoever.

Truth is that media and police force are two alpha males that never got along. They, at best, politely tolerate each other, and that is how it should be: one's negatives highlighted and checked by the other. Truth, also, is that the media conferences added nothing. Yes, the public had a right to know, but not hear everything over the loudspeakers or in bold highlighted text. And the public didn't need to know something if no harm was to come to them, did they? Why scare the living daylights out of the common man who was already carrying the load of an uncomfortable existence in most cases?

Sexy, Rita knew, would have carefully choreographed the press conference and fed the scribes his manicured vocabulary. Or possibly he served them a generous dose of superglue in the only press conference they had managed to organize and they went quiet. Maybe, due to the cold shoulder given by the police, the sources of stories and alleged expert views on this murder had dried up or perhaps the media had lost interest. They had shut up. And that reminded her she hadn't submitted the weekly log to *Sexy* for the week. It was Saturday today, and it was long due.

Rita realized she had been cinching her jaw so long that it ached, like she had being chewing gum for a few hours till Nene called her to say that a new set of informants had been corralled and briefed with the candid-shot of Sishir Singh/Honey Singh from the elevator. He was expecting some results in a day or two.

Maybe they'd get lucky this time around?

Every circle had to close at some point.

TWENTY-FIVE

It was panic, then anger, frustration before despair for Handlebar. He sweated like a pig in a swamp even though the air-conditioning in the room was set to eighteen. He had logged into the account to check if his client had read the message he had left in the Drafts folder. His client had read and deleted his update from the previous evening, but there was a message waiting for him. People know when they are guilt-ridden; he knew he was guilty of acting as advised by the police and omitting the mention of discovering the second Honey Singh. If his client had somehow been versed about that from another source – if the past record was any indicator, he was convinced the news would have been transmitted to the client – it wouldn't be easy to explain this time around. In his report he had, in his defence, told his client that he had been delayed in setting up the surveillance the other day as he had had a flat tyre while he was on his way to Honey Singh's office, which was partly true. If Handlebar had been the only one on the job and some team hadn't been keeping a watch on him, it was a good enough reason to exonerate oneself. He was late because of a valid reason and hence, missed the other Honey Singh. However, the occurrence of two Honey Singhs had happened much later and the other team might also have conveyed the time of the event and the fact that they had seen him beholding and photographing the two Honey Singhs. He decided to procrastinate. If he didn't open the client's message, maybe the client would assume that he hadn't seen it yet, and not take some drastic action straightaway. Maybe, he should call the police. Weren't they the ones who got him in this mess in the first place? Had they not come along at his door, things would have been as simple and pleasant as they were before, so it was only right that they should be the ones taking the brunt now.

The room was dark. Curtains drawn purposefully to prevent any light coming into it, like someone wanted to call it a night when it was day.

'It's time to pack up and run,' Honey Singh – or someone who looked like him – was on the phone almost whispering into the mouthpiece.

There was crackling from the other side. The person on the other line said something.

'I know I said that, but I didn't know the local police would come so close so soon ... yes, Veer's dead and that is a major concern now, as nothing can be blamed on him any longer. We didn't think it through, and we don't have another fall guy.' The voice diminuendoed as the conversation went on.

The line crackled again.

'We need a getaway plan before it all blows up ...'

Crackle.

'… no you listen to me. I have covered all bases till now but it will get increasingly difficult to hold for very long especially if the police come around with a search warrant—'

Crackle.

'Yes, everything is encrypted, but it's not some Morse code, and even that damn code got broken in the end. Remember they have brains in the Interpol. If the police get hold of all our computers, we are in deep shit. You don't know what we miss and what they might find.'

Another long crackle.

'How can I destroy everything? Torch my office?' The testiness was palpable in the voice now.

Crackle again.

'OK, let's see how this week pans out. I'm booking tickets for as early as possible. Pack light and pack only what you cannot do without. Ciao for now.'

Rita sat in her office post lunch ruminating on all theories they had conjured up so far and a few other new ones passing through her tired brain. There is always, they said, a reason behind the reason. She didn't know which one of Honey Singhs yet, but one of them conclusively had some implicit reason to action the stakeout by Handlebar on the other after Ron Jogani's murder in the Brussels hotel. If the police had a photograph – which they must have figured a day later from the news – it was not beyond an average brain to cotton on that the police would come to the door sooner or later. Like her team had voiced, the reason behind that might have been to know when and which department of the police and their subsequent movements. Crime Branch, that she was part of, wasn't the primary response unit so they were the last entity the murderers would have anticipated. But once

Interpol got involved, it actually merited *Sexy* giving the case to her than to some local constabulary, since one didn't know which bailiwick to hand the case over to. Hell, they still didn't know where to look. Perhaps the previous diamond burglaries might have gone undetected – as they looked unrelated on the surface – if one uniformed police station was appointed for the job. Unfortunately, for the offenders the case being handed over to Crime Branch wasn't a good thing; Crime Branch came with more resources than a local police station and with all the powers that the Commissioner of Mumbai Police could put behind.

However, there was still something eating Rita up: if only one Honey Singh went to Brussels, who assisted him in Brussels?

She debated in her mind.

But how could they be certain only one Honey Singh went to Brussels?

The other one did not have a passport.

Big fucking deal!

He could have gone under an alias. Just like the second Honey Singh – who she was confident – wasn't known as Sishir Singh in real life. There was no one following either of the Honey Singhs before the incident so if he had gone out of the country for a few days, who would have known?

Kitty Varghese wouldn't tell. That is, if she knew. She was out of the country so maybe she had no idea really.

Mrs Lucky Singh might not even know. Her son didn't have to say he was not coming home for a couple of days. He could have called regularly.

What about the phone records? And emails from Blackberry?

That was hardly enigmatic to comprehend. For someone who could penetrate hotel networks, destroy Jogani's computer remotely, mask his IP address that even the trained police technicians couldn't infiltrate, how formidable would it be to run some code to manipulate the geolocation of his Blackberry such that it was routed through India even while he was abroad?

Simple as ABC.

And if some camera did catch Honey Singh, no one would even question which one of them got captured simply because two Honey Singhs were neither expected nor imagined nor acknowledged. Bloody dazzling.

Sad part: Honey Singh and the crew were now acquainted with who was looking for them in Mumbai. Not just that, they were more than sufficiently aware that the police were asking questions about Veer Singh, which had spelt more than the proverbial doom for the poor guy. Veer Singh may or may not have opened some door to the mystery, but his murder had practically convinced Rita that Honey Singh and/or Kitty Varghese were involved. If Kitty Varghese was at all involved, Honey Singh was in it too. However, the converse wasn't a certainty: Kitty Varghese might just be a bystander in the game unless she had been assisting the concealment of the second Honey Singh. Possible, even probable; it was too soon to rule out either way.

Jaded and exhausted thrashing theories, Rita decided to call Ash. She had totally forgotten that he was in town, and in her bed, when she had left him in the morning.

Ash was chomping on chop-suey when Rita called. He told her he had been in the apartment all day, listening to music. Mumbai was blessed with room service for everything. One phone call and most of the grocery and meals could be delivered at your doorstep within minutes and without any delivery cost. Rita's refrigerator had a lot of menus and shop cards and he had called for some beer and a Chinese take-away.

'I was feeling guilty of having left you behind ...'

'I guess you'll have to make up for it tonight.'

Here cometh cheesy onslaught.

'Ash, I'm in the office.' Despite anticipating some prurient comment, she nevertheless blushed.

'That's precisely why I said you'll have to make up for it tonight, not now DCP Miss Hottie.'

'I wanted to run some things by you.'

'Shoot.'

Rita gave him a summary of what had happened since the morning. Their conviction that the two Honey Singhs were known to each other, that their undercover was actually stalked by the Honey Singh lookalike, the dumping of Veer Singh and the surmise that Honey Singh number two was the mysterious client of Handlebar.

'Too many suppositions in the surmise, my girl. You have no evidence. It all sounds like a highly enthusiastic exercise in speculation. Even if he's guilty he'll walk away, believe me. You need veridical evidence not conjectures at this late stage.'

'What do you mean?'

Ash was right in some way, but …

'Without any evidence, you can join the dots in any warped constellation your mind directs you to. A million minds could provide a million and one hunches. Don't get me wrong. I know you are correct up to a level as even I found it ridiculous to believe that everyone and their dog missed being tailed – unless, of course, it was done by someone invisible – remember? So if it was actually the doppelgänger following your guys, he would have taken excessive precaution, maybe he didn't follow them all the way. Just saw everyone leave after one another and extrapolated the rest. But you need to have data to support it. Imagine taking your hypothesis to court. Honey Singh, from what you've told me, has a rock-solid alibi – he doesn't have a passport on record, he's configured his phones to seem they were in Mumbai when he called or answered them or emailed with the device. To top that he has a doppelgänger that only Mr Handlebar has seen, and who, in my opinion – based on what you've told me about him – would have less than zero credibility in court. The whole thing will sound like Don Quixote's fanciful dream. You see what I mean?'

Rita kept quiet. Ash had valid points to ponder.

'The only way you can break this case is by ferreting out both the Honey Singhs and sweat them simultaneously.'

Ash was referring to Prisoner's Dilemma, an age-old technique practised by most law-enforcement agencies around the world. Capture two people of the same group on some lesser charge and take them to solitary confinement where they cannot exchange messages between them. Then sweat them out. Ask them to cooperate separately by providing them with incentives to betray their partner. In more cases than not, one of them breaks, squeals when they realize the police have enough on them.

'However, 'Ash continued, 'I would strongly urge you to keep this under wraps. Honey Singh shouldn't know you're looking for his doppelgänger.'

'That's not possible. Handlebar omitting the spotting of Honey Singh's duplicate in his report would have tipped them off that Handlebar is operating under someone's orders or influence.'

'Maybe, but does he know that Handlebar has done this on *your* instructions?'

'I'm pretty sure he is smart enough to twig who could behind it but us.'

'Yep, I guess so. You'll have to find some other way.'

There was a brief silence again.

'What time are you coming home?'

'I don't know, Ash. I'll call you a bit later. Sorry.'

'No worries.'

Rita's mind returned to the conundrum at hand. Handlebar had already submitted the report so the cat was not only out of the bag, it had jumped in full sight of the client by now. He would have read the message and found the sighting of second Honey Singh excluded. If the second Honey Singh had been deliberately planted outside the office for detection, Handlebar would get reprimanded again. No doubt there. If the doppelgänger's outing at the wrong place had been a genuine slip-up, the client – if it were either of the Honey Singhs – would only be too happy that Handlebar missed it. Ash was right; it was in Rita's interest to feign that *they* weren't exposed to the double.

She was in the middle of her thoughts when the mighty private investigator, Mr Handlebar Raja, called.

'Hello madam, myself Raja. We met when you came to see me regarding the case.'

How would I have met you otherwise? At the prom?

'Yes Mr Han … Mr Raja,' Rita almost slipped, 'of course we met. Hope you are keeping well. What can I do for you?'

'I was trying to reach Inspector Jatin, but could not get through. I have received another message from my client.'

Rita waited for him to read out the message or explain but nothing came; all she heard was heavy breathing on the other side.

'What did you client have to say now, Mr Raja?'

'I haven't opened it, madam, that's what I am calling to check. Should I open it? I'm very scared.'

He can't shoot you through the computer screen.

'You have nothing to be scared of, Mr Raja. You're working with us and your safety is our responsibility. Open the message and tell me.'

What a big moppet.

There was loud clacking of keyboard that was heard via the earpiece. Rita could visualize Handlebar's fat fingers and fatter head logging in and navigating to the Drafts folder.

'Read it to me verbatim, Mr Raja.'

'Am I really safe?' Handlebar confirmed.

Should I come and sleep in your bed with you to make you feel safe?

'Yes you are,' she assuaged his fears yet again before another attack of paranoia could erupt. 'We have people in place to see no harm comes to you or your family. You should not be concerned, just go around like nothing's happened.'

'OK.'

Then Handlebar read the message verbatim:

> *So you arrived late for surveillance because you had a flat tyre? Are you sure it was the tyre? Because if I find out that you got waylaid because of something else, it would not be good for you and your family. OK – you say you were late, but did you return early too? Did you not see anything unusual that needed reporting? I have another report from my other agents and it says they saw a lookalike of the target. Am I to believe that you missed him altogether? What I want to know is why are you feeding me piffle? I give you twenty-four hours to confirm to me what you really saw – with pictures, I know you snapped a few – or I'm coming for you, and I'll make you pay. Which body part do you want to lose first ...?*

Handlebar Raja's voice quivered. Rita could sense the guy was frightened. Petrified. And if Honey Singh & Co. were the clients and they were the ones behind the cold-blooded murder of Veer Singh, it wasn't so empty a threat. Taking body parts sounded a bit drastic and melodramatic though, but a bullet through Handlebar's massive head couldn't be ruled out. And it couldn't be risked.

Rita pondered if she should ask Handlebar to tell his client the truth. However, what would that construe? The client, whoever it was, obviously knew it already. All it would suggest is that Handlebar had been dishonest in his original report and now that his evasion had been picked up, the investigator had regurgitated the truth when was threatened? That might land Mr Handlebar Raja in an even bigger mess.

'What … should I … do now?' Handlebar almost whispered in staccato, his voice wavering, almost child-like as if he was about to cry.

Rita could empathize, she felt sorry for the guy. Whatever he had been, he hadn't been evil or wicked. Agreed, he had come across as self-confident and conceited in the beginning, but he had meant no harm. And the situation he was in now was primarily a result of following her orders to censor information from his client. And now the client had threatened. And threatened big time. Fact was, she could triangulate who that creepy client was, but she had no evidence to take him out. Not yet.

She had to do something that was visible to him for his sanity.

'Mr Raja, we have twenty-four hours before your client will take any action, like he's said in his message. I'll arrange upright security for you, leave that to me—'

'But it's not just me and my wife, madam, in his last message, he had also threatened my kids and grandchildren.'

Shit.

'Why didn't you say so before?'

'Because he had only warned me at the time that I should not make mistakes again, it was more a warning, not a direct threat.'

'I'll ask Jatin to get addresses of your children too. I'll get security for them too.'

'How ... can you ... guard all our lives?'

'I can and I will, I promise. And I'll get to this client of yours sooner than you think.'

'You know who it is?' There was a bit of optimism in the voice now, like a dehydrated leaf looking up at the sky and finding promising rain clouds. If his client was apprehended, his ordeal would be over, forever.

'We are not a hundred per cent certain, but we'll get to it soon.'

'How soon?'

'Very soon, and don't you worry about anything. Jatin will visit you and Mrs Raja today itself.'

'Thank you, madam. And when you catch this client, please call me. I want to slap his face.'

Conversation over, Rita was back to where she was. Still no clue except the fact that Raja's client knew there was a duplicate, which wasn't anything new. If Honey Singh was the client and his lookalike was a party in his criminal activities, it was understandable they had figured out that Handlebar Raja had lied to them for a second time. Evidence against either one would crack the case open. Trouble was she couldn't find either.

TWENTY-SIX

Veer Singh dead. Another murder. Was she responsible for it? If you took your police job merely as a job then no, of course not; the murder had occurred out of her bailiwick. But if you were Rita, and police was your calling, then any murder or any crime that any policeman – or woman – failed to impede was a failure for the whole police community. Poor Veer Singh, according to Rita, might have paid the price of the Mumbai Crime Branch getting too close to the agents of Ron Jogani's murder, and as such she was, in some indirect way, responsible for it. She made it a point to ask someone in the team to check who had made the call to Veer Singh that Mumbai Police had been looking for him. That could be a cue.

On that note she looked at the time: 9:13 p.m. Her three reports had long left the office.

She felt guilty of having left Ash alone all day. She called Ash, apologized, shut the computer, and left the office.

Ash was home. He had ordered some pizza from the local Italian and was waiting for it when Rita walked in.

Hug. Kiss.

'Tired?'

'Yes. And I'm really, really sorry for having left you alone on a weekend,' she said.

'And I forgive you yet again. Though I don't see why you should apologize in the first place. I'm here on a vacation now, and you're working on a murder case. According to me that should be your priority; I know I would attend to that before my personal interests.'

'You are a gentleman.'

'What took you so long to make that one out?'

'Ha-ha.'

'Anyway, did you discover anything more?'

'Less than nothing,' Rita uttered, the voice giving away her frustration.

'Don't fret, don't lose hope. No one can fly below the radar screen forever, Rita. At some point they all get caught out, whoever they are. That's a fact. I'm not quoting some fiction writer.'

Before Ash could start with his smarms or cheesy one-liners, the bell rang. The pizza guy had arrived.

'Coke?' Rita smiled when Ash walked in with the pizza and a large bottle of Diet Coke in his hands, after paying the guy.

'It was free with the pizza, so why wouldn't I take it?'

'Fair point.'

'I know you must be tired, so let's have a quick drink, finish our dinner and then I'll give you a massage and you can tell me about your day?'

'Massage? You are a masseuse now?'

'Massager. Masseuse is generally used for a female.'

'Oh, I didn't realize that. Are you a massager now?'

'Well, I can do wonders with my hands.'

Here cometh the sleazy lines.

A shot of Jim, pizza with Diet Coke and back to Jim Beam – it was all in a span of twenty minutes, all the time it took Rita to narrate the day's findings to Ash Mattel.

'Veer Singh's murder tells us one thing,' Ash began after he had cleared the dishes. Good man. 'Insipid as it might sound, but it's the truth: when hope begins to die, desperation skyrockets. People panic, become reckless. Some make compromises, others lash out. Veer's murder is an indication that the culprits are freaking out, to say the least, don't you think?'

'I know, we concluded that too. In a way it indicates we are on the right track. However, finding two Honey Singhs does expand the possibilities, which, sadly, doesn't always mean positive.'

'That depends—'

'On?'

'The half of eight is four or three or a zero depending on who asks the question, isn't it? Mathematically, it has to be four, but if you are in some art class then you could cut the figure of eight sideways or vertically and respectively make up a three or a sphere. It's the same with expanding possibilities. While I agree that two Honey Singhs are double the menace, it should also be easier to search for two needles in the proverbial haystack than one.'

'I've ordered a fresh search for the other Honey Singh. If we're lucky, the search should lead us to the duplicate or maybe we will end up with the already known Honey Singh yet again. Fingers crossed.'

'Great.'

'Do you think Honey Singh knows about the duplicate?' Rita wanted an expert opinion.

'Of course. They are working in collusion, no doubt about that.'

'One thing bothers me ...' Rita got up, put on *The Doors* debut album, walked to the bottle of Jim Beam kept at the table and carried it back on to the couch where the two of them snuggled.

They tinkled their glasses.

'So what bothers you?'

'I know we dwelled on this before but it still bothers me as we have no explanation. The private investigator – Mr Raja – has been trailing Honey Singh for months now. How come, then, he never witnessed the second Honey Singh ever before? Don't you find it a bit surprising?'

'It could be one of the two things. I've never met him but from what you've told me, this Mr Raja isn't one of the shiniest and sharpest tools in the box, so it's entirely possible that he missed the duplicate before. Maybe he saw both of them but since he didn't see them together, it never occurred to him there were two. That's the simplest explanation. The other reason could be that with Veer Singh having gone from the scene – or if Honey Singh & Co. knew it was about to happen, which shouldn't surprise any of us since our premise is that they ordered the killing – they had to reveal the duplicate to lead you astray. My speculation would be that the duplicate, now, established, he will vanish from the scene forever. So—'

'We leave Honey Singh alone and chase someone who's disappeared from Mumbai. And they can meet after the interval and live prosperously after the police have closed the case or relegated it to a cold case and parked it in some deep freezer.'

'It is a brilliant plan, isn't it?'

'Bloody brilliant, I have to say. In which case we should refrain from admitting there is a duplicate at any expense.'

'That's the difficulty. If Mr Raja has been threatened, it means that they know he's witnessed the duplicate, taken photographs and deliberately omitted it from his weekly log. And they claim someone else has seen the duplicate so they have that confirmation from someone else and maybe photographs, maybe some other evidence to tilt the game in their favour.'

The rest of the evening passed discussing the case. Jim Beam was in top form and Jim Morrison echoed that *'it was the end, my friend'*, apt lyrics for Rita and Ash, as Ash would be gone in a day. This was the end until next time.

Ash brought Rita the morning coffee. She realized she was being pampered. Ash would be gone tomorrow and then, it would be her, in her apartment, all by herself. She closed her mind to his imminent farewell. 'But medically speaking, how is it even possible for a doppelgänger from another set of parents?' Rita asked even before she opened her eyes.

'It could be plastic as you've worked out.'

'What else could it be?'

'I could use the cliché that everything happens for the first time at some point, but in this case it's already happened before, so it can indeed happen again. There have been some known cases before.'

'Really?' her eyes popped open.

'Do you know when fingerprinting of criminals started?'

'Early nineteenth century … I think.'

'It was in 1903, somewhere in Kansas in the United States. They used something called the Bertillon system before that, which was nothing but physical measurements of individuals to establish their identity, till they found two African-American inmates that were a mirror image of each other, serving their sentences in the same prison at the same time. I know all of us who work for or with law-enforcement agencies always discount coincidences, but here's another one: they even had the same name: one was Will West and the other was William West. On probing further, they found no familial relationship whatsoever between Will West and William West. It was only fingerprints that told them apart.'

'So Honey Singh two may well be a genuine doppelgänger?'

'It hardly makes a difference in your case. Plastic or genuine, you still need to find them both before you know if they are an anomaly of nature or handcrafted. Though, there is yet another rung of coincidence if they are true lookalikes …'

'That they both end up being in Mumbai and know each other well enough to collude in crimes.'

'Bingo! You're a smart girl. Now, should we make love and eat breakfast or have breakfast first?'

'What's the plan for the rest of the day?'

'I don't know. What do other couples do on a day off?'

'I've got limited experience, but how about cuddling up to watch a film?'

'Let's do that then, but only on one condition.'

'And what pray could that condition be?' Rita could predict something lewd was about to come out in response.

'No clothes under the sheets. I want to research how your body reacts while watching a film. Purely for research reasons, I promise.'

'You're such a perv.'

Oh, now I'm a perv, am I?'

TWENTY-SEVEN

They say if you do not remember any dreams when you wake up, chances are you didn't have one. The resulting consequence is you have a clear head in the morning. In fact, the night you have a deep sleep you do not dream. Dreams occur in shallow sleep. Dreamless slumber is a positive thing. Rita had slept like a baby. It was Ash's last night in Mumbai before he flew off on Monday. They dressed up in silence, the sadness hanging in the atmosphere, and then Rita dropped him at the airport before heading to the office.

Rita once again wallowed in her case, staring at the two photographs. Frowning, concentrating on them. Not looking at them for something specific, but merely taking in everything as a whole. Her gaze skipped from one photograph of Honey Singh to the other. Both clicked minutes apart. In fact, a little over nine minutes apart. Two of them, twice the problem. Puzzle heaped upon puzzle. Then, a random flash occurred and she discerned they weren't two distinct puzzles; they were like two pieces of the same one. And they were coming together for her only now.

Buy two for one. The Americans called it twofer. She surmised that it might have been part of the plan from the beginning – it wasn't some accessory planted after the event. It must have been carefully thought of before, albeit they didn't need that to be uncovered in the past thefts.

Her eyes went up in desperation but she remembered Woody Allen: *you can't be an atheist and look at God with imploring eyes.* You can't be a deist and expect God to intervene on trivial earthly issues either. This was her battle; she had to fight it herself.

Looking for something. Anything.

Hoping for something. Anything.

She intermittently got up, walked a bit and looked out of the window, then returned to her desk. There were cables a floor below where she stood. Pigeons sat chatting or just singing, making noises. A lot of them looked alike like two Honey Singhs, no way to discern. Pigeons, unlike pet dogs, didn't wear collars or else you could identify them with the collar colour or any number or other tags. Irony was the only way the police had identified two Honey Singhs was by their different coloured shirts. What else did they have to look for? Thoughts fluttered around in her brain. Thoughts are no different from a person taking a walk in a small room. They go up to a point, hit the wall and then spin around to travel back. And like that person, they notice some things they might have missed on the way. Rita's thoughts were not different. And she saw something she had missed earlier.

And suddenly, like a picture that had been shot a while ago, it started to develop in her eyes. Gradually, like it emerges in the dark room. Bit by bit. A vault of realization cracked open, by reflex.

The eyes can miss a thousand details because they only get to see something once. Then there's always a question of who's seeing the subject. Perhaps, they got too engrossed in some part of the subject that they ignored the rest. There could be a certain shock element that the mind could get distracted by, thereby letting the eyes lose focus. Eyes are merely a lens, it's the brain that processes and analyses what we see. Isn't it? Also, sometimes the spectator's mind has already decided on something so it obliterates what it doesn't want to see. But the camera is different. It captures and freezes the moment as it was. No scope for emotions. No filters whatsoever. It captures as-is. It seizes every detail. What is even better is the captured moment can be enlarged if the capturing lens' quality is good. And you had to give it to those clever folks at Samsung for the zoom they offered in their Galaxy phone that Handlebar carried. That was one decision that Handlebar had taken wisely for which he would always be applauded. The enlarged picture of the two Honey Singhs – seen and snapped only minutes apart – had one more commonality than their being replicas of one another.

The veracity of the entire drama was bewildering. How could she have missed it when she saw the photographs first time around? It jibed at her.

Both Honey Singhs wore the same watch. Rita had an eidetic memory – a blessing or curse to remember everything like a photograph once seen – she remembered having seen the same Omega Seamaster on Honey Singh's wrist; he had flashed it when she had met him at his office. The same blue dial. She took out a lens from her drawer and looked at the photographs closely. On both the watches worn by the two Honey Singhs there were identical striations from a few years of use on the visible metal strap, and the matching small dent on the case near the winder in the watch in both the pictures.

Could it be?

They had been anti-Sherlock all this while – theorizing before they had the facts. She now knew she had the possible missing link.

There were never two Honey Singhs.

Honey Singh had finally made a mistake. The diamond robberies were committed with complete *sang-froid* because they had been planned to perfection. This outing to mislead Handlebar hadn't been. Honey Singh had donned a different shirt, but he had forgotten to take off his wristwatch.

Omega is one of the most respected watch brands in the world. It was on the wrist of Mr Armstrong when he took that giant leap for all of us mankind. It was the first watch in space. But when your time is bad, even an Omega cannot save your ass.

She picked up the photographs and the lens and walked to the Operations Room where the guys had been working.

'They never had a tail.' Rita didn't realize she had blurted out till she did. The glee had ensured the tongue was ahead of her brain.

'Who didn't have a tail, ma'am?' Jatin asked.

'Our police guys who tailed Handlebar did not have a tail.'

'Then how did Handlebar's client know what handlebar had missed to report.'

'They weren't spotted through the windscreen; they were sighted in the rear-view mirror.' She passed on the photographs and the lens. 'Look at the wristwatch on both the guys.'

Jatin, Vikram and Nene inspected the photographs under the lens. They got it instantly.

'It's the *Doosra* – like in cricket? The other one. It's the same delivery, but it goes the other way. It's not two separate deliveries. Cutely done.'

'You mean? Vikram got it, but it was still a shock.

'It could be that they bought the watches together?'

Really, Jatin? Are you for real?

'No it is the same watch – look at the indentations and striations on the watch and metal strap. He didn't think anyone would spot that. There is only one Honey Singh.'

'But we've got the photographs of both only minutes apart ...'

'Minutes apart' – those are the operative words. They are not in the same frame though.'

'You mean ...' Nene looked up.

'In the little time he had he only changed the shirt. Shoes and jeans, he knew wouldn't be visible as he would only be seen in the car when he travelled with Kitty Varghese. No reason to change. Watch, it either didn't occur to him or he got sloppy.'

'That's very unlike them.'

'Yes. I think they did play a ghost double but didn't plan it as meticulously as they planned their burglaries. Either that or they brought forward the sighting of the second one when we got closer than they had anticipated.'

'What do we do?'

'You do the rerun. See how long it takes for you to drive out of sight from the front entrance of Honey Singh's office, then find a way into the building from the rear door and walk back out front to be seen. Time it with the time stamps on these photographs. These photographs were taken nine minutes and fifty-three seconds apart. See what's the best time you can do that in, they should be a close match. The course needs to be done sooner rather than later. Tonight itself.'

Rajesh Nene, still scathing about not being allowed to get Honey Singh into the police lock-up and grill him hard enough to get the truth out of his dishonest mouth, wanted to nail the little exercise perfectly, that Rita had outlined. He decided to carry the cross himself rather than delegate it to someone in his team or to the local constabulary. He agreed to meet Jatin at the Bandra Kurla Complex after dinner. The plan was to reconstruct Honey Singh's movement and time it.

It was 9:23 when the two met at the closed tea stall that Handlebar had mentioned in the report. The lights in the offices around looked exhausted after having burnt the long day, but some of the offices were still lit up indicating that some of them still had people working the late shifts. BKC had some offices that were back-office operations for companies based abroad and, intrinsically, worked twenty-four/seven to accommodate the working hours in the US or whichever country was awake at the hour. Despite the time of the day, there were still a few people on the roads, albeit the crowd density was far lower than in the daytime. The streetlights were alight and vehicles moved in and out of the buildings without being questioned by the building security. That was good. It meant Nene's personal car would not be unnecessarily conspicuous or challenged when it drove in and quickly drove out of Honey Singh's office building either. The car's registration number might be noted by the personnel but even so, what? Honey Singh wouldn't be checking who came into the building he had his office in; it wasn't that he owned the damn building; he was just another one of the many occupants.

Nene scanned the area with his fox-paced eyes. One 360 and he had all in. There was no sight of anyone he knew or who could possibly know him or recognize him without the uniform. Some keen eyes would, evidently, recognize him by his haircut and mannerisms. A policeman was, above all, a policeman. The uniform was for the amateurs to identify the police; the professionals didn't need that – they would be familiar with people like Nene from a mile. The only precaution was to check if Honey Singh wasn't still in the office and bumped into Nene or Jatin driving in or out. That would cause suspicion. Nene pulled out his mobile, called the police control room that he knew someone in and asked him to connect to Honey Singh's office. The call he knew was secure even for someone like Honey Singh, since his call would get routed through the police control room's stringent encryption that could overcome any software that attempted to unmask the number or origin of the call. The desk phone at Honey Singh's office rang a few times and went into voicemail. Nene hung up. They waited another ten minutes to see if anyone came out of the building, in case someone had left only seconds back. No one. Once assured they sprang into action.

They agreed Jatin would hang around the tea stall like Handlebar, and like Handlebar take photographs from an identical Samsung mobile phone despite the cosmic drop in the lighting conditions. The idea was not to play *find-the-difference* with separate photographs of Nene here; the photographs would capture the time elapsed between the sighting of Nene after he drove off and when he reappeared at the gates of the building.

Parking Jatin's car by the roadside the two men drove away from Honey Singh's building to check which could be the closet point where Honey could have possibly dropped off from the car and walked his way into his own building through the rear gate. A short drive of barely two minutes – crossing the bank building where Handlebar had parked his car – the road turned left towards Kalina, and their car was indeed out of sight from where Handlebar had camped. Then there was another left turn – that Kitty and Honey would have apparently taken – only a few metres later into another office complex that also housed a South Indian café providing a perfect reason for a couple to drive in to. The building with the South Indian café had separate entry and exit points in front and a pedestrian passage in the rear, similar to the one in Honey Singh's office building. Nene steered into the building and stopped. All buildings were interconnected to walk between them, it seemed. Bingo!

The two policemen drove back to the start point. Jatin dropped off at the closed tea stall and Nene drove into Honey Singh's building, parked and walked out. Jatin spotted him and snapped a few pictures.10:12 p.m., before he disappeared into the building. Jatin snapped Nene again, in the car this time, at 10:16 p.m.

Nene drove the little circuit they had only just reconnoitred, found a parking on the other side of the building with the South Indian café, briskly walked – almost ran without anyone raising eyebrows – into the neighbouring building and crossed over into Honey Singh's office premises and walked out of the main entrance for Jatin to see him again. 10:33.

The time difference between the two sightings of Honey Singhs was a fraction over nine minutes.

Nene had, even with his super-efficient driving, achieved the same in approximately fifteen minutes.

Nene and Jatin sat in Nene's car wondering how Honey Singh had shaved off approximately six minutes from his mystic act. Especially since Kitty and Honey had perceptibly done the same course in the crowded daytime. The journey should have taken longer.

Could it be that DCP Rita Ferreira had misjudged this one? Were there actually two Honey Singhs with identical watches?

'Maybe he knows another route that we missed. Should be do another recce?' Jatin suggested.

'I guess so. Let's do that on foot. Maybe it's a foot passage that we overlooked.'

'Good idea.'

They walked the length of the road till the turn. Handlebar would have seen if the car had stopped before the turn. He would have certainly reported that Honey Singh got down if he had viewed that. The first left turn that could take anyone back was the entrance of the building with the café, there wasn't any other route.

As they stood in the parking lot of the building with the café, it struck Jatin first.

'With so many cars still in this complex, it must have taken you a while to find an empty parking slot first?' he queried.

Nene clutched on immediately. 'And Kitty Varghese, on the other hand, would have dropped Honey Singh at the gate and rushed off, so … in case Handlebar had driven out behind them, he would have chased the car not knowing that his target was no longer in the vehicle …'

'And Honey Singh would have jogged through this crowd, which would be quicker than you driving into this place to begin with and then the time it took for you to park.'

'Gotcha.' Nene gave a two-finger mock salute. He had missed that the additional time he took to get to the front of Honey Singh's building was the time he had taken to drive into the café and find a parking slot. Those unassuming four/five minutes probably made up the crucial difference between Honey Singh's charmed manoeuvre and Nene's rerun.

'Let's do another run.'

'I'll drive this time. I'll drop you by the gate and then take a U-turn and go to the tea stall, then time you again.'

'Done.'

This time they achieved the manoeuvre in ten minutes.

'Should we call up ma'am or just email?' He glanced at his watch: 11:04.

'I'd say just email at this hour. Anyway, this isn't any discovery, this is only a validation of her own conjecture. If this run was to override or negate her promise, then I'd have certainly called. I mean we only know what we already knew, right?'

'I guess so. I'll email her.'

The guys had walked back to their parked cars talking.

'Good night. See you tomorrow then.'

'Good night.'

Nene shot off immediately. He was a married man with family and it was late. Jatin sat there scrolling his phone for the photographs he had taken of Nene in the last hour and smiled. Honey Singh was quite an item playing a double role when there wasn't a lookalike. He wondered how Honey and/or Kitty had creatively imagined the whole thing in the first place. And why?

He started his motor and drove slowly to the end of the road.

Ever noticed that when you come across a new word it suddenly appears in all the prose you read? Everywhere? It isn't that the word has been included in the Oxford dictionary only after you encountered it. It's just that you're more conscious of it. It's the same with everything else. If someone points out something new, good or bad, you end up spotting it more. It wasn't that there was a sudden flood of reckless motorcyclists in Mumbai. But after Rita had pointed out one reckless rider, Jatin had noticed that it was some kind of an epidemic on the streets. The motorcyclist he saw here wasn't even the same one. Engrossed in his wonderment, he totally missed a motorbike coming from his right. Then he realized he wasn't the only one. What was it with the motorcyclists in this city? Brakes screeched. Almost twenty drivers blew their horns simultaneously, even at this hour. Expletives were shot from open windows and even from shut ones. The motorcyclist didn't care, just sped. He could have hit something, died or killed someone but he didn't stop, he just didn't care. Though Jatin couldn't take down the registration details as it was dark and it was the wrong angle for spotting the plate or following the motorcyclist, but he could see that the colour of the machine was green and not red that he had noted down the registration number of when he was with Rita. And he had also received the task to find who it was and ask the local police station to pay them a courtesy visit and some sincere advice on riding. Shit! He was late on the assignment. Today. Definitely!

He knew Rita Ferreira never forgot anything; it might have slipped in her priorities due to the urgency of the current Ron Jogani murder case. He made a mental note to pull up the vehicle registration database to search for the number he had noted previously. A letter should actually be sent to local police stations to impose a fine on such rashness. This was beginning to become a menace. With that in mind he drove off too.

Rita's Blackberry pinged at 11:24.

Yes, her guys had done the same circuit in almost the same time that Handlebar had recorded. However, it was still an assumption and assumptions cannot be validated or proven or even taken to court. Trouble was, how do you prove a negative? How can you prove that Honey Singh had no lookalike in the world till you had seen and eliminated the entire world's population? You could prove a double if you saw one, not disprove if you couldn't see one.

Rita had inherited the light sleep from her father. He never slept soundly and never slept more than six hours a day. Books and music filled up all his spare moments. He had told her of the 'day the music died,' how Maclean had immortalized his idol Buddy Holly and that February day in 1959. He had, in fact, given his interpretation of the entire American Pie and how Don had covered Dylan, Elvis, The Beatles, Lennon, Rolling Stones, Leonard Cohen …

But all that was before alcohol overshadowed everything else. Addiction, he never admitted to. Talking of inheritance, he had bequeathed his music collection to his only child too. All on vinyl. Pristine. And Rita had always cherished that far more than the land and property her parents had left behind. Enough that if she didn't want to work ever, she could live on rental income alone. However, her work, now, was what she lived for, especially when she was in the middle of any investigation like this, not the boring bureaucracy.

She was up, bored, sipping Jim, missing Ash. *He must still be in the skies*, she thought.

Before calling it a night she emailed the team calling for an emergency meeting early morning at nine.

'Tickets booked for day after,' Honey Singh was on the phone again. He was in his bedroom but he spoke in undertones like he was concerned someone would overhear him.

There was crackle on the other side.

'Yes, Wednesday evening. I have your passport and all the relevant papers … no just a small bag, please.'

Another crackle. Another question.

'We fly from Delhi to London, then to Miami and then to our heaven … yes, that's the best route, there is no direct flight. Our flight is early morning, so get to the airport like I've told you. Yes, I know it's too early but trust me. The earlier we get there, the better.'

The person on the other side asked something more.

'Take as circuitous route as possible. Change cabs if you have to. We can't fail now.'

TWENTY-EIGHT

The entire circus had been incredibly planned. Rita's brain was clouded: it wouldn't be the first time some criminal got away. Police files around the world are full of cold cases. Unsolved crimes.

There was no duplicate Honey Singh. Nene's next set of informers had found the only Honey Singh they already knew about. Take it to a court of law and say: 'there isn't another one because we can't find him,' and the case is over. That is, if it can even be filed in the first place.

Veer Singh's death could conjecturally be linked to Honey Singh and, perhaps, Kitty Varghese. No evidence there either.

Rita and team were confident it was Honey Singh. Kitty could be an accomplice, but they weren't certain.

'I cannot fathom how one person could fly into another country and manage a burglary in that manner all by himself … we thought there were two Honey Singhs, which, unbelievable as much as it was, offered some credibility to our theory.' Rita couldn't come up with any.

'It has to be Kitty,' Vikram said.

'My gut feel tells me that too, but we know she was in Köln. And we also know she was never out of sight of someone in the group for more than an hour or so. How could she have made it to Brussels and back without being missed?'

'Let me get Honey Singh in a lock-up ma'am and I'll get him to speak,' Nene offered.

Jatin smiled. He knew that given the opportunity Nene was more than capable of making Honey Singh talk. He also recognized Rita wouldn't permit any of those old police tactics.

'Let's go and talk to him once more.' Rita stood up. She had no more patience. 'Who's coming?'

Nene and Vikram stood up.

'I think Nene should come with me this time. A fresh pair of eyes.'

Rita and Nene stormed into Honey Singh's office like on the previous occasion. No calling ahead, no notice. The little receptionist guy sat there, but he didn't as much as make the effort of asking who they were, what they wanted or check if his boss had time to see them.

'Good morning, Mr Singh.' Rita opened Honey Singh's office door and entered, followed by Nene.

'You, again?' He sounded irritated.

'Do we stink?' Nene asked impolitely.

'I didn't say that—'

'What is the problem in seeing us again then?'

'Look, I didn't mean to be disrespectful, it was just something uttered.' Honey Singh's countenance shouted that he comprehended this meeting wasn't going to be another soft-spoken one. The body, the posture was confident; his eyes were nervous. 'I'm sorry. Sit down please. What can I do for you?'

'We can have this conversation back at the police station of your choice if you want.'

'I said I'm sorry.'

'Apology accepted.' Rita took over. She realized Nene had rankled him enough. 'God, my watch stopped. What time is it?' She intentionally looked at Honey Singh. Honey Singh was working on a laptop and there was a big-screen computer behind him, and Rita caught a partial reflection of some brochure but she couldn't see the full screen as his body was in between the two screens. It was some place beginning with CA …

'11:04.' Honey closed his laptop.

Yep. Same watch. She could see the slight dent from across the desk where she sat. The scratches on the chain weren't visible; they weren't required to confirm either. If she had any evidence, only then the watch could be confiscated and compared to the photographs. Getting a warrant based on photographs to prove that the two were one. It didn't make someone guilty of murder or burglary.

'Any leads on the murder investigation you were working on?' Honey Singh started.

'Yes, very concrete ones in fact. But that's not what we are here to discuss.'

'How may I help you DCP Ferreira, and …' he looked at Nene who hadn't found Honey Singh worthy enough to introduce himself.

Nene still didn't say his name or rank.

'Your friend Veer Singh died.' Rita broke the news calmly.

No remorse. No shock. Honey Singh stayed poker face.

'I don't see why you've come to inform me of a death of someone who, as I mentioned when you were here last time with

Senior Inspector Patil,' Honey Singh ensured he looked at Nene when he mentioned Vikram's name, '… that Veer Singh and I we split ages ago—'

'Wasn't he a close friend at one point in your life?'

'He was, indeed, but I have had no contact with him for years now.'

'Do you know if he has any distant relatives?'

'No.'

'I guess it was a wasted visit then.'

'What part of India was he killed in?"

Guilt, besides being an extremely strong emotion, is also a fantastic phenomenon. You can, of course, hide it if you're a serial offender or a good actor like Honey Singh. But – and here's the thing – it spills out in other ways. If someone fed you partial information on a situation that you are fully aware of, it can put you in a quandary sometime. Did I hear that? Or do I know that? There is a fragile line. You need to keep a record of everything because you're living a lie.

'I didn't say he was killed, did I?'

'Well …' Honey stopped, but only for a split second. 'If he had died a natural death I wouldn't be hearing it from you DCP Ferreira.'

Great comeback on the question Rita had asked.

How could Honey Singh have known Veer Singh had been killed in India? A crucial thought had pushed through and she got up without a warning.

'We'll be seeing you soon, Mr Singh.'

'And don't you even try leaving this city till I tell you or you'll be sorry you tried,' Nene shot before they walked out.

Rita and Nene updated on their short meeting with Honey Singh. Both confirmed that the watch was a giveaway. Rita also revealed that she had sighted holiday brochure of some country on Honey Singh's screen when they barged in unannounced. He had subsequently closed his laptop, but the initial two letters of the place were C and A; she hadn't caught anything else.

'The plan is on the mark: to put as much geographical distance between them and their crimes,' Rita concluded.

'Europe?'

'No, it can't be Europe, not when the Belgian police is looking for him. I want a list of countries starting with C, second letter A.'

'Canada.'

'I said the whole list. Canada is too risky. Even if he has a passport and visa, he still has to return at some point. Get a list. There can't be that many ...'

'I'm on it.' For once Vikram didn't note the task down. He started typing on his computer pronto. 'Cambodia, Cameroon, Canada, Cape Verde, and that's it.'

'Jatin, call up our sources – ask Commissioner Saxena's secretary to make calls if required – and check the names of people who've been granted visas to these countries in the last six months. Save for Canada, I can't imagine too many Indians flying to the other three countries for vacations or business.'

'But surely they would have been issued under aliases.'

'We have non-disclosure agreements in place with embassies for security reasons. Share the description, photographs of Honey and Kitty, their backgrounds, addresses. They cannot beat all the scrutiny.'

Jatin rushed out.

There was no indication when – if it were actually happening at all – that Honey Singh and Kitty Varghese were flying out, but with this entire discovery there was a *certain* urgency in the team. Like they were close to the finish line somehow. They had got Honey Singh, but still they hadn't. And that frustration, that anger was pushing the adrenaline.

Save for the Canadian Embassy, which asked for a court order before revealing any personal information on the visas they granted, the other three embassies didn't require much cajoling. Or arm-twisting. A simple request from the Mumbai Police Commissioner's Office was treated with urgency. Cape Verde and Cambodian Embassies were in New Delhi; all info was sent to them digitally. Being the only offices in India, they didn't take long in coming back with a negative response. No one who remotely resembled Honey Singh or Kitty Varghese – physically, financially or professionally – had applied for a visa for either country. No one by the name Sishir Singh either. Rita knew that it was next to impossible for any national to apply for a visa to a nation when they were out of their native country. Honey Singh couldn't just fly to Dubai or Singapore and apply for a Cape Verde visa there. You had to show residency in a country to use the local embassy.

Cameroon didn't have an embassy in India. Indians can apply for tourist visas when they land. It isn't one of the countries you escaped to, though the nation not having diplomatic ties with India might be an advantage. How do you ask them to extradite a criminal? Cameroon is right above the equator in West Africa, and Rita couldn't imagine that after making all the money that they had, Honey Singh was desirous of spending the rest of his life in Cameroon. Although, it wasn't a bad stopgap before seeking asylum somewhere in the South American nation Uruguay, which had harboured and sheltered criminal refugees including Nazis from World War II. It was a long shot, but a shot nevertheless. She made it a point to ask Vikram to check the flight connections to Cameroon. She was quite certain that there wouldn't be any direct flights. The team would have to watch pretty much every flight out of Mumbai. Also, domestic flights to other international airports in India.

The Canadian Embassy finally, after a lot of pressure from some minister *Sexy* knew, promised to send over their response the following day. The whole running around for embassy confirmations took the best part of the day.

Jatin confirmed that besides the unapparent security, now a visible team had also been contrived and put in place for Handlebar Raja and his extended family. As such, it wasn't essential for Mr Raja to capitulate in the face of threats issued by his elusive client and alter his last report.

Rita sat in her apartment, laptop switched on. The half-empty bottle of Jim Beam lay exactly where she and Ash had left it on Sunday night. She waited for the temptation to pass and then filled her glass with the Diet Coke that had come free with the pizza that Ash had ordered.

Google is a magnificent phenomenon. It can find you anything you want on the web – and these days almost everything is on the web – it can also make suggestions and recommendations based on what you search. It even starts serving, what it thinks are relevant, ads. Conversely, what it lacks is human brain and eyes to look at you and around you to determine why are you rummaging for something particular. It can be extremely irritating at times, but it can be exceptionally valuable. You search for information on Care Verde and Google deduces that you are looking for your next holiday destination though Rita wasn't planning on one, but there is no way Google knew that. How could it? So if Rita Ferreira was viewing pages on Cape Verde the dazzling algorithm processed that Miss Ferreira was seeking a vacation on some islands. What's better it deliberated that Miss Ferreira aspired a vacation in a warm climate with lots of sun and sea. Cape Verde is a small island country. And if Miss Ferreira was keen on an island what better than throw up an offer for holidays in the Caribbean Sea? Cayman Islands popped up, and they caught Rita's eye. They weren't in the list of countries beginning with CA only because Cayman Islands are a territory of three islands in the Caribbean. Though located south of Cuba they, at independence, voted to remain a British Overseas Territory, and remain under the jurisdiction and sovereignty of the United Kingdom taking the British monarch as the head of state, but there's the catch: they do not form a part of UK, ergo, they have their own government, their own leadership and are not governed or regulated by the UK.

Everyone and their dog knows that the Islands are known to be a major financial centre with 300 banks, sixty-thousand local population in approximately 100 square miles of total area. So, it's simple maths who these banks service? Besides international players like Deutsche Bank, UBS, Goldman Sachs and HSBC, there are a plethora of local and regional players stealing assets and accounts from the ever-secretive Swiss. Same principles of banking, equal anonymity is guaranteed.

But.

What everyone or their dog does not know is that, unlike Switzerland, moving to Cayman Islands and taking up residency is as simple as stealing a lollypop from the baby. All you need is money and patience.

$1.6 million – Cayman Island Dollar is almost the same value as a Euro – of investment gets you permanent residency on the islands. There are enough consultants around the globe to help you invest that money in the right mix of assets to get you started in the right direction. Once the countdown begins, living five years on the Islands grants you citizenship of British Overseas Territory. Indian Police can only watch the contrails of your flight thereafter.

Rita had been, for a long time, a preponderant of syllogism: an ancient Greek logical deduction that combines two separate pieces of information. She was well aware that none of those who burgled had declared the total extent of their loss due to tax reasons. Extrapolating the declared loss, she did some woolly maths on fingertips – Mumbai: $525K, New Delhi: $790K and Brussels: $10m – whoever was behind them could easily afford a resident permit right away with enough left in the bank to build it from there. The fact that it hadn't happened yet meant there was some delay caused on account of pending paperwork. Or else, if they were close to their target wouldn't they jump and finish the game they started?

Rita still held her hypothesis that none of the three heists were carried out by a single individual. It was a team. Small team. You needed as less links in the chain as possible to keep it strong. A secret needs as less people as possible to keep it under wraps. Not finding any other players to benefit from these capers besides Honey Singh and Kitty Varghese, she inferred it was a two-person team. They could have flown under the radar but for collateral damage: Ron Jogani.

The only gap was how it was possible with Kitty's alibi in Germany.

Doubt crept in when she couldn't find the answers. *Am I doing it right? Am I even on the right track?*

She was so exhausted she was in a state of fugue. She had lost track of time, and Jim she reasoned wouldn't help. It was midnight when she shut her laptop and tapped on her Blackberry to pick up any new messages. There were a few. She scanned till she saw one from Jatin. He had finally found the owner of the reckless motorcycle rider they had encountered a few weeks prior. Nothing major.

Switching off the lights she slipped out of her jeans and wore the shirt to bed.

A stray thought floated along like a latent dandelion suddenly chartering up and down in the gentle wind: a reckless motorcyclist drifting through lined cars, missing traffic lights, disregarding the risk to his own life in the process. Was he doing it for kicks or was he rushing to accomplish something? What could be worth endangering one's own life? You might be closer to the treasure, but dead.

She switched on the bedside light and got up with a jolt, sweating. Without bothering to put on her jeans she walked into the living room and switched on the lights. The tunnel was ending; the light was turning from hazy to bright.

Hadn't they already risked their lives for diamonds? Would a wee bit compromise like reckless motorcycling halt anyone from staying away from diamonds worth ten million Euros?

She poured herself Jim Beam and restarted her laptop and waited for it to reboot.

And what made *her* so sexist to think that a motorcycle rider can only be a male?

You only need an Einstein to break a cipher. For everything else there's mathematics. As per Google Maps, Dom Hotel in Köln, Germany, where Kitty Varghese resided for her fashion show, was approximately 214 kilometres from Crown Plaza hotel in Brussels where Ron Jogani had gotten killed. A distance that Google Maps showed could be covered in over two-and-a-half hours in a car, which could take a reckless motorcyclist much less. One hour thirty minutes, give or take. But the whole premise hinged on one single posit: Kitty Varghese rode a motorbike …

Rita ran both her hands through her hair in frustration. Frustration sired by months of failure that had been boring holes in her forbearance. For a long time, nothing, they hadn't had a single break in the case. Now, when her instinct told her that she was on the right track, she did not have access to the office file. She winced at the taste of despondence that had suddenly dried her mouth. She took a sip of Jim and looked at the time on her screen: 01:17. She couldn't call anyone at this hour for the files. If only she had the report for Kitty Varghese's alibi – what time did the fashion shows culminate in the evenings and when did the group split for the night? All Kitty needed was a clean seven/eight hours. Less than a two-hour bike ride to Brussels, a three-hour halt, which was adequate to collect the gun and other gadgets, deliver at Crowne Plaza, maybe collect the diamonds, return or dispose of the gun and race back to her hotel. If she left after nine in the evening, she can be back in bed by five the following morning. Presto! But, all this was conjecture. She needed confirmation that would only be possible in the morning. 0117 hours in New Delhi meant it was still 2147 hours in Brussels. She called Victor, who picked up his mobile on the third ring.

'Good evening, Victor, I'm sorry to bother you.'

'Hello, Rita.' Victor must have stored her number, as she didn't have to introduce herself. 'It must be quite late in India.'

'It is one-twenty in the morning.'

'Then it must be urgent. How may I help you?'

'I'm wondering if you knew: could someone ride a motorcycle from Köln to Brussels and back in a night?'

'Twice.'

'I beg your pardon?'

'I mean any good motorcyclist can do that journey twice in a night. You see some of the Autobahns in Germany had no speed limits, so that part could be covered at, say 140–150 kilometres an hour. What is this regarding?'

'Victor, I think the accomplice in the Brussels murder did exactly that.'

'Do we have any evidence?'

'Precisely the reason I called at this hour. There was a lady that could have hired a motorbike from Germany for the commute—'

'A woman?'

Sexist.

'Yes. I can send you all the details and photographs. I'd want you to use your resources to check if that was the case.'

'I'll get this checked at first light tomorrow, Rita. Send me the details.'

They traded their exasperations and agreed to touch base in the morning.

Rita made a note to check if Kitty Varghese even had a valid driving licence for a motorcycle. With that thought she shut her computer once again, finished her shot of Jim and anticipated it to induce some somnolence in her anxiety-filled interminable night.

TWENTY-NINE

Nene, Vikram and Jatin had all read the urgent email Rita had sent the night before to meet early in the Ops Room on Wednesday. She hadn't divulged either of her surmise or compiled a list of tasks in the mail, but all four were in office at 7:30. Nene, as always, had picked up much-needed four hot coffees in Styrofoam cups on the way.

Rita's eyes felt gritty reminding her of the sleepless night she'd had. She took fifteen minutes to update the team on the inferences she had drawn the night before. Her luck in finding out about the Cayman Islands, her speculation that it might be the destination given that it provided residency for a cost.

'The reason we missed it is because Cayman Islands aren't listed as a single country, it's a cluster of three separate island countries.' Rita waited for the guys to digest the complexity. 'I got lucky, guys. And thank you, Jatin, for sending me the email on the reckless motorcyclist last night.'

'I'm sorry I couldn't do that simple thing earlier, but—'

'No, I think the delay was appropriate. Had the email come at some other time it might not have set me off in the direction, who knows?'

The guys sipped their coffee and listened intently; their countenances telling Rita that they had an inkling that she had the ace by its shorts.

'The only fracture in our theory till now was how was it possible for one person to accomplish the Brussels burglary and get away. And we kept looking for another guy besides Honey Singh. We never thought it could have been Kitty—'

'But she was in Germany at the time, wasn't she?'

'She was and she wasn't. I checked on Google Maps and then with Victor that any motorcyclist – and the person does not even need to be reckless – can do the return journey twice in seven hours plus. I bet it was Kitty.'

Mouths gaped and closed. Eyes widened, eyebrows raised and dropped.

'Jatin – check the alibi reports we have on Kitty Varghese. Check what time the fashion show ended in the evening, and what time the group dissembled and retreated to their respective rooms, specifically on 2nd April evening.'

Nod.

'Vikram, could you check with the licencing authorities if Kitty Varghese has a motorcycle licence. Also, please check if she has a motorcycle.'

Vikram didn't waste a minute. He picked up his coffee and left on the double.

'And Nene, Mr Handlebar Raja is not on the job any longer. I want you to organize twenty-four/seven surveillance on Honey Singh and Kitty Varghese, both. Ideally, it should be oblivious to them, but I don't care if our guys are spotted. Any diversion either of them take from their usual routes today, they should call you.'

The guys left for their respective assignments, and Rita decided it was time to fill in the case log and go meet *Sexy* personally: a plenary verbal update to the Commissioner before requesting him to call up the CBI headquarters in New Delhi to dispatch a guy for Cayman Islands High Commission in Chanakyapuri.

Sexy sat behind the vast desk in his office. Cool, casual and calm demeanour, not a hair out place, which wasn't abnormal when you only moved directly from a chauffeur-driven air-conditioned car to an air-conditioned office. His hair pomaded with some matt paste. Sedate. Like he'd jaywalked out of a meditation. Panache personified. Rita wondered if his hair ever got ruffled, like when he was at the golf course.

'Good morning, Miss Ferreira,' he said jubilantly.

Cheerful mood.

'Good morning, sir.'

'My assistant expressed a few minutes ago that you wanted to consult me urgently. What can I do to facilitate?'

Rita narrated the whole case without the big man interrupting, thinking that *Sexy* might term the entire investigation as botched or as some phantasmagoria: the murderer was Honey Singh, then his double that was non-existent came into the picture and now it was Honey Singh again!

'Ingenious,' *Sexy* summarized her long spiel. 'Brilliant subterfuge, a picaresque feat, we have to admit. So, since he got captured on the camera he fabricated a fairy tale of a private detective following him on behest of an unknown client only to discover a non-existent double. We have to acknowledge his originality that he let us discover the duplicate through a third party to make you feel clever when he was. Essentially, bamboozling you ...'

'Yes sir. And he succeeded in bambooz ...' Rita stopped herself; it wasn't the smartest thing to repeat *Sexy*'s lexicon; it never sounded natural from anyone else's mouth, '... fooling us for quite some time by subtly propagating the theory of an old friend Veer Singh who he and his girlfriend had fallen out with.'

'And what makes you contemplate they're fleeing the country?'

'It was a bit surprising for someone to be looking a holiday brochures of a foreign country when that someone does not have a valid passport.'

Rita was right. Most cases crack open because something does not fit. One wrong piece in a puzzle and it stood out like an Ogre's thumb.

'I have to give it to you, Miss Ferreira. I'm glad I took the right decision to hand this case to you.'

'I got lucky, sir.'

For the first time since Rita had known him, *Sexy* stood up and shook hands to commend her. 'I'll call up Delhi right away,' he said.

Luck is like salt. It is not a condiment kept somewhere in the spice cupboard only to be pulled out when required. You need salt in every meal. You need luck in every investigation like you need it in almost everything you do. In the race between smart criminals and police, it is luck that decides the final outcome. The final roll of dice got Rita and her team the six they so desperately needed.

All the searches came up positive.

Kitty Varghese had a motorcycle driving licence issued in Mumbai. She even owned a Kawasaki Ninja 650R, which she had disposed of only two months ago.

Victor called back to say that a woman by the name of Shivani had hired a motorcycle from a local motorbike rental on the evening of 1st April and returned it on the evening of 3rd April. The odometer records confirmed that the hirer had travelled a little over nine hundred kilometres. This meant she had possibly done the journey twice, on two consecutive nights, to arrange for everything at Brussels. What's more, the CCTV images – B&W, through the helmet visor and extremely blurry even after professional clean up – showed that Shivani was Kitty Varghese. This wasn't conjecture; this was evidence.

Cayman Islands High Commission had issues no visa in any category to anyone called Honey Singh or Kitty Varghese. However, with the profiles that were sent across to them, there was an exact match with a couple: Mrs Shivani Malhotra and Mr Ajay Malhotra. Bingo!

There was one unusual pattern reported though. Neither Honey Singh nor Kitty Varghese had ventured out of their respective homes today.

'It's three in the afternoon on a Wednesday,' Rita looked at the three men in the Ops Room. 'I can understand Kitty having a lie-in, but why wouldn't Honey Singh go to work today? Call one of your guys, Nene, and ask them to go to his office right away. If he isn't there, ask someone to go to his home in Andheri and check. This isn't good news.'

Rita asked Jatin to prepare the papers for arrests.

'Vikram, ask someone to get in touch with four or five travel agents. I can't imagine there is a direct flight to any of the three Cayman Islands. We need to know from various sources which possible connection these guys might take.'

Vikram made notes.

'And we have the names of the passengers, maybe we strike lucky to find the bookings from some travel agent. It must all be interconnected now, won't it?'

'Not sure ma'am, but if we knew possible routes and the airline, then I'm pretty sure we can find them.'

Chhatrapati Shivaji International Airport
1700 Hours

'I'm tired now,' Kitty said looking around.

'Already?' We have another few hours before we check and go through the security,' explained Honey Singh.

'I think you're paranoid, getting to the airport a full day before the flight. No one can even imagine we managed to pull this caper, much less believe it or prove it. Plus they have no evidence. Why would anyone come after us?'

'You never know. We hadn't imagined they'd ever get so close either, but the DCP and her team did. Eliminating Veer Singh backfired; there was no other possible fall guy so they could close in any minute. And I didn't want them to seize us when we were getting to the airport. Best to come here in the cover of the night – at least, now both of us are in the airport …'

'What did you tell your mom?'

'Nothing whatsoever. Telling her might have endangered her and the plan. If she doesn't know anything, she's safe. I'll only call after we land at the final destination. I might send for her after a year or two – when all this heat goes away – to pick her up. I've left enough money for her to cover expenses.'

'Have you checked the money?'

'All secured in private banks on Grand Cayman. I'm carrying all relevant papers. Don't you worry, Mrs Malhotra.'

'First thing we do when we get there is to get married.'

'I can't wait.'

Police Headquarters, Crawford Market, Mumbai 1930 Hours

It was now evident that Honey Singh and Kitty Varghese were missing from their respective residences since the night before. Absconding, Rita summarized. They had stressed the suspects enough for them to panic, to make a move, to pick their stash and run. So someone finally got their panties in the wad. Honey's mother had told the police that he hadn't come home from work the night before and hadn't called either, which was not unusual. He did that many times.

Must be with some friend or with that girl, she had claimed.

The local police guy that went into Honey Singh's office had slapped the little ruffian Titu a few times, but the statement had remained what he had originally given to the police. *Sahib did not come to office today*. He was made to call Honey Singh's mobile a few times but it went straight to voicemail. It wasn't common for the *sahib* to not inform him, but it wasn't something that had never happened before. Honey Singh didn't owe Titu any explanation if he didn't attend office.

Rita was tense. A torrent of expletives flooded her mind. They had finally uncovered the whole mystery only to discover that the perpetrators had successfully got away. They had been late by mere hours. She glowered in her defeat. There was still a chance to halt the travel midway at London if they had left the Indian shores. She could call up Victor and ask Interpol to intervene, take over the case and bring down Sishir Singh aka Honey Singh aka Ajay Malhotra and his floozy. But it won't be the same thing as making the arrest herself. And it would be difficult to extradite the killers of Veer Singh: the Belgian Police would certainly try them for Jogani's murder before anything else. It would still be a success but a victory is something else. It's when you held the trophy.

Vikram rushed in with the possible travel itineraries to Cayman Islands.

The flights to Cayman would have layovers in London or Paris, and Miami, unless the phoney Malhotras had deliberately selected an offbeat route.

Jet Airways, British Airways, Air France and United flights made the best and fastest connections.

If they hadn't flown out already, the earliest flight was only after midnight, barely five-and-half hours away.

Security and check-in was two-and-half hours away.

'OK … here's what we do. Call up the travel agent to check all these four airlines if we have Mrs Shivani Malhotra and/or Mr Ajay Malhotra. They might not be booked on the same flight, so be careful they do not miss.'

Chhatrapati Shivaji International Airport
2130 Hours

Jet Airways opened the check-in for Flight 9W118 to London Heathrow a tad early. First in the queue were Mrs and Mr Malhotra. Kitty alias Shivani Malhotra stayed behind her husband, looking around. She, being a known face that could be recognized, was best not standing upfront the airline check-in guy who could see a discrepancy in the name if he acknowledged her.

Checked-in.

Boarding passes issued.

Without wasting any time, the couple passed through the security and walked in at 2130 hours.

Police Headquarters, Crawford Market, Mumbai
2345 Hours

No Malhotras were booked on any sector on Air France or British Airways.

Rita and team still hadn't heard back from United and Jet Airways. It seemed there was some technical glitch and the cumulative bookings for the entire flight from various sources weren't coming through.

United returned empty at five minutes to midnight.

Jet Airways confirmed that Mrs Shivani Malhotra and Mr Ajay Malhotra were booked on Flight 9W118 to London Heathrow.

'What time does the flight leave?'

'In twenty-five minutes, ma'am.'

'Jatin, Vikram, Nene – call up every police station in the vicinity of the airport. Ask them to get to the airport authorities to offload these two passengers. You know the drill.'

Chhatrapati Shivaji International Airport
0045 Hours

The gates had been closed a while back. The flight attendants had finished the safety briefing.

'Ten more minutes,' Shivani Malhotra put her hand in her husband's hand as they sat in the window and aisle seats in economy with no one in between. A last-minute ticket wasn't available in upper classes. They were booked in First Class from London onwards.

'I always knew the risk, but this got close.'

The aeroplane was being taxied on the asphalt, making its way to the runway.

Minutes to departure.

Bandra-Worli Sea Link
0046 Hours

Rita was in the front seat, with Nene driving; the red beacon on the roof, siren blazing. Vikram and Jatin were behind them, followed by another police car full of uniformed cohort.

'Good evening, sir,' Rita finally got through to *Sexy* on his unlisted home phone. 'Apologies, but it was an emergency, sir. Our suspects are on the flight leaving Mumbai in next ten minutes. We need to stop the flight.' Rita gave the details.

'Let me call in my debts. Call me as soon as you get there.'

Chhatrapati Shivaji International Airport
0050 Hours

The engines had started. The pilot had asked the flight personnel to take their seats.

That was when the call came in from Air-Traffic Control.

The Commissioner of Mumbai Police has no legal jurisdiction over Air-Traffic Control. But here's the thing: you do not say 'no' to him under normal circumstances. And if that

Police Commissioner is Sanjay Saxena, you do not say 'no' to him under any kind of circumstances. Or the next call will be from the Home Minister of the State. *Sexy* could press pause on Mumbai like you pressed pause on a film on your Tata Sky or your DVD player.

The Air-Traffic Control officer-in-charge had made all excuses not to stop an aircraft on the runway, as that would mean many subsequent flights would be delayed. He had begged.

Sorry, that is not an option was the response.

The pilot had protested vehemently, stifling the epithets he had in his throat. If they missed this take-off slot, he calculated, they might be put at the back of the queue. *Why, what's the problem?* He had asked, but he got no response. He was told to declare 'technical glitch', keep the doors locked and wait for further orders. Not negotiable.

0052 Hours

The police sirens were silenced before the approach. The local Assistant Superintendent of Police on the scene had asked his team to switch off the red beacons on the vehicles too. Three police vehicles were parked in front of the aircraft that only the pilots could see. Everyone waited till Rita and Nene followed by the other units arrived at the runway.

The time was 0117 hours. The police had enough evidence to make the arrests.

The Reason Behind the Reason

The police machinery took over. It took six officers and two advocates three days to break Honey Singh and Kitty Varghese.

DCP Rita Ferreira's theory was on the mark. They admitted to the earlier burglaries in Mumbai and Delhi, the multi-million Euro heist at Brussels, to the culpable homicide of Ron Jogani and to the ensuing hired killing of Veer Singh – another collateral damage.

The murder of Ron Jogani had sired the subsequent events, which propagated the despicability when the local police got involved and started knocking on their doors. The original idea was never to flee Mumbai or India. Honey Singh and his mother had been grossly fleeced of their inheritance by the so-called family members due to early bereavement of Honey's father. Honey Singh, deprived of the riches that were rightfully his, needed money so he could get back by anonymously buying back his father's business and reducing the others into a life of penury and penance: an equally nasty plan to reprimand those detestable. That it wasn't a noble end-goal got further aggrandized by the means he wanted to achieve it. The whole yarn of Honey Singh clandestinely working on some software that could change the face of financial accounting and bring in millions was fabricated. He was good at what he did – computer maintenance and writing simple computer programmes – but he wasn't a genius as he claimed to be; he did not have any outstanding epochal ideas to conceive that no one else had thought of. The story was a façade to legitimize the money if he succeeded – and he had, to some extent, gotten away; well, almost – in pocketing the millions. How else would he have attributed his sudden inheritance? It was all thought-through. The idea of fleeing was recent, premature. The i's hadn't been dotted. When Rita & Co. increased the heat, he shortlisted the places he could get away without having to return. Research told him that getting to Cayman Islands appeared straight as a rifle shot and well within reach.

Kitty Varghese was a complicit accomplice in all the crimes. She wasn't indoctrinated, she didn't need to be. She was equally guilty. She was a runaway from a Catholic seminary because she didn't want to waste her life by becoming a holy sister. She looked extra-terrestrial in the environment: far too attractive to be of any assistance to God or His worshippers. If anything, she believed, she would only be a distraction to men if she stayed back. She hadn't broken off with Veer Singh because of what she had admitted to Rita: that Veer Singh did not accept her modelling career was nonsense. Honey Singh was the man who had a precarious plan. The risk was so enthralling it paled all worries, all consequences. She relished cheap thrills a little too much for her own good. Running from seminary and getting away once had given her the confidence and the impetus to up the stakes. It engendered a false fortitude. Aware that her modelling career will expire with her youth, the diamond larcenies, the threat of getting caught only pushed the adrenaline higher. Risqué that she was, men always went out of their way to succour. Like the guy who told her how old and grand the building was of Zaveri Jewellers; it even had a glass dome on top. Like the guy who helped her hire a motorcycle in Germany without too many questions or papers …

They could have left the game after the first burglary or the second. Hadn't they made enough dough? The murder wasn't planned, and it could have been very much avoided. Honey Singh could have apologized to Ron Jogani, given some hogwash how he accidently entered the wrong room, blamed the hotel clerk or locks and keys, gotten away. Maybe he could have merely shown the gun to Jogani to shut up and run away without the diamonds. Maybe Jogani wouldn't have reported. Of course, no one will even know what *could* have happened. The fact was that Honey Singh couldn't control himself: when the stakes are that high, people do unprecedented things. And that, precisely, is the problem with avarice. No one always wins. No one always loses. The art is to win more than you lose. Or at least stop playing till it's a zero-sum. Then leave the table. But when you start descending into the darkness of evil, you see no reason, you stop nowhere or at nothing. In their lust for more, most people make sure they lose everything they've already got. That's how Devil plays; he always blinds you and suspends you in some fifth dimension where everything sounds like a lament. There is no restitution.

The plan of concocting the theory of a duplicate, and establishing a specious spoor to implicate Veer Singh was Kitty's idea to save her Honey by zeroing in on the private detective, Mr Raja – the dingbat, as she referred to him – follow Honey Singh so in case someone came asking they would think: *poor Honey Singh*. The lie worked for some time before it decalcified.

The money – most of it unspent yet – was recovered from four separate anonymous offshore accounts in the Cayman Islands. No diamonds.

Kitty Varghese got six years for being a willing accomplice to the break-ins and thefts. Honey Singh admitted, under oath, that Kitty Varghese was never an accomplice in either of the two murders. The judge still saw her as an 'accessory after the event'; she should have reported the heinous crimes, but she didn't. Six years was too harsh for burglary, too less for murder, people thought. The media hawks got new material to deliberate for weeks.

Honey Singh committed suicide, two months after he was sentenced to life imprisonment.

As expected, Mrs Lucky Singh was distraught. She had no idea her son had a deep-rooted hatred for her in-laws for fleecing her when she, herself, had long been over the grudge.

There are times when you know what's happened is correct, but it's tragic nevertheless. Sad, Rita thought. Two mislaid souls. It would have been akin to explaining laws of gravity to a couple of potatoes falling from a skyscraper. Too complex. And, now, perhaps too late.

ABOUT THE AUTHOR

Vish Dhamija is the bestselling author of eight crime fiction books. He is frequently referred to in the press as the 'master of crime and courtroom drama' in India. In August 2015, at the release of his first legal fiction, *Deja Karma*, *Glimpse* magazine called him 'India's John Grisham' for stimulating the genre of legal fiction in India, which was almost non-existent before his arrival on the scene. Vish lives in London with his wife, Nidhi.